"You've got a lot of courage, Stormy."

She gave Guy a long, level look. "Courage? Most of the time, I'm running scared. I put on a good act, but—" She broke off, looking annoyed. "Now why did I say that? I don't know what got into me, talking so much about myself. You couldn't possibly be interested."

"But I am. It helps me to understand you better."

"Why would you want to do that?" she said, sounding puzzled.

"Because—God, you must know how I feel about you!"

The bewilderment on her face surprised him. Was this some kind of game she was playing? He met her eyes and he knew it wasn't a game. He saw a hunger to match his own, and suddenly, without thinking it through, he pulled her into his arms and kissed her....

ABOUT THE AUTHOR

Successful novelist Irma Walker set much of her seventh Superromance in Bolinas in her home state of California. Bolinas, she reports, "is a little jewel of a place. The San Andreas fault goes right through the middle of Bolinas Bay, and you can see it in the rock formations at the mouth of the bay." Irma enjoyed writing *Stormy Weather*, and especially liked the character of Tommy, who in many ways reminds her of her own grandson, Mickey.

Books by Irma Walker

HARLEQUIN SUPERROMANCE

104–SONATA FOR MY LOVE
147–THROUGH NIGHT AND DAY
163–SPANGLES
210–GAMES
247–MASKS
339–CRYSTAL CLEAR

Stormy Weather

IRMA WALKER

Harlequin Books

TORONTO • NEW YORK • LONDON
AMSTERDAM • PARIS • SYDNEY • HAMBURG
STOCKHOLM • ATHENS • TOKYO • MILAN

Published August 1990

ISBN 0-373-70417-8

Printed in U.S.A.

To my friend,
Helen Marcia,
who is Lola Ruth's other grandmother.

CHAPTER ONE

IT WAS LATE FRIDAY AFTERNOON and the supermarket aisles were thronged with people doing their weekend shopping. Stormy Todd ignored the crowds. She concentrated on the bag of cat food in her hand, comparing its contents with the house brand, which was thirty cents cheaper. She had just about come to a decision when a very large woman careened around a corner and bumped into her cart, almost knocking her down.

Pretending not to hear the woman's comment about "damned teenagers, always getting in the way," Stormy decided the cheaper house brand was a better buy and dropped it into her grocery cart. As she moved on down the aisle, she reflected that she rightfully could have told the woman that not only was she twenty-four, five years past being a teenager, with two school-age kids of her own, but that *she* hadn't been the one who wasn't watching where she was going.

At one time, she probably would have done just that, but she'd learned to hold her tongue in the past couple of years. So she returned to her grocery shopping, hurrying because she was eager to get home.

With the ease of long experience, she added a large carton of oatmeal, a box of Cream of Wheat, a two-pound package of navy beans, two loaves of whole wheat bread from the day-old table, a large jar of peanut butter and a carton of dried milk to her cart. She hesitated a long time at the meat counter, finally choosing a small but plump fryer. The fryer would put a strain on the week's food budget, but she would economize somewhere else—and besides, maybe she could stretch it out for two meals.

And anyway, this was a very special day, wasn't it? Her first paycheck in more than two years . . .

A sudden rush of joy made her smile. A job—how wonderful to be working again and earning her own way. Of course, the job, in a take-out pizza parlor, only paid minimum wage plus very scanty tips, which meant tightening the belt even more than when the welfare check and food stamps had been coming in every month.

She wasn't bitter about that. After all, you couldn't expect high wages when you hadn't even finished high school and had no particular job skills. She would have to pay for the family's health insurance, which would really hurt, and there'd be no more food stamps, but to be off welfare was a relief that only someone who had been living on other people's charity for two years could possibly understand.

Minimum wage was hardly enough to exist on, not with three people to feed and clothe and pay rent for, but she had her pride back—and somehow she'd find a way to meet her bills, even if she had to take on an extra night at work eventually.

Everything's coming up roses, she thought as she pushed the cart toward the shortest of the checkout lines.

Some of her optimism evaporated when she saw that her nemesis, a sharp-tongued cashier who made it very plain that she disapproved of welfare recipients, was on duty today.

"In the future, have your food stamps ready, lady," had been the woman's latest zinger, spoken in an unnecessarily loud voice—and then she'd smirked at the woman behind Stormy in line as if to say, "I really put *this* freeloader in her place, didn't I?"

Stormy had bitten her tongue hard although she'd wanted to point out that no one in her right mind would go on welfare unless there was no other choice. And she *had* gone back to work just as soon as Laurie was well enough that she didn't have to be watched every minute for fear she would strain her already weak heart. So what if her job at the fast-food place left her with less money to live on than welfare by the time she paid for health insurance? Someday that would all change. Someday she'd get on with her education, learn a marketable skill, get a really good job...

She reached the cashier and waited silently while her groceries were being rung up. The woman gave her a hostile look and told her, "Let me have your food stamps, lady."

"I'm paying by check," Stormy said with satisfaction, and held out her paycheck and her driver's licence as ID.

The woman examined the check with insulting thoroughness. "I need a second ID," she said finally. "A credit card will do."

"I don't have any credit cards," Stormy said. "My driver's license is valid identification. You've taken it before—and I've been shopping here for several years."

Something in her voice—or maybe it was the cool stare she leveled at the cashier—made the woman flush.

"Well, I guess it's okay," she said ungraciously.

She took the check, stamped the back and gave Stormy her change, counting it out on the counter instead of dropping it into her hand.

Stormy picked up the change and packed her groceries into the mesh bags she'd brought with her and stalked out of the store, feeling surprisingly good in spite of that final insult. Things were looking up. Yes, they really were....

Three blocks later, she turned off the busy avenue onto a quiet street lined with the small, pre-World War II cottages that Californians call bungalows. In the late May sun, the houses looked very neglected and forlorn, with their windows boarded up and Keep Out signs nailed on the front doors.

At one time, when Stormy had first moved there, April Street, although undeniably shabby and run-down, had teemed with life—children playing ball in the front yards, women gossiping with each other over their back fences, dogs barking, old people taking their daily walks, a multitude of aging cars in driveways and parked at the curbs.

It had been an interracial, blue-collar neighborhood, where everybody minded their own business but also lived in harmony with each other. She could still remember how thankful she'd been that she could afford, just barely, to live there instead of in an inner-city flat or in one of the city's public housing complexes.

That's when she'd been working at a child-care center, the only job she could find where she could keep her preschool kids with her during the day. For a long time, she had survived, had even managed to save a small nest egg for a rainy day. And then the rainy day had come and the nest egg hadn't been enough, after all.

Laurie's illness had been diagnosed as rheumatic fever, following a mild case of strep throat that had been misdiagnosed as a simple sore throat. Those black days when Laurie had hovered between life and death, her slight body burning with fever, was a time Stormy tried never to think about now. When the fever had broken and the doctors told Stormy that her daughter must have constant supervision to make sure she stayed quietly in bed, that even the least bit of exertion could overtax Laurie's weakened heart, she had quit her job, knowing that she had no other choice.

For a while, her savings had supported the three of them. She'd practiced the most stringent economies, had augmented her savings with small jobs she could do at home, taking in ironing, doing plain sewing, anything that would bring in a few extra dollars.

But it hadn't been enough, and when the rent was overdue and eviction hung over her head, and the knowledge penetrated that without a job, she had no health insurance for any future medical emergency, she had swallowed her pride and applied for welfare.

Stormy grimaced, her eyes haunted, as she remembered the humiliation of the day she'd gone in to fill out the papers that would put her on the welfare rolls. She had felt diminished, shamed, a total failure. Sitting there in that harshly lit waiting room with its hard benches, its odor of dust and human despair, waiting to be interviewed by a social worker, she had vowed that someday she would pay back every penny, even while she knew that that day would be a long time in coming....

Suddenly impatient with the direction of her thoughts, Stormy hastened her step. This wasn't the time to be thinking of the past, of the bad days. Today there was a cause for celebration, her first paycheck. Just last week, she had notified her caseworker that she'd found a job and would be going off welfare, and it had been one of the most gratifying moments of her life. Oddly, the woman had tried to dissuade her.

"I'm not sure this is a good idea, Ms. Todd," she'd said. "Without food stamps and medicare—well, you are taking a really big chance. Even a few days' illness could mean you wouldn't be able to pay your bills, and if it doesn't work out and you lose your job, you know it takes time to get back on the welfare rolls. Maybe you should at least keep food stamps. With two children to support and just drawing minimum wage as you are, I'm sure you still qualify for them."

"I won't need them. I can make it," Stormy told her. "I know I'll be earning less than welfare at the Pizza King at first, but eventually, I'm sure I can work my way up to some kind of better paying job. And we're used to living on very little. I know all the tricks."

"Well, good luck, my dear. I do wish you the best."

And even while Stormy had nodded and thanked her, she'd known that she would need all the luck she could get.

Stormy shifted the position of the mesh bags, moving the heaviest one so it rested on her hip, and the buoyancy, the feeling of euphoria returned. *What a wonderful day,* she thought, and knew that even if it were raining, she'd still feel the same way.

A middle-aged man passed her, his sidelong glance approving. She knew what he saw—a small, too-thin woman who looked like a teenager, with ivory-fair skin, eyes so dark a green that they sometimes looked black, and the kind of face people called heart-shaped. At various times, she'd been told that she was pretty or cute or even, on occasion, beautiful, but she was too realistic to believe it. Not that she had an inferiority complex. No, she knew her own worth, and it was when people tried to put her down, that her name, Stormy, was appropriate.

Yes, she could stand up for herself when it was necessary. When hadn't she been forced to do just that, even before she'd reached her teens? Briefly, an image of her grandmother, that too-gentle, unworldly, helpless woman who had given her so much love, formed in her mind.

Her eyes smarted, and Stormy shook her head impatiently. What the *hell* was wrong with her today? She had every reason to be hopeful about the future and yet the past kept getting in her way. Next thing you knew, she'd be thinking about Eric and the worst betrayal of her life. And that she refused to do. She'd reconciled that hurt a long time ago, reasoning that since he'd given her two wonderful kids, the family that she'd always longed for, she had to forgive him for the other things he'd done to her—such as neglecting to tell her that he already had a wife when he proposed marriage to her and later, when she was pregnant with their second child, deserting her....

She reached the cottage where she'd been living for the past four years and turned in at the gate. The front yard, unlike the lawns of its boarded-up neighbors, was well cared for and neatly trimmed, with a riot of spring annuals adding a fringe of color around the edges and along the path.

The condition of the cottage itself was a different matter. It had been years since it had seen a fresh coat of paint and the roof had several telltale patches while streaks of rust stained the cement drain under the end of a drain pipe.

Stormy stared worriedly at a patch of mold in one corner of the porch, then shrugged. There was nothing she could do about that now. Ever since the cottage and its neighbors had been sold to a conglomerate, the street had gone downhill. No amount of complaints to the real-estate company who handled the property had produced any repairs and gradually, over the past two years, the other tenants had moved out. As soon as a cottage was vacated, it was boarded up, adding to the street's aura of neglect, and intensifying its deserted look. Now only she and her two children remained.

In fact, she was lucky her cottage was still inhabitable. Most of the other tenants hadn't been so lucky, which was why they had moved out. Her latest complaint, about the deficiencies of the gas floor furnace, had resulted in a caustic letter from the real-estate company about people who were constant complainers.

Which was grossly unfair. She had done all the repairs she was capable of, including patching the roof and the front steps, and repairing the screens. When things she couldn't repair stopped working, she just did without. Which was why the front doorbell didn't ring and the heat in the bedrooms was nonexistent.

Last December, when the plumbing had backed up, she'd been forced to pay the plumber out of her own pocket, which had meant an even slimmer Christmas than usual.

Well, as soon as she could manage, she would follow the others who had given up and moved away. And then the whole block would be deserted. She had sworn, when she was a kid living in a San Jose public housing project, that she would never live in one as an adult, but she'd been forced a few months ago to swallow her pride and put her name on the waiting list for public housing. Eventually, unless she found a way to better herself, she would raise her kids in a city housing project, thus perpetuating the family tradition.

She heard the kids even before she inserted her key in the front door lock. Tommy must have talked Laurie into playing one of the games he was always inventing because, as she moved down the hall, she heard Laurie complaining that he kept changing the rules to suit himself.

Typical Tommy, she thought, but she was smiling as she put the mesh bags of groceries on the sink drain board, then unnoticed, turned into the living room. She pulled off her head scarf and slid out of her all-weather coat. Absently rubbing the circulation back into her numb arms, she watched her two kids, her heart swelling with pride.

Laurie was seven—a golden-haired, fairy-tale princess of a child with her mother's green eyes and her father's fair hair—and a deep cheek dimple that was all her own. Tommy, who had his mother's coloring, was nine, going on ten. His whip-lean body had the grace of a born athlete, but this was deceptive because his interests lay in another direction: in anything that challenged his mind. Games, the more difficult the better, were his passion, and already he was doing sixth grade math although he was only in the third grade.

Stormy sometimes worried about that, about him not fitting the norm, but she was also inordinately proud of his clever, always curious mind.

"Hi, kids—how about a hug for your mom?" she said.

Laurie and Tommy abandoned their game and pounced on Stormy, collecting their evening kiss and hug. Stormy gave Laurie an extra hug. There had been so many months that she'd lived with fear. Now Laurie was almost back to normal, well enough to go to school again, but she herself still had mental relapses into those dark times.

Which was why her voice came out a little husky when she asked, "Whose turn is it to help me get supper?"

"Laurie's," Tommy said.

"Tommy's," Laurie said, just as promptly.

"Oh? So we've lost track, have we? So both of you can help. Laurie, you set the table, and Tommy, you can help me in the kitchen."

"What's for supper?" Tommy, who was always hungry, asked.

"Beans and rice," she said.

"Aw, Mom, we've had beans twice already this week," he complained.

"So how about spaghetti?"

"What kind of sauce?"

"Tomato."

"We had that once already—last Monday."

Stormy smiled at him. "Then how about fried chicken and mashed potatoes?" she said.

Tommy's eyes, as green as her own behind large, round glasses that dwarfed his face, lit up. "Wow! You hit the lotto or something, Mom?"

"I should be so lucky. As it happens I got my first paycheck today. How about that?"

"Hey, great." He fixed her with a surprisingly mature stare. "Does this mean we don't have to sign up for free school lunches anymore?"

She swallowed hard. "Tommy—you know the reason for that. I'm working again but we still have to tighten—"

"—our belts," he said, grinning at her.

"Okay, okay. So I use trite phrases. Better than cursing."

"Right. Hey, Mom, you got a letter. I had to sign for it," he said importantly. "It's on the kitchen table. It's real, y'know, official looking."

Stormy's heart sank. Official-looking letters, especially ones that came by registered mail, meant trouble. Was it an overdue bill? But she'd paid her bills at the beginning of the month. It probably was some kind of advertising gimmick....

But it wasn't an advertisement. She stared at the return address for a long time, summoning her nerve. South San Jose Realty—was it another raise in the rent? Even a small increase would be a disaster.

She took a long breath and opened the envelope. With growing disbelief, she read the letter inside.

Eviction? How was that possible—and not only an eviction notice, but a final one. What did this sentence mean, that she'd already had two notices and had been given two extensions?

"But—that's not true," she said aloud. "I don't owe three months' rent—I have receipts to prove I pay my rent on time every month."

She groped backward for a chair, her legs suddenly weak. Fear, instinctive and sharp, washed through her. *Homeless....* That terrible word, the dread she lived with every day of her life. For a while, she'd been one of them, the homeless living on the streets of San Jose who couldn't even qualify for public relief because she'd had no address. The ones who slept in shelters, as she had, or lived in cars or in cardboard boxes in some alley, their eyes empty and lost.

In the richest country in the world, the homeless were a reproach to everyone, so many of them people who once having fallen between the cracks just couldn't get back out. Stormy took a deep breath, using reason to fight back the fear and panic. It was a mistake, one of those crazy things that happen in a computerized world. All she had to do was prove it. She'd always managed to scrape together rent money, even when they did without other things, because she had this deep, overwhelming fear of being homeless again.

Her outrage soared, and she was tempted to tear the letter in two and throw it in the garbage. But of course she didn't. No matter that it was a mistake, it still had to be dealt with.

She read the letter again, hoping that she'd misread it or perhaps misunderstood what it was saying. But she hadn't made a mistake. It was a final eviction notice and it gave her three days to vacate the cottage or be forcibly evicted.

Swallowing hard and fighting nausea, she folded the letter and stuffed it into the back pocket of her jeans. With Tommy's insatiable curiosity, it wouldn't do to leave it lying around.

She began putting away the groceries, and when Tommy came into help with supper preparations, she even managed to produce a credible smile. The novelty of having chicken for a weekday meal kept Tommy occupied and diverted his attention from the letter, for which she was devoutly grateful.

Afterward, when the dishes were done and their cat, Magic, had been fed a special chopped chicken liver dinner, they played a lively game of gin rummy, and since Stormy found it impossible to concentrate, even Laurie swamped her tonight.

For the rest of the evening, while the kids watched their favorite sitcom on the black-and-white TV that a former neighbor had given them, she was silent and lost in thought. After the children were in bed, she sat for a long time, pencil in hand, making a list of the things she must do the next day to straighten out the eviction-notice mess. At least tomorrow was a Saturday, her day off since she was working Sunday this week.

But the next day, when she went to a phone kiosk in the nearby shopping mall, and called the real-estate company, all she got was the runaround.

"Sorry, Ms. Todd. No one's available to talk to you about an eviction notice. You'll have to call back Monday," the woman who answered the phone told her brusquely.

"But the notice only gives me three days and I need to straighten it out right away—"

"I am sorry, but there's nothing I can do. Mr. Mitchell takes care of such matters—and he's left for the day. Like I say, you'll have to call back Monday morning."

The sound of the phone clicking in her ear made Stormy wince. Grimly she deposited more coins into the pay phone and dialed again, but this time there was no answer, and she was finally forced to give up. Three days, the notice had said—which meant that she must reach someone, do something by Monday morning, because what if the letter didn't mean three business days? What if Monday was eviction day?

Well, she couldn't just wait around and hope for the best. She would have to take matters into her own hands and—and what? How could she get the attention of those people? She was sure the woman at the real-estate office had deliberately brushed her off. As soon as she'd given her name, even before she'd stated her business, it seemed the temperature at the other end of the line had dropped fifty degrees.

One thing they couldn't very well ignore was bad publicity, only—who could she turn to? Who gave a damn about the problems of one single mother?

A memory stirred, then crystallized in her mind. There *was* that woman columnist—what was her name? Clara—no, Claudia Benson. She had a daily column in the *Bayside News* and she was always taking up the causes of people in trouble who had nowhere else to turn. Maybe, if she could interest the columnist in her problem, something could be done to straighten things out.

Stormy dropped more coins into the slot, dialed information and got the number of the *Bayside News*. When she reached the newspaper and asked for Claudia Benson, she was connected immediately.

"Yes?" a feminine voice asked.

"You don't know me, Ms. Benson—"

"Oh, do call me Claudia. How can I help you? Start by telling me your name."

"Todd. Stormy Todd."

"Stormy? Are you in show business?"

"No—that's my legal name."

"Interesting...so how can I help you, Stormy?"

"I understand that you sometimes assist people who—well, who are in trouble and have no place else to turn to."

"Sometimes. So what's your story?"

Quickly, Stormy related the circumstances—the eviction notice, her attempts to reach the real-estate company, her suspicion that she had just been given the runaround. The woman listened silently, and when she didn't interrupt with any questions, Stormy knew, even before Claudia spoke, what her answer would be.

"Well, you certainly have a beef. The trouble is that I have any number of similar stories and I can't print them all. Why don't you contact the sheriff's department at city hall? They handle evictions—they're the people you want to talk to."

Stormy thanked her dully and was about to hang up when Claudia added, "Leave your phone number and I'll see what I can do. I can't promise anything, of course."

"I don't have a phone but you can reach me at..." Stormy gave her address, even though she knew from the disinterest in the columnist's voice that she was merely being polite.

After all, how important could the problems of one single mother be when dozens just like her were being evicted from apartments and other rentals in the city every year? Well, that didn't mean that she was going to give up. There had to be some way to stop this eviction—and wasn't it strange that when the chips were down, she always had to solve her own troubles?

CHAPTER TWO

CLAUDIA BENSON wasn't really her name. It was a generic name, adopted for convenience by a series of writers who had taken over the column called "Claudia Speaks" at the *Bayside News* from time to time. She'd been born Sylvia Frost and she was young, ambitious and, at present, very frustrated because, in her opinion, she'd been stuck far too long in a dead-end job.

What she wanted, yearned for, was to be one of the boys, to share in the camaraderie of the paper's journalists, the "real" reporters. Writing sob stories about little old ladies who had lost their dogs—or single mothers being evicted for nonpayment of rent—was just not her bag.

Although she'd been polite to Stormy Todd, and had even taken down her address, she had no interest in pursuing what she considered to be a humdrum and unimportant story. She had already dismissed Stormy Todd from her mind and was taking her hobo-bag purse from a desk drawer, preparing to leave for an early lunch, when Bob Ryder, her immediate boss and the assistant city editor of the *Bayside News*, spoke behind her.

"What was that all about, Syl? You sure brushed her off quick."

Sylvia shrugged. "Nothing important. Another eviction case. I get a couple of them every week. The lady claims she doesn't owe any back rent and that she didn't get the first two eviction notices. Have you noticed? Nobody ever does—or so they always claim. Even if it's true in this case, it isn't worth following up."

She gave him her best smile. "I'm on my way out, boss. I've got a hot lunch date with a new man and I'm already late. He's waiting for me at that new Thai place near the plaza...."

Her voice trailed off since it was obvious Bob wasn't listening.

"That address you took down—didn't I hear you say April Street?"

Hiding her impatience, Syliva glanced down at her pad. "Right, 423 April Street. That mean anything to you, Bob?"

"It might. Seems to me... wait here a minute. I want to look something up." He disappeared into his office. Sylvia glanced down at her watch and made a face. She was already twelve minutes late—and her new boyfriend was the impatient type. On the other hand, Bob Ryder *was* her boss, the man who handed out hot assignments, pay raises and all that jazz.

As soon as Bob reappeared, she knew he was on to something. There was a gleam in his eye that only appeared when he was going for someone's jugular. Who was it this time? Thank God it wasn't her....

"Got it. That's one of the streets Guy Harris's new housing project is slated for. It's controlled by—hell, what's the name of that real-estate company? South San Jose Realty, I think it is. It's part of the blind trust Harris set up last year when he went into politics and decided to run for mayor. But it's still one of his holdings, all right. Now I wonder what the hell's going on? Evicting that woman—what did she tell you about herself, Syl?"

"Single mother, two small kids, works at a take-out pizza parlor." Her voice was cool because she hated being called Syl. "Claims her rent is paid up, that she never got even one notice, much less two, which could or could not be the truth. Take your pick."

"Too bad she isn't an elderly widow. Now that'd really make it a weeper. But a single mother, working at a minimum wage job, two kids to support—yeah, that's not bad. Not bad at all."

Sylvia was silent, already knowing what was coming—and resenting it in advance. Bob fixed her with a hard look. "I want you to get out there to that address and interview her. And I'm talking about right now. Get whatever you can that will put Harris in a bad light. If it's something solid, I want it out in tomorrow's paper. Meanwhile, I'll contact the old man and see what he thinks. This is bound to interest him, the kind of grudge he's got about Harris. And who knows? Maybe both of us can score some points over this."

At her suddenly interested stare, he grinned wolfishly. "It's just possible that we've finally got something to hang on that bastard, Harris. Let's see the great white political hope wriggle out of this. When we get through with him, he's going to look like a real dyed-in-the-wool jerk, the most insensitive money-grubber in California."

GUY HARRIS stood with his back to his spacious office, staring out one of the ceiling-to-floor windows that overlooked the busy downtown streets of San Jose. His reflection, against a dark, rain-drenched sky, stared back at him, reminding him of the time a reporter from *Financial Beat* had taken a picture, not of him, but of his image as it appeared in that very same window looking dark-hued and, Guy thought at the time, a little sinister.

The piece the reporter had written about him had described his craggy features, his powerful build, his thick, dark red hair. Then it had gone on to say that Guy Harris was something of a mystery man among other real-estate titans, that he was especially effective in his financial dealings because he had no weaknesses, no Achilles' heel.

Now, as Guy studied his image in the window, he reflected that the article had been wrong. He did have weaknesses. And what were those weaknesses? Too much pride, impatience with people who didn't see things his way, the determination to never again be caught in the position of having to take orders from other people. God knows he'd had his fill of that sort of helplessness when he was a kid.

He took no particular pride in the wealth and power he'd accumulated in his thirty-six years of life, but only in the fact that he had fought back relentlessly every step of the way, had achieved his success all on his own, and had never retreated from any battle, no matter how large or how small....

The other occupant of the room spoke, asking him a question, and he turned his head to look at her. Marilyn—his good right arm, the woman who had become, if not indispensable, at least more important than any other person in his life.

But did he want more? It was no secret that Marilyn expected him to propose eventually—not that he'd given her any reason to believe she would become Mrs. Harris someday and share his life. No, he'd played it cool—as always.

The object was to win, whether in business or at games or even when courting a woman's favors. Those early years, when he'd struggled so hard, working at a dozen part-time jobs while carrying a full load of classes at San Jose State, he'd lost as often as he'd won. But that had changed once he learned how to handle his priorities. He'd made a lot of mistakes, but he'd never made the same one twice.

Friendships and serious relationships with women had been things he'd put on hold. Only one woman, back in college, had ever gotten past his guard. She'd been sexy, bright, a real charmer, and he'd fallen hard for her only to have her zap him for all she was worth and go off with another man. It had taken him a long time to get over his disillusionment—and he'd never made the mistake of letting down his guard with a woman since.

But his single excursion into love, at an age and time in his life when he was most vulnerable, had left its scars—along with earlier encounters with the female sex. Even before his one youthful lapse, he'd never had any good reason to trust the female half of the population.

The first woman in his life had been his natural mother—who ever she had been. An hour after his birth, she had dumped him into a trash can, left him there to die of exposure—or to be eaten alive by alley rats. That someone had heard his cry and rescued him in time, she couldn't possibly have known would happen.

And later, the various foster mothers who'd taken care of him along the way hadn't given him any reason to believe in the essential goodness of women. A rational part of his mind told him that he'd had a series of unlucky draws, that there were plenty of fine, compassionate women who took in foster children to raise and gave them the best of loving care. But this realization had come later, when he was an adult. As a child, he had been convinced that all women were manipulators, predators, tricky to deal with, dangerous to trust.

Which was why he had never committed himself to a woman, not even, come to think of it, to that girl in college. Was that why she'd ditched him and married another man?

Oh, he had romanced his share—maybe more than his share—of women. He was a normal man, maybe even more highly sexed than others, but he never became involved in a relationship with the expectation that it would be permanent. Some women may have wanted marriage, even expected it, but that wasn't his concern. He was always up-front with them right from the first date, had never lied or pretended a commitment he couldn't fulfill.

And none of them had been hurt. He would swear that not one of the women he'd become involved with had come away with anything more than pique that they hadn't managed to land—what was it one reporter had called him?—the most eligible bachelor in San Jose?

His eyes brooded on Marilyn now as she read aloud the results of a recent opinion poll. She was undeniably beautiful, with her well-coiffed blond hair, her slender body, her exquisite face. Was she the one he should marry? A wife, the right one, would be invaluable to him if he won the mayor's race, especially someone like Marilyn, who was practical, capable, and who shared his goals. That she'd chosen him as her entry to the kind of life she wanted rather than from any deeper personal feeling for him didn't turn him off. Hell, what was wrong with being ambitious?

Yes, she fit the bill, all right. She was beautiful and smart, good company—and also great in bed. She even had a sense of humor—or at least she laughed at his jokes. Just what he wanted, right? A helpmate who would work at his side to bring his dreams to fruition.

And he did have his dreams. Some would call them his ambitions, but he didn't see it that way. He wanted to be mayor of San Jose, but not for personal glory. He had a real commitment to the city, to bettering it. He'd worked hard for everything he'd acquired, but would his success have been possible in another town, one cast in stone like San Francisco, their glamorous neighbor to the north? No, it had been pure luck that he'd been born in San Jose, a bustling, hustling, upward moving, open town. So he owed his hometown a lot—and he always paid his debts. This was one characteristic that reporter from *Financial Beat* had forgotten to list....

"Did you hear me, Guy?" There was a hint of exasperation in Marilyn's cool voice. "I asked what you want me to do with this report?"

"Report?"

"The latest opinion poll. Do you want me to file it away with the other?"

"What else? Why are you asking me that when you know the answer?" he said, smiling at her.

"To get your attention. You haven't heard a word I've said for the past five minutes."

"Sorry about that. My mind seems to be wandering today."

"Well, that's understandable. This poll puts you right on top."

"For now. Election is still six months away," he said dryly. "My worthy opponent hasn't even officially announced his candidacy yet."

"Maybe he's afraid to. This poll shows how the wind is blowing. Out with the old and in with the new." She picked up the report and put it away in a file-cabinet drawer.

Guy eyed her thoughtfully. She always looked so unruffled, so unapproachable, but that was an illusion. When he made love to her, she returned his passion with surprising energy. Or was *that* the real illusion? Strange—usually he could tell when a woman was faking it. With Marilyn, it was impossible to be sure...

The office door swung open and a short, stocky man came bustling in. Guy felt a sting of annoyance. He'd always been jealous of his privacy, having had so little of it as a kid. And Larry Singer, his campaign manager, had developed a tendency lately of barging into his office at will without bothering to knock. Even though Larry was a long-time business associate, as well as his campaign manager, a knock was surely called for.

"Did you see this?" Larry demanded, waving a newspaper at Guy. His normally pale face was flushed, and his eyes, usually so cold, were blazing with strong emotion. "The nerve of this *Bayside News* rag—it's obviously a setup. Ever since the polls started going your way, the rats have been coming out of the woodwork."

He slapped the paper down on the desk in front of Guy and pointed at a column. "Read it—it's enough to make you throw up."

Guy read the column, and his own anger stirred. The columnist—Claudia Benson she called herself—specialized in "human interest" stories, and this one was a real tearjerker. A young single mother with two kids, no money or family to rely on, turned out of her home by a ruthless and insensitive landlord. Oh, it was cleverly worded. No grounds here for a libel suit. But its sly innuendoes made it very clear that he, Guy Harris, was the evil landlord who had done this wicked deed. It was so overdone and melodramatic that it should have been funny. Not so surprisingly, he didn't feel like laughing.

"Hell," he said explosively.

"Hell is right. A real hatchet job by that scum bag, Harvey Cummins. He's never forgotten that you won that lawsuit against him. Thought that with his newspaper behind him and a tribe of top lawyers representing him, he could have things his own way in this town. Well, he lost that suit, but he makes a bad enemy, Guy. I wonder how far he intends to go with this business?"

"No one's going to pay any attention to this kind of trash," Guy said, his tone deliberately mild.

He wasn't surprised at Larry's short, explosive expletive. "You think not? Your honored opponent, the mayor, is probably rubbing his hands with glee right now. And others will be paying attention to it—the other party, for instance. There's a lot of voters out there who believe anything they read in the papers. What we need is a retraction from Claudia Benson."

"We'll never get that," Guy said with conviction.

"Right. So we'll have to use a different tactic. What we have to do is expose this as a bunch of lies—and as quickly as possible. And for that, we need documentation that this woman, who is several months arrears in her rent, was given two chances to pay up and didn't take advantage of either of them."

"You're sure this part is true?"

"It's true." Larry slapped a brown folder on the desk in front of Guy. "This is a private investigator's report Clyde Farris sent over from South San Jose Realty. He ran a check on the woman after she ignored the first overdue rent notice. When he read that piece in the *Bayside News* this morning, he sent this over by messenger. He knew we'd want to see this—he's one shrewd dude."

Guy nodded his agreement. Clyde Farris was the manager of South San Jose Realty, one of the businesses he'd put in the blind trust two years ago when he'd decided to run for mayor. The man was indeed a shrewd businessman. For the past three years, even before the realty company went into the trust, Farris had been in charge of the

April Street development project. So far, he'd done more than a credible job of gradually vacating the property.

Guy scanned the report on Stormy Todd quickly. Two eviction notices, sent by registered mail and both signed for by Stormy Todd; two extensions, each giving her three months to pay her back rent or vacate the cottage on April Street. There was also a report on the woman, dated several months ago, signed by a reputable local detective agency. Single, two kids, a seven-year-old girl and a nine-year-old boy, an unwed mother—or at least there was no evidence that she'd ever been married, no job, on county welfare...

"Not a very impressive record," he said, finally looking up from the report. He handed it to Marilyn to read.

"A freeloader, out to get all she can. You'll notice that notation in her welfare record. Something about a charge of fraud—which was dropped," Larry said contemptuously. "If you ask me, she's hanging on there, refusing to vacate in hopes of getting a big relocation settlement. Clyde Farris tells me she's the only holdout now. Got tired of waiting for a big plum to drop in her lap, so she went public. Someone's put her up to this, told her that you're vulnerable because you're running for mayor. Now she's trying a little blackmail. Well, it won't work. Once we air this report—and we should get on it as quickly as possible—the ball will be in our court. After all, your holdings are in a blind trust. You didn't have anything to do with the eviction notices."

Guy started to speak, but Marilyn put her hand on his arm, stopping him. "Why don't we let Uncle Clyde handle it, Guy? You know that you can trust him to do what's right."

Guy started to nod agreement, then changed his mind. Clyde Farris was Marilyn's uncle, and while he'd never found any reason to distrust the man's judgment, he discovered he was unwilling to turn this business over to him—at least, not until he'd satisfied his own curiosity.

"I think I'll go have a talk with this—uh, Stormy Todd," he said aloud. "It's just possible it's some kind of mistake that can be cleared up without any fuss."

"Come on! You don't want to get involved," Larry said, sounding shocked.

"I agree," Marilyn chimed in. "It can only cause more gossip. Let Uncle Clyde handle it."

Suddenly it occurred to Guy how often, these days, the two of them agreed on just how he should conduct himself. It may have been this or his own gut instincts, honed on the meaner streets of San Jose, that made him decide to talk to the woman. After all, it was his hide she was trying to nail to the wall.

"I'm going to have a talk with her," he said. "It might be as easy as offering to forget the past-due rent if she vacates immediately. We could even pay her moving expenses."

Larry made a gesture, as if washing his hands of the whole business. "Yeah, and if that fails, you can always exert that legendary charm of yours," he said.

CHAPTER THREE

IT HAD BEEN A LONG TIME since Guy had been on April Street. He remembered it as a friendly neighborhood of small families, old people in retirement and young couples just getting started in life. He'd purchased the holdings, including two adjacent streets and a wide undeveloped area, from an entrepreneur who had bought up the cottages, one by one, with the plan of razing them and then using the land for an industrial park. Because of city zoning problems, and a gross overextension of credit, the man had gone bankrupt instead.

Since the price of the property was irresistible, Guy had bought it with the idea of renovating the bungalows and turning them into quality rentals. Then the new California earthquake standards bill had been passed, and he'd put his engineers to work, surveying and evaluating the cottages, most of which had been built during the building boom that followed World War II. When the results of the survey came in, he'd quickly realized that the cost of upgrading them to meet the new standards would be prohibitive.

It was then he'd decided to utilize the prime location of the site, within easy commuting distance of the city's downtown business district, to eventually construct a complex of luxury town houses. Since he'd been in the midst of several other projects, including a new shopping center, there had been no need for mass evictions. Instead he'd decided to use natural attrition to vacate the cottages.

Only absolutely necessary repairs would be made, and when people moved out, the cottages they'd occupied would immediately be boarded up. Eventually, seeing the handwriting on the wall, they would all move—and there'd be few hard feelings because they wouldn't be under any particular pressure.

Having made this decision, he turned the property over to Clyde Farris, the manager of one of his real-estate companies, to handle. It had been a costly process, both in time and lost rent revenues, but it was obvious from the rows of empty bungalows he was now driving past that it was finally coming to fruition. In a few minutes, he would find out to his satisfaction what was behind this sudden snag in the plan that, until now, had proceeded without too many problems.

Larry was probably right about the woman, that she was a freeloader, he reflected. If she was the lone holdout, something suspicious could very well be going on. Either she was an opportunist, hoping for a large relocation settlement, or she was in cahoots with Harvey Cumins, the owner of the *Bayside News*, who was using this situation to smear the man who'd bested him in an important landmark court case.

Larry, Guy reflected a little ruefully, was also right to question his personal interference. He wasn't even sure, come to think of it, if it was legal, his coming here. After all, he *had* established that blind trust, which prohibited him from direct involvement with the businesses he owned, to forestall any accusations that his judgment as mayor, should he be elected, was self-serving.

When he'd decided to run for office, he'd checked into the problem of conflict of interest thoroughly. Since he was mainly in the construction and real-estate business, he was particularly vulnerable. Hence the blind trust. Until now, there had been no problems.

Briefly he brooded over his wisdom in coming here, then shrugged it off. He'd been accused often of stubbornness—and something stubborn in him refused to retreat. The truth was that he detested freeloaders, opportunists who took advantage of other people's vulnerabilities. He seldom played their game, but in this case—yes, maybe he could see his way clear to pay the Todd woman a reasonable relocation fee, provided she was willing to retract the accusation she'd made against him in that gossip column.

Just thinking of that blasted column made the back of his neck burn. Hell, he wasn't any of the things she'd called him. A shrewd and competent businessman, yes. A slumlord, no. Someone who knew what he wanted and thrived on competition, yes. But he'd never knowingly cheated anyone in his life. The opposite, in fact. Not that he intended to defend himself to this—this Stormy Todd. Now *that* sounded like a phony name if he'd ever heard one.

He didn't have to search for the address. Up ahead, he saw a postage-stamp-size yard of lush grass and the cheery color of spring annuals. Sandwiched between the dried-up years of its neighbors, it looked like a small oasis. So the Todd woman was a green thumber. The pertinent question here: what else was Stormy Todd?

He parked his Mercedes in front of the cottage, and got out. The gate was standing open, and as he went up a path of worn red brick, he was bemused by the sight of a bird feeder, obviously homemade, that dangled from the ferny branch of a mimosa tree. So the Todd woman also like birds—or someone here did.

The cheeriness of the yard ended at the porch. Not only was the paint weathered and peeling, but the top step had been recently repaired. The cottage, too, was long overdue for a paint job, and when he rang the doorbell, there was no sound inside. He finally resorted to knocking, waited for a few moments, and then knocked again.

The door swung open, revealing a small, dark-haired boy. Although Guy's experience with children was minimal, he assumed the boy was nine, as stated in the investigator's report on Stormy Todd. He was holding a cat, which was limply draped over his arm. It had a black mask of a face and two very blue, slightly crossed eyes.

The boy stared at him, not speaking; his eyes, dark green and obviously very curious, were owllike behind round glasses that swamped his small, triangular face. His build was on the slight side, but there was something mature—or maybe it was knowing—in his steady regard that reminded Guy of himself at that age.

Nine going on forty, he thought, suppressing a smile.

"I'd like to speak to your mother," he said.

The boy hesitated, looking wary. The cat wriggled free, bounded to the floor and came over to sniff Guy's ankle. Since his experience with cats was as limited as his experience with children, he was a little nonplussed when a rough purr emitted from the cat's throat and it began rubbing its face against his pant leg.

Evidently passing muster with the cat made him acceptable to the boy because he stood back to let Guy enter.

He pointed down the hall. "She's in the living room," he said.

Although Guy was silent as he followed the boy down the hall, he was tempted to chide him for letting a stranger into the house so easily. He couldn't help wondering, from the boy's quick acceptance, how many strange men Stormy

Todd, single welfare mother, had entertained through the years.

The boy disappeared through a door at the end of the hall. When Guy followed him through the open doorway, he paused, staring into a small, sparsely furnished room. A teenage girl and a small child were sitting on a shabby couch, their heads close together. The teenager, dressed in washed-out jeans and a voluminous sweatshirt, was telling the child a story. From what Guy could hear it involved a girl named Laurie who lived in a barn with a large population of farm animals, all of whom could speak.

As she talked, the girl illustrated the story with drawings on a pad of yellow paper that rested on her knees. Completely absorbed in the story, neither noticed him, and Guy had the random thought that the kids were lucky to have such a devoted—and imaginative—baby-sitter.

He looked around the shabby room, taking in its tidiness, and the attempts to beautify it with a profusion of what he recognized as sweet potato vines in mason jars and a series of black-and-white charcoal drawings, matted but unframed, on the wall. Most of the sketches were animals, some domesticated but mostly wild, with a few clever human caricatures mixed in.

Unexpectedly a mental picture of the last of his numerous foster homes, a barren, ill-smelling flat on the fringes of the city's downtown area, flashed through his mind. The slovenly woman who'd been his foster mother had made no attempts to make things more cheerful, not even with a sweet potato vine in a mason jar of water....

Oddly the memory activated his irritation at the Todd woman. Not stopping to figure out why, he took a step forward, into the room, prepared to demand to see Mrs.—no, *Miss* Todd. It didn't help his mood that when the teenager looked up and saw him, she immediately jumped to her feet, her hands balled into fists.

"Who the hell are you—and what are you doing here?" she demanded.

"Ah, he's okay," the boy said.

It only took Guy a few seconds to pull out his wallet and show her his ID. He assured her that he was not a thief, that he had come here to see Stormy Todd about a business matter.

"I'm Stormy Todd," she said. "What kind of business matter are you talking about?"

Now that he was closer, Guy could see that she was a grown woman, although slightly built. She also had the greenest eyes he'd ever seen and a skin that could rival any teenager's. As for her hair—the words "polished ebony" came to his mind.

"I'm here to discuss the eviction order," he said.

Her eyes darkened almost to black. "You're Mr. Mitchell? That wasn't the name on your ID card. In fact—of course! Guy Harris—you're the slumlord who's been trying to evict me."

Her face, which had looked pale, took on an ominous flush now. "Well, it won't work," she said, her eyes flashing. "My rent is paid up until the first of next month. I was only behind that one time, and that was two years ago. I don't know what your game is, but I have no intention of leaving, even if this dump *is* falling down around our heads, not until I find another place I can afford. And I didn't get any prior notices, not even one, so you can just get on out of here. I don't know how you have the nerve to come here, anyway. You're nothing but a racketeer—"

"Now hold on. You did get prior notice to vacate. The letters were sent by registered mail and you signed for both of them. You've had ample time to find a place."

"The only registered letters from that—that real-estate company I ever signed were responses to complaints about the condition of the bungalow. Even if your accusations were true, which they absolutely are not, where am I supposed to move to? I can barely afford the rent here, what with a four percent rent raise every year. And I *have* looked everywhere. There just isn't anything in my price range."

"What about public housing? You must qualify, being on welfare—"

Her eyes blazed; for a moment he was sure she would attack him. She turned her head stiffly and looked at her children, both of whom were listening with solemn faces. "Go to your room, kids," she said. "I want to talk to Mr. Harris in private."

"Aw, Mom, I wanna stay. What if you need help, like you have to throw this turkey out?" the boy protested.

The girl took her thumb out of her mouth long enough to say, "I wanna stay, too."

"No arguing. Off you go, kids—and close the door behind you."

"You should have a witness, Mom," the boy said earnestly. "You know, in case he says something you can sue him over."

"Out—both of you," she said, pointing at the door.

She waited until they were gone before she swung back to Guy.

"How come you know so much about my private business?" she demanded. "Claudia Benson's column didn't say anything about me being on welfare. Anyway, it isn't true, not any longer. I got a job last week—and besides, that letter your company sent was a lie. I don't owe you any rent. And how many times do I have to tell you that I did *not* get any eviction notices, much less sign for them?"

"Are you saying you aren't six months behind on your rent?"

"I am not. I have the rent receipts to prove it, too. It's all a big lie."

Guy was silent, studying her and wishing he could read her mind. How strange—she wore no makeup, and her clothes were worn-to-the-nub, but she still was a knockout. Her black hair, glossy and thick, covered her head in a mass of curls, which he was sure were natural; her eyelids were as lineless and creamy smooth as a baby's, and her mouth tilted up at the corners as if it was more used to smiling than frowning.

As for the rest of her, she was small, yes, but she was all woman with those high, cone-shaped breasts, narrow waist and long slender legs. How old was she, anyway? Certainly, not a teenager, not with a nine-year-old son...

"What is it?" she said sharply. "You're looking at me like I have two heads. If you don't believe me, I can show you the rent receipts."

"I believe you. And I was thinking that—well, that it's obvious there's been some sort of mix-up. And since you've been put through so much stress, I want to apologize and assure you that my—that the real-estate company will drop the eviction proceedings. In fact, I can guarantee that you won't be bothered again."

He hadn't realized how much of her belligerence stemmed from fear until her whole body sagged with relief and her eyes took on a brightness that he suspected were tears.

"Thank you, Mr. Harris." She swallowed hard and then came up with a smile. "Would you like some tea and cookies?"

Before he could answer, the kids were back in the room. He realized that they must have been listening—and from the expression on their mother's face, so did she. But she didn't scold them. Instead she told Tommy to put the kettle on for tea and Laurie to get out some of those oatmeal cookies she'd made yesterday.

The boy gave Guy a sheepish look and sidled up to whisper something in his mother's ear.

"I'm afraid we're out of cookies," she said. "But we do have tea."

"Tea will be fine," he said and then wondered why he was prolonging his visit.

After the children left the room, he settled himself, at Stormy's invitation, on the lumpy couch. The cat promptly appropriated his lap and began making bread on his knee, purring loudly.

"You can push her off if you like," Stormy said. "She doesn't usually make up to strangers so quickly."

"I don't mind if she doesn't," he said. "She's rather—unusual, isn't she? What breed is this?"

"I'm not really sure. I just call her a long-haired Siamese. She turned up on the doorstep a couple of years ago. That tag on her neck said Magic, so that's what we call her." She smiled suddenly. "It's really an appropriate name. There's something—well, magical about her at times. I guess she'd been abandoned, but it seemed strange when she's such a—a loving cat."

Laurie came back into the room. She was holding a rather bedraggled doll. "This is Flame," she said. "I adopted her at Christmas 'stead of getting a new dolly."

"She's very nice," he said, staring at the doll's faded, slightly battered face. Did adopted mean that she was secondhand—like from a Salvation Army store? If so, Flame was a lot luckier in foster mothers than he'd ever been.

Tommy came back into the room, carefully balancing two cups of tea on a tray.

"You wanna play some cards?" he asked hopefully after Guy had tasted the tea and declared it neither too strong nor too weak. "There's this new game I just made up. You use a regular deck of cards, but the idea is to add up the numbers in your hand. Clubs get an extra point and hearts the lowest..."

He went on to describe what seemed to be a rather complicated set of rules. His voice was casual, but there was a predatory gleam in his green eyes that alerted Guy. He wasn't surprised when Tommy added, his voice elaborately casual, "If you wanna make it more interesting, we can play for money. Say, a penny a point?"

His mother gave him a hard look. "Knock it off, Tommy. He's a real card shark, Mr. Harris," she told Guy. "If he gets the chance, he'll end up with all your change."

"I'm not so bad at cards myself," Guy said amused.

By the time he left, an hour later, it was obvious to Guy that Stormy had been right. If they had been playing for money, he would have lost all the change in his pocket—and a couple of bills, too. He'd also made a judgment of sorts about Stormy Todd. Unwed mother or not, he would swear that she wasn't a woman who jumped into bed with any man that came along. Her attitude toward him had been one of friendly reserve, and there'd been no come-ons, no man-woman games, which was more than he could say about most of the women he met.

Maybe he was being softheaded, but he believed that she really hadn't received those first two eviction notices. Nor did he need the receipts she insisted on showing him to believe that her rent was paid up-to-date. In fact, he intended to investigate this whole business as soon as possible. It could be an honest mistake, a clerical error—or it could be overzealousness on the part of Clyde Farris. Either way, he intended to find out the truth.

He was driving across town, headed home, when he spotted a toy shop that was still open for business. On impulse he parked and went inside. The shop was almost empty and there was only one clerk, a middle-aged woman who directed him to the doll section in the rear of the store.

One doll caught his fancy immediately. It had a cloth body, a porcelain head and was wearing a calico dress, straight out of the Old West. It also had blue eyes, golden hair, and the same wistful expression as Laurie Todd.

He was carrying it to the cash register when he passed a display of games. He stopped to browse through them, finally chose a new version of Trivia, which was touted as being suitable for "twelve and up." Of course, Tommy was three years younger, but somehow he was sure the game would be just right for the boy.

The next evening, when he was leaving his apartment, on his way to pick up Marilyn for a dinner date, he decided, on impulse, to drop the toys off at the Todd house. He told himself that it would be killing two birds with one stone since he wanted to tell Stormy that he'd ordered his assistant to contact Clyde Farris, the manager of South San Jose Realty, with instructions to immediately withdraw the eviction action.

The rain that had been threatening all day came down in earnest just as he turned into April Street. Again, it occurred to him how uninviting the street was with the houses boarded up, their windows unlighted. Surely the Todd woman and her kids would be better off, certainly safer, in another neighborhood. He'd have to see if something couldn't be done about relocating her. The company could afford to pay her moving expenses and any rent deposits needed. After all, it would be advantageous to both parties.

His first thought when he saw that the windows of her cottage were dark was disappointment—and then a surprisingly sharp stab of fear. When he realized how inappropriate both emotions were, he told himself to shape up. The woman certainly must have friends, a social life of some kind. Why shouldn't she and the kids be out somewhere? They might even be shopping. After all, it was only a little after eight o'clock...

He was turning the car around in the middle of the street when he saw something else that made him slam on the brakes. Piled on the curb in the deep shadows of a tree was a heap of—what? He squinted, staring, but it was too dark and he couldn't make out any details. Whatever was there under the tree had been covered with what looked to be plastic drop cloths. Inside the opaque plastic, he caught the murky glow of either a candle or a flashlight.

"What the hell—!" he said aloud.

He got out of the car and approached cautiously, unconsciously hunching his shoulders against the pelting rain. Inside the plastic, rippling its wet surface, something was moving. Against the glow of the flashlight, he could make out the outline of a head—was it Stormy? If so, what was she doing, sitting out there on the curb in the rain?

As if he'd spoken the question aloud, a voice rang out. Along with bravado, it held a slight quaver but it was unmistakably Stormy Todd's husky voice.

"I've got a gun. Don't you come any closer or I'll shoot out your lights," she said.

CHAPTER FOUR

STORMY'S EMPLOYER, who was all business and never wasted compliments or smiles on mere employees, had called Stormy into his office as she was punching out at the end of her shift. After first assuring Stormy that her work was satisfactory, he told her that the restaurant was cutting back on its employees. Since she'd been the latest one hired... He ended the sentence with a shrug, avoiding her eyes as if embarrassed.

Stormy stared at him in dismay. There was a hollowness in the pit of her stomach and a sudden lump in her throat that was all too familiar. All her life, she had responded to bad news this way, so she had to swallow hard before she could ask, "You mean you're laying me off?"

"I'm afraid so. As I say, your work is okay. You're a hard worker. As soon as business picks up, I'll contact you and if you're still available, I'll put you back on the payroll."

His face softened, making him look more human. "You can pick up the pay you got coming today before you leave. I told Aggie to add a couple days—sort of a bonus, see? I'm sorry about this, Stormy. It's that street construction the city's doing outside. It's been cutting into our drop-in trade. Of course—" he gave Stormy a wintry smile "—I can probably use you as a temp. You know, when someone calls in sick or takes a vacation."

"But I—" Stormy broke off. After all, why would the fact that she was barely making it on a forty-hour-a-week wage matter to this man? With business slow, he had his own troubles.

"I don't have a phone," she said instead. "But I'll keep in touch."

Somehow she got out of the office without crying, but afterward, she went into the women's rest room, hid herself in a stall for a while, and let the tears come. Laid off...what next? she thought, and then had to smile through her tears because what could possibly top losing your first job in two years just two days after you'd drawn your first paycheck?

But losing her job wasn't the worst, after all. Half an hour later, when she reached home and came up the brick walk, moving slowly while she assumed her "happy" face for the benefit of the kids, three men came around the corner of the house toward her.

They were husky men, dressed in rough work clothes, and her first reaction was fear. When they stopped a few feet away, she realized that they were just as uncomfortable as she, and her fear turned to apprehension. What now? she thought.

One of them, a black man with salt-and-pepper hair, seemed to be having trouble looking at her as he identified himself.

"I'm from the sheriff's department, ma'am. Are you Ms. Todd?"

The blood rushed from her head and she reeled back a step. "My kids—"

"They're fine." He handed her a piece of paper. "Sorry, ma'am. This is an eviction order. We're gonna have to put your things outside on the curb and board up the house."

"But—but that was all taken care of by—" She broke off as realization swept through her. Her disillusionment was almost too much to bear. Another broken promise—how stupid she'd been to believe Guy Harris! But why had he bothered to lie? To make sure she wouldn't call the newspaper to send out a reporter—or maybe so she wouldn't have time to raise the money to pay the past-due rent they claimed she owed them? Or just because he'd found it embarrassing to face her and tell her in front of her kids that he was putting her out on the street?

And I believed him, she thought angrily. *I really did believe him....*

"Our orders were to clear you out immediately," the man was saying, "but since only the kids were here, we decided to wait until you got home. Don't want to be responsible for turning two little kids out in the street."

"But it's too late now to arrange for—for storage," she said. "Can't you wait until morning?"

"Sorry, ma'am. You'll hafta arrange for a friend to keep an eye on your stuff tonight. Orders is orders, you know."

She bit hard on her lower lip. She wanted to scream at him, use some of the language she'd learned as a project kid. But what would be the point of yelling at this man who was only doing his job? The person to blame was Guy Harris. Damn the man anyway! She had actually *believed* his lies. She'd even liked him, thought he was nice....

But she couldn't resist looking the man in the eye and saying, "I wouldn't like to have your job. I'd starve before I took money for evicting people from their homes."

"It's honest work," he said shortly.

She didn't answer, afraid of what else she might say if she lost control of her temper. She unlocked the door and went inside, the men following her. Laurie and Tommy were sitting side by side on the living-room couch. Laurie was sucking her thumb, and Tommy had his arm around her shoulders. From the relief on their faces when she came through the door, Stormy knew how frightened they were. Even so, Tommy tried to brazen it out.

"Those guys said they're from the sheriff's department. You rob a bank or something, Mom?"

Laurie began to cry, and then both of them were in Stormy's arms, huddled up against her. Stormy put her own anger aside and set about explaining there'd been a mistake, but there was nothing they could do about it this late in the day.

"So we're going to have an adventure," she said brightly. "We'll sleep on the street tonight—how about that? We'll curl up on the couch—hey, how about a picnic supper? And in the morning, we'll get this whole mess cleared up."

She set Tommy to work making peanut butter and cheese sandwiches and diverted Laurie's attention by telling her to choose several books and her favorite doll to sleep with. She got out her old canvas suitcase and began packing changes of clothing for herself and the kids.

In the morning, we'll get this whole mess cleared up. How glibly she'd said that—and how unlikely that things would be that easy. When had anything ever been easy for her? Yet—she had weathered worse things, hadn't she? And she'd weather this. A mistake had been made. That she knew for sure. But what if there was no way to clear it up? What if it had been deliberate, Guy Harris's way to get her out of the way?

It clouded up just as the men were piling the last boxes of household goods on the curb. By now, Stormy was numb. The rage that had sustained her as she watched her possessions being carried out through the front door and deposited under the ginkgo tree at the curb had gradually been dulled by despair. Only the necessity of keeping up a front for the sake of the kids kept her from giving up altogether, just walking off down the street, abandoning everything she owned to the threatening rain.

Something in her eyes, although she was sure she was hiding her feelings well, must have given her away to the man in charge of the crew. Silently he went to his pickup truck, got out several plastic drop cloths and began covering her furniture.

"It'll keep out the rain," he said gruffly when he was finished.

She swallowed hard. "How much do I owe you for the drop cloths?" she said.

"They're on the house." He hesitated, then added, "Look, lady, I've got five kids at home to feed or I never would have taken this lousy job. And you gotta realize—most people we evict are total deadbeats. They take advantage of the law to stay as long as they can in a place without paying any rent. Then they move on to the next place and do it all over again. I've evicted some people three, four times. I don't know how you got in this fix, but I don't figure you for a deadbeat. So, good luck. I hope things work out for you, okay."

He was gone before Stormy could thank him.

She took a deep breath, then let it out slowly. When she was sure she wouldn't cry, she turned to grin at the kids.

"Let's boogie," she said, and then when they laughed, she lost the battle and had to turn away again, this time busying herself with making a nest for them for the night.

She made a game of it. She put Tommy to work piling boxes on each side of the couch, then tucked the plastic over it all to form a small enclosed space with plenty of headroom. The rain started in earnest as they were munching the sandwiches Tommy had made, washing them down with milk. Magic, who had vanished when the men appeared, still hadn't turned up, but at Laurie's insistence, Stormy sat a bowl of dry cat food and some milk at the edge of the couch for her.

With a child curled up on each side, so close that she found it hard to move, Stormy read to them from the books Laurie had selected, and then Tommy invented a game that involved naming as many animals as possible, which he won, hands down. Magic appeared, ate her food and drank the milk, then curled up with Laurie at one end of the couch. Both kids fell asleep quickly, but Stormy stayed awake, sitting upright in the middle, afraid to sleep.

The rain, which had slowed to a drizzle, had a somnolent effect on her as it pattered against the plastic covering overhead. She knew she should turn off the flashlight to save the batteries, but there was something so comforting about the light that she left it on.

A question kept haunting her. What if someone came to rip her off? How could she stop them? Who would hear her if she screamed? The street was empty, the last house now boarded up. Well, if anyone came, she'd just have to fake it, bluff her way out of trouble. Meanwhile, there was the long night ahead to get through.

In the morning, she'd—well, she'd think of *something* to do, a way to put their possessions into storage until she needed them again. As for a place to stay, which had to be her first priority tomorrow, she only had what was left of the week's wages, plus the bonus her boss at Pizza King had given her. There was enough to pay for a night at a cheap hotel and—well, things would work out. She had to keep believing that.

The rain stopped and she was acutely aware of the silence. It seemed almost to be alive, harboring all sorts of menace. Since the men had left, only two cars had turned into the street, and both of them had gone right back out again, obviously having made a wrong turn. Of course, it was still pretty early. It was the heavy overcast that made it so dark. Well, the night would pass, and then it would be morning. Everything always looked so much better in the morning, didn't it?

She must have dozed despite her resolve to stay awake because she didn't realize there was a car until it turned around in the street and its headlights fell on her face through the plastic drop cloth. Her heart gave a panicky leap, and began pumping very fast as she heard a car door slam and then the sound of footsteps on the sidewalk, coming up fast.

When the footsteps stopped, just a few feet away, she summoned up all her courage.

"I've got a gun," she said. "Don't you come any closer or I'll shoot out your lights."

GUY WAS COMPLETELY nonplussed when he recognized Stormy's voice although why he should be when it was obvious what had happened, he wasn't sure.

"It's me—Guy Harris," he said. "What the hell are you doing out here on the street?"

The plastic rustled and then Stormy was outside, confronting him. In the beam from the car's headlights, her face was contorted with outrage. Involuntarily he took a step backward, and her lips twisted with contempt.

"Don't worry. I don't really have a gun—lucky for you, you bastard!"

"Okay, I asked a stupid question. It's obvious what happened. Look, I didn't lie to you, Stormy. I gave my assistant explicit orders to cancel that eviction order. Something must have gone wrong—a clerical error or bureaucratic snafu. It takes time to—"

"Liar," she said, her voice so even he might have been fooled if it hadn't been for her clenched fists. "You'd better clear out before I do something I'll regret later—"

"Look, I want to help you. I have no idea what went wrong, but I swear to you that—"

"What went wrong was you lied to me. Don't give me that—that garbage about a clerical error. Okay, you've got what you want. Now you can raze your cottages and build—whatever it is you want to build. But that doesn't mean I have to listen to any more of your lies. Not that I believed you. I knew you were lying all along."

"But you did believe me. And now you feel like a fool. Listen to me—I was telling the truth. And I'm going to fix things up."

"Right. Oh, I'm sure you'll fix things up. Tell me—why did you come here tonight? To make sure the sheriff's men followed orders and put me out? Or maybe you came to gloat. You were really steamed up when that column about you came out, weren't you? As for taking me in with your lies—okay, maybe I did believe you. Big deal. You aren't the first guy who did and I suspect you won't be the last. When it comes to men, I've got rotten judgment."

He started to speak, but her voice overrode his. "Okay, you win. So why don't you shove off? Tomorrow, I'll get someone to cart my junk away and then I'll be out of your hair. Just what you planned when you came snooping around yesterday. And don't take too much credit for this. All the big guns were on your side. It isn't hard to fool a born loser."

"You're not a born loser," he said with conviction. "You're a born fighter. But you don't have to fight me because I wasn't lying to you. I'm going to straighten things out in the morning. But for now—you can't stay out here all night alone—"

"I'm not alone. The kids are with me," she said, her voice tight. "And if you didn't know about this, why are you here?"

"I bought a couple of presents for Tommy and Laurie. I came by to drop them off. We can talk about that later, after I take you to a motel—"

Her whole body seemed to swell. She raised her arm and pointed to his car. "Get the hell out of here before I scratch your eyes out, you bastard!"

"I didn't mean—look, you're going to wake the kids."

As if his words were a signal, Tommy poked his head through the opening in the plastic. "Hey, Mom, what's going down out here?"

"Mr. Harris is just leaving," she said.

"But first I have something for you and your sister," Guy said quickly. He walked away, a little stiff-legged because he hadn't liked her verbal attack—and her assumption. Did she *really* think he'd make a pass at her under these circumstances? Under *any* circumstances? After all, she wasn't exactly his idea of a raving beauty even with those eyes and that mouth. No way was he going to let a feisty-tempered, unreasonable and totally irritating female like that get under his skin....

He got the toys out of the car and returned to Stormy and her kids.

"Here," he said to Tommy, handing him the game. He gave the doll box to Stormy, who for a wonder, was silent now. But not sorry, he thought sourly. No, she wasn't one bit sorry that she'd cussed him out. Nor was she going to apologize...

He watched as Tommy tore the paper off his gift. When the boy's eyes took on a bright shine, he discovered that he didn't mind the water dripping off the tree branch overhead and running down inside the collar of his trench coat.

Without his glasses, Tommy's eyes were strangely vulnerable, and he felt a sudden catch in his throat that startled him.

"Wow," Tommy said softly.

Stormy watched him for a few seconds and then her face softened and she turned to Guy. "So what went wrong?" she asked briskly, and Guy knew he'd won her over—at least, for the moment.

"You can be sure I'm going to make it my business to find out tomorrow," he said grimly. He hesitated briefly, then added, "When I mentioned a motel, I only meant you and the kids needed a place to stay tonight. I wasn't trying to—"

"I know. I was just being bitchy. Why would you come on to me when you can probably have your pick of women?" she said with a reasonableness in her voice that told him she wasn't fishing for compliments. Since this was pretty much what he himself had been thinking earlier, he decided to let it drop.

"Why don't we move to the car?" he said. "It's much more comfortable and I can turn on the heater. I'll call my assistant on the car phone, and have her get someone from the real-estate office down here to guard your belongings until morning. Then I'll take you to a nice quiet motel near that caters to families."

"Hey, that's neat," Tommy said enthusiastically. "I've never been to a motel. We lived in a hotel for a while when I was a real little kid, but it was pretty crummy, lots of roaches and rats, like that. A motel's a lot nicer, right?"

"Right," Stormy said hastily. "Why don't you get our suitcase—and bring Laurie's books and doll, too. She's sleeping so soundly I'll have to carry her to the car."

But it was Guy who carried the sleeping child to the car. She felt so light, almost weightless in his arms, that it occurred to him that even for a seven-year-old girl she was very small. Come to think of it, Tommy was small for his age, too. Heredity? Or didn't the woman feed them properly, for God's sake?

After the kids were settled in the back seat, Laurie still asleep and Tommy reading the game instructions via the dome light, he asked Stormy, "What crummy hotel?"

At first he thought she wasn't going to answer, which wasn't surprising since it was none of his business. In the overhead dome light, her face looked drawn, too pale, and she kept blinking her eyes as if they hurt.

"The Paradise Hotel," she said with obvious reluctance. "It's downtown. The people who live there call it Roach Haven, which is a pretty appropriate name."

Guy nodded his agreement. He knew the hotel, one of several that catered to people on welfare. It was probably the worst of the lot.

"You'd better make that call," she said.

"Right," he answered, but he didn't reach for the phone yet. The rain had started again; it drummed against the roof of the car, and already the windows were beginning to steam up. It came to him that to a passerby, they would look like any ordinary family: father and mother in front, kids in back. Any ordinary family who could afford a Mercedes Benz, he amended.

Tommy, holding the game tightly in his lap as if afraid it might be snatched away, was examining the interior of the car now. "Are you rich, Mr. Harris?" he asked.

"Tommy—that's none of your business," Stormy said sharply.

"It's a natural question," Guy said. "And yes, some people would call me that, Tommy. Others would say I was comfortably off."

"Yeah, that's what I figured. This game cost you thirty-seven dollars plus tax. Man, that's more than Mom makes all day at her job. She's supposed to get tips but people don't tip much in those fast-food places."

"Tommy, Mr. Harris isn't interested in our private affairs."

Tommy grinned at her cheerfully, then returned to his examination of the game. From his absorption in reading the directions, Guy expected him to be an instant expert. He knew he needn't have worried about the game being too advanced for the nine-year-old....

He picked up the phone and reached Marilyn in a matter of minutes.

"Yes?" she said crisply.

"This is Guy. I've run into a problem—you remember the—uh, Ms. Todd, the woman who lives on April Street? Well, I dropped by to leave a couple of toys for her kids and there's been one helluva mix-up. You did notify your uncle that I wanted the eviction notice dropped, didn't you?"

There was a long silence. "Yes, I did. Is something wrong?"

"Very wrong. She's been evicted—her things are sitting on the curb. I want you to call your uncle and tell him, loud and clear, to get someone over here to guard her possessions until morning."

"Doesn't she have friends to do it for her? Why should you get involved?"

He counted to ten, then said, "If you can't handle it, then maybe I'd better call someone else who can, Marilyn."

Again, there was a long silence. "Very well. I know when I've been put in my place. I'll call Uncle Clyde immediately. And what about dinner? Our reservation is for eight—or are you canceling it, Guy?"

Guy resisted the impulse to slap his forehead. "I'll be a little late. I want to get Stormy and her kids settled in a motel for the night—"

"Stormy?"

"Ms. Todd. It shouldn't take very long."

"I certainly hope not."

She didn't say goodbye. The click in his ear made him wince. He dropped the phone back in its cradle and told Stormy, "Okay, it's all arranged. She'll have someone here shortly."

"I hafta go to the bathroom," Laurie said from the back seat. She was sitting up, rubbing her eyes. Tommy put the gift-wrapped box in her lap, and she stared at it with solemn eyes.

"Well, open it, knothead," Tommy said. "It's a present from Mr. Harris. I bet I know what it is—"

"Tommy," Stormy said warningly. "Go ahead, honey. Open it."

Laurie struggled with the wrapping, finally accepting Tommy's help. When she opened the box, her eyes widened, and a flush rose to her pale cheeks. Wordlessly she took out the doll, held it out at arm's length so she could examine it thoroughly, and then hugged it up against her chest. When Tommy reached out to lift the hem of its long calico skirt, she slapped his hand away. "Don't," she said sharply.

"Just looking to see it she's got on long bloomers," he said, shrugging.

Stormy and Guy exchanged glances; Guy sought manfully not to laugh, but lost the battle.

A plaintive voice stopped him. "Mama—I really have to go," Laurie said.

"Can't you wait for just a few minutes until—"

"No, I hafta go real bad," Laurie said firmly.

"No problem," Guy told Stormy. "No one's going to rip off your furniture in the middle of a rainstorm. I had already passed your house and was turning the car around to leave before I saw your furniture piled on the curb under the tree. If your flashlight hadn't been on, I probably wouldn't have noticed it at all. Why don't we find a filling station and then come back?"

"Okay," she said, but her consent was so reluctant that he knew she wasn't convinced. Remembering the collection of junk her house had been furnished with, he wanted to smile. On the other hand—well, when you have so little, even a sweet potato plant in a mason jar could be important to you....

It was several minutes later that they pulled into a filling station. Guy felt a stab of pleasure when he noticed how Laurie clung to her new doll, taking it with her into the women's rest room. He took the opportunity of privacy to call Marilyn again. She assured him, a little tartly, that her uncle had promised to send one of the clerks from his office to April Street, and he relayed the information to Stormy on her return.

She smiled at him, a genuine, six-carat smile, and his breath caught in his throat. Had he been thinking of her as looking like a waif? Well, if waifs had knockout smiles like that, he was all for more of them. What would she look like dressed in decent clothes, with her hair arranged in a more fashionable style? With her face made up and—no, with that complexion, her naturally dark eyelashes and brows, that pink mouth, she didn't need any makeup. Come to think of it, he liked her hair that way, curling all over her head....

They drove back to April Street and found the street empty of cars. Even though Guy knew her possessions were there, under the branches of the ginkgo tree, it was almost impossible to make out the plastic-covered pile because of the rain and the lack of light.

"You're shivering," he said to Stormy. "And I could use some coffee. That guard should be here any minute. Why don't we stop somewhere for a bite before we check you into a motel?"

"I'm hungry. Can we have Big Macs, Mr. Harris?" Tommy said hopefully.

"Sure. Keep an eye out for the yellow arches," Guy said, hiding his amusement. Trust the little guy to immediately take advantage of his suggestion. Who knows, he might be entertaining the future president of General Motors—or the United States—in the back seat of his Mercedes tonight....

"Don't take advantage of Mr. Harris," Stormy said.

"Please. Call me Guy," he said.

She didn't answer, but he knew she'd heard. Did this insistence on formality mean she still didn't trust him? Well, so be it. He wasn't really sure he trusted her, either, not totally.

They located a McDonald's several blocks away. Guy, who hadn't eaten fast food in years, found himself champing happily on a Big Mac, polishing off a bag of French fries and a strawberry shake.

Stormy, who was busy with her own burger and fries, seemed disinclined to talk. There were dark circles under her eyes, and she rubbed her eyes a couple of times, blinking hard. Guy, who had never been drawn to girlish women, wondered what there was about her that got under his skin.

Like a burr, he thought, and found himself smiling again. He gave the kids some change, pointed to a video game in one corner of the large, crowded room, and they were soon absorbed in the game.

"You feeling okay?" he asked Stormy then.

"What do you think? That I take things like being evicted in stride? Well, I don't—but don't worry. I'm not going to cry on your shoulder and tell you my life story. All I want from you is that you keep your promise to cancel that eviction notice. In return, I promise to move out as soon as I can manage it."

She hesitated, then added with obvious reluctance. "That probably won't be real soon. I got laid off today. Even if I had the first and last month's rent and a cleaning deposit, landlords won't rent to you unless you've got a job or some kind of steady income. But I'm sure I can get a job right away. Maybe I could get one here." She looked around the busy restaurant with appraising eyes.

"Don't rush into it. Surely you can do something better than—"

"Look, if I could get a job working in an office or a bank or anything that has some kind of future, don't you think I'd do it? But I didn't finish high school and I've only held low-paying jobs—and besides," she added belatedly, "what business is it of yours? So butt out, okay?"

"Butting out," he said with a straight face. "Sorry for being so nosy."

From the expression on her face, he knew she wasn't placated, so he was surprised when she said, "I'm sorry, too. That wasn't called for. I just—well, sometimes I say things without thinking. You've been really decent—and I'm sure now that the eviction wasn't your fault. But if you ask me, you oughta keep a closer eye on your assistant and her uncle. They could be playing some kind of game."

Now it was his turn to be tempted to tell her to butt out of his business. But then he looked at her closer and caught the droop of her shoulders, the nervous twitch in one eyelid, and it came to him that she'd been crying recently. "You could be right," he said agreeably.

For a while, they watched the kids, who were taking turns with the video game. Laurie's scores seldom rose above the lowest level, but Tommy had already won ten free games, which he was sharing with his sister. If they were sleepy, it didn't show. It was obvious to Guy that whatever her character flaws might be, Stormy Todd loved her two children and was a good mother. So why hadn't she married their father and given them a real home? Or did they have the same father? It was even possible that she didn't know who had fathered her kids.

"Do Laurie and Tommy see their father often?" he asked, his tone casual.

"He's dead. He was killed in a truck accident."

He felt a small shock. "Then you're a widow? Shouldn't you be covered by his social security?"

"No. We weren't married. He took off long before he was killed—several months before Laurie was born, in fact."

Guy concealed his shock. "You must have been pretty young," he said.

"I turned sixteen soon after Tommy was born."

"My God—and you kept him?"

She looked at him with surprise. "Kept him? What else would—oh, you mean why didn't I give him up for adoption? Or are you asking me why I didn't have an abortion?"

"Women do it all the time," he pointed out, not bothering to conceal the sudden bitterness in his voice. "Or if they do go to term, sometimes they do other things, like dumping their babies in trash cans with the umbilical cord still dangling.''

''You're talking about—that couldn't have happened to you!''

''Why not?''

''Because you're too—too self-confident. Like you were born with a platinum spoon in your mouth.''

''No platinum spoon. Not even a silver one. I started at rock bottom. Any success I've had, I did on my own.''

''And now you think everybody else could do the same?'' she said. ''You think I must be lazy or stupid or I wouldn't be living on the edge all the time? Listen, I do the best I can. I didn't go on the street or take on an uncle to pay the rent, and I wouldn't think of eating that hamburger you paid for except I figure you owe me. I don't believe you lied to me now. But you did dump off your promise to me on someone else to handle and you didn't bother to check up to see if your orders had been carried out. Okay, you're an important man with lots of important things to do. You're also very rich. You can call it comfortable if you like, but you're rich, all right—and the worst kind of snob. You came up from nothing and you've only got contempt for people like me who didn't do as well. Did it ever occur to you that maybe luck had a little something to do with it, that you got a couple of breaks back there somewhere? And I'll just bet that you had some help from someone along the way, too, no matter what you say about doing it all yourself.''

Guy felt the heat of anger rush to his head. He wanted to blast her, wanted to tell her how wrong she was, but something, the combatant look in her eyes, warned him off. He could have said that at least he'd never gone on welfare, but then she could rightfully point out that he hadn't been left, at eighteen, with a toddler and another baby on the way.

Without anyone dependent upon him, he'd been free to work at odd jobs while he put himself through school, free to take chances and get ahead without anything to distract him from his goals. As for having help—yeah, there had been a few teachers, even a couple of bosses, who had given him a lift up along the way. Was he, as she said, a snob? It was possible—not that she had any right to judge him.

Any more than you have a right to judge her....

So he was silent, and instead of being placated, Stormy looked even more upset. It was obvious that not only wasn't she going to apologize, but that his silence annoyed her. Stormy—oh, yes, that was a proper name for this quick-tempered little female. And why the hell did it matter to him what she thought of him? She was not a problem, but she was swiftly becoming a headache.

The kids played off their last free game and then returned. Laurie slid into her mother's side of the booth and leaned against her arm, her eyes half-closed.

"Time to get you settled for the night, Laurie," Guy said. He looked at Stormy. "That motel I was telling you about is not far from here. We should be able to get you a room there."

"Is it—do you know what the rates are?" she asked.

"South San Jose Realty will spring for this," he said.

He knew she wanted to argue, but she must have had second thoughts because she only nodded.

"Don't worry," he said. "We owe it to you."

She didn't answer. They bundled the kids into the car, and a few minutes later he was carrying Stormy's suitcase into a comfortably furnished motel room.

Tommy looked around with interest. "Hey, this is great." He disappeared into the bathroom, soon came out with his hands full of complimentary shampoo, soap, lotion and a shower cap. "Hey, look at all this cool stuff. Can we keep it, Uncle Guy?"

"Don't call Mr. Harris that," Stormy said.

"It's okay with me," Guy said quickly. "And yes, anything you don't use up you can take it with you when you check out, Tommy." He looked at Stormy. "I'll let you get some rest, Stormy. And don't worry. Everything will be fine in the morning."

She nodded, but he couldn't rightfully blame her for the wariness in her eyes.

"Why don't I pick the kids up in the morning and take them to school?"

"That's too much trouble. I'll take them on the bus," she said.

"It won't be any trouble. We can have breakfast together first."

This time she didn't argue. She followed him outside, and then stood looking up at him, obviously ill at ease.

"Thank you for stopping when you saw my things on the curb," she said abruptly. "You could've just driven away. And I'm sorry I jumped on you in the restaurant. It's been a rough day."

Now did that hurt, Stormy? he thought, but he didn't make the mistake of saying it aloud. He told her she was welcome, said he'd see her in the morning, and left. It wasn't until he was almost home that it came to him that while she'd apologized, she hadn't retracted what she'd said.

EARLY THE NEXT MORNING, even before he took a shower, dressed for the day and went into the kitchen for his first cup of morning coffee, Guy called Marilyn.

"Guy here," he said. "Did you take care of that business with your uncle last night?"

Marilyn took so long answering that he thought they'd been disconnected. "Uncle Clyde called me just now," she said finally. "He sent one of his security men to the April Street address, but he had a hard time finding the place. No street sign, he said. Just after he got there, a moving van came to pick up the woman's furniture. It seems she hired someone to move her things to a storage warehouse. Uncle Clyde tried to contact you, but you had your answering service on. Didn't you get his message?"

"Damn—I didn't check it when I got up. I don't understand any of this. When did Stormy arrange for a storage warehouse to pick up her stuff? Is Clyde sure the trucker was legitimate?"

"Oh, yes." She named a well-known local trucking firm. "The manifest was signed by Stormy Todd. It was strictly on the up-and-up. I would assume she arranged for the pickup from the motel. It's strange she didn't tell you what she planned to do."

The coolness in her voice finally penetrated, and he asked her, "What else is bugging you, Marilyn?"

"Bugging me? What could possibly be bugging me? It wasn't a bit inconvenient when you didn't turn up for our dinner date. I heated some tomato soup after I finally gave up. This was about eleven o'clock."

"Oh, God—look, I'm sorry, Marilyn. I got tied up with—well, the kids were hungry and we stopped for hamburgers and fries, and then sat there talking for a while. And it took time, getting them settled in that motel. I had a lot on my mind—hell, I'm sorry!"

"I *quite* understand," she said. "You felt responsible for the woman and her kids. How old is she, anyway?"

"Old? Why do you ask?"

"Just curious."

"She's in her early twenties—look, I have to hang up. I want to call her and—"

"Of course, Guy. I wouldn't dream of tying up your line when you have so many important things to do." The phone clicked in his ear.

Absently he made a metal note to make it up to Marilyn for the messed up dinner date as soon as possible, then put her out of his mind. He called the motel, but when he asked to be connected to Stormy's room, the desk clerk told him she had already checked out.

"Checked out? But it's only seven—"

"She left early, about—wait a minute." But it was several minutes before the desk clerk came back on the line. "My wife works the night shift here at the desk. She tells me your friend went out less than an hour after she checked in. Said it was an emergency and asked the wife to keep an eye on her kids for a bit—you can see the door of their room from the desk, see?"

"How long was she gone?"

"Oh, about half an hour. She called a cab, and when she came back, she popped her head in the door to thank the missus. She was all wet, like she'd been out in the rain without an umbrella. The wife asked if she was all right and she says everything was just peachy dandy, which is normal since she led a charmed life. Which was some kind of crazy thing to say, right?"

"And she left early this morning, you say?"

"Yeah. About six o'clock, she paid her bill and took off down the street with her kids. The little girl was lugging a cat. We don't allow pets in the rooms, so they musta smuggled it in."

"She paid you, you say?"

"In cash. Most people pay with credit cards these days, but she plunked down the sixty-five bucks in cash."

"Did she leave a message?"

"Well, yes, she did. Said someone might be by, looking for her—say, you aren't Guy Harris, are you?"

"That's my name."

"Well, she left this note for you. You want to stop by for it or I can read it to you—"

"I'd appreciate that," Guy said tightly.

There was the rustle of paper, then a brief pause. "This is kind of embarrassing, but—well, what it says is, 'Go to hell, Mr. Harris.' She must really be ticked off at you—say, you've got the same name as the guy that's running for mayor. You related to him?"

"No. I'm a stranger in town," Guy said.

He dropped the phone back in its cradle as if it were suddenly too hot to hold, then sat there, staring down at it. What had happened last night? Had she gone out in the middle of the night to arrange for someone to pick up her furniture? But why not use the phone? It just didn't make sense. None of this made sense....

And why the hostile note? Had she been playing games last night, pretending she believed him? Why had she paid for the room when he'd told her the real-estate company would pick up the tab? Had she been looking ahead? Maybe this was the prelude to a lawsuit. Yes, that was possible. It was even possible that she'd left the motel last night to go talk to a lawyer....

Well, the hell with her. The hell with trying to be a good guy. He was going to put the whole thing out of his mind.

He'd made a mistake, just like Larry and Marilyn had warned him he was doing. As far as he was concerned, the little witch could sink or swim on her own now. And good riddance.

CHAPTER FIVE

THE RESTAURANT was crowded, noisy, not particularly clean, but their busy waitress hadn't protested when Stormy slid the cardboard box that held Magic under the table even though she must have realized from the air holes in its sides and the scratching sounds the indignant cat was making that something alive was inside. For the first time since Magic had come to live with them, Stormy was glad for the inherited genes that had rendered the cat naturally mute.

Although she was acutely aware of the diminished amount of money in her wallet, Stormy hadn't had the heart to caution the children about the amount of expensive restaurant food they had ordered and were now hungrily consuming. It was enough that they had stopped asking painful questions that she was unwilling—or unable—to answer, that Tommy was sounding like his old self, that Laurie's eyes had regained their sparkle.

Acutely aware of how inadequately she'd handled the shock of finding out that once again she had been taken in by Guy Harris, she was feeling guilty. When, at the first light of day, she'd aroused Laurie and Tommy, telling them to take their showers, brush their teeth and get dressed, she'd been so angry that she'd infected them with her agitation. Now that they were back to normal, busy stuffing themselves with pancakes and eggs and sausage, it was time to put aside her rage and her disillusionment and—yes, admit it!—her disappointment, and decide what to do next.

She stared down at the barely touched food on her plate, and despite her resolution to put this latest disaster behind her, a new rush of anger made it hard to breathe.

After Guy Harris had left last night, she had been getting ready for bed, so bone-weary that she'd felt nauseous. Then Laurie had called out Magic's name in her sleep, and she'd realized that she had completely forgotten about the cat.

She had almost finished undressing and gone to bed, leaving the whole situation to be handled in the morning. It was the knowledge that when Laurie awoke, she would expect to find Magic sleeping at the foot of her bed, that finally decided it for her. The children had been through so much; if Magic disappeared, how could she face them?

So she put her shoes back, on, and went to the registration desk to tell the woman desk clerk that there'd been a family emergency and to ask if she would keep a close eye on her room, which was in sight of the desk, until she returned.

The woman, middle-aged and comfortable looking, had been very sympathetic. She had promised that she would look out for Laurie and Tommy, check the room every few minutes, and she'd even called a cab for Stormy from the registration desk phone.

A few minutes later, when the cab pulled up in front of the cottage on April Street, Stormy had made the sickening discovery that her furniture and everything else she owned was gone, and she had wanted to scream, to keep on screaming. Nothing was left, not a piece of scrap paper, not even the plastic drop cloths—nothing! The one bright spot was Magic, who drifted out of the shadows and rubbed against her leg, giving one of her silent cries.

Stormy hadn't screamed nor had she cried. On the short ride back to the motel, she'd sat with Magic curled up in her lap, her eyes closed, fighting the turmoil inside. And even now, hours later, she still was racked with anger and the feeling of being cast adrift, of being impotent and helpless, all the things she'd vowed she would never feel again.

"Hey, Mom, you aren't eating," Tommy said, looking at her plate.

"I'm full—why don't you finish this off?" she said, forcing a smile.

Briefly something very adult peeked out at her from Tommy's eyes and she knew he'd guessed how desperate things were even though she hadn't yet told them that everything they owned except a couple of changes of clothing each and a few toys and books had been stolen during the night.

What am I doing to my kids? she thought in despair. She had failed them so many times, had barely provided them with food and clothes and shelter, certainly not with anything else of value—except her love. But was that enough? Maybe she should have given them up when they were still babies to people who could provide them with the security they deserved.

If she'd done that—would Laurie have contracted rheumatic fever? The free clinic she had taken her daughter to when she'd developed that sore throat had been vastly understaffed. Was that why they hadn't tested Laurie for strep throat?

"You okay, Mom?" Tommy said, and because he sounded so uncharacteristically worried, she put her own doubts aside and smiled at him.

"I'm great—and it's obvious you are, too, from the amount of pancakes you're putting away."

"What are we going to do next, Mom?" he asked lowering his voice so Laurie couldn't hear.

"I'm thinking, I'm thinking," she said, trying to sound cheerful. "You got any ideas?"

"It'll be real great at the beach today, but I guess that's out," he said. "You've gotta go to work and we hafta go to school, right?"

She started to tell him that they would be skipping school for the day, and then the rest of his words sank in. The beach—Guy Harris had said something about the beach last night. He had been telling Tommy about the place he owned at Bolinas. Tommy had asked where that was and he'd explained it was just a little north of Stinson Beach in Marin County, across the San Franciso Bay's Golden Gate Bridge. "I go to my beach house at Bolinas to get away from people," he'd said. "But I'm afraid I won't get much chance to use it this summer. I'm up to my ears in the—in other projects."

Other projects—like running for mayor of San Jose, she'd thought. Oh, yes, he'd be busy all right. So why not take advantage of the situation and move into his beach house for a while? It would serve that bastard right if she—what did they call it? Squatting? It would solve so many problems—not permanently, of course, but maybe long enough to give her a breather.

The thing was—Bolinas was a long drive up the coast from San Jose by car. Lord knew how long it would be by bus—if there *was* bus service to such an isolated place. It would probably take most of the day. And then there was bus fare. Even if she had enough money left for bus tickets after paying for the motel room and breakfast, what about Magic? Animals weren't allowed on public transportation.

Which left hitchhiking, a very dangerous way to travel these days. On the other hand, if she was careful, and accepted only rides from women or an older couple, surely it should be safe enough. Yes, that's what she'd do—the next problem was finding someone who was going to Bolinas.

She took a deep breath, realizing Tommy was still waiting for an answer to his question.

"How would you like to go to the beach for a few days, kids? Mr. Harris—" her voice wavered briefly "—is letting us use his beach house for a while. What do you say—should we take him up on his offer?"

Any doubts she had were banished when Laurie squealed and clapped her hands, and Tommy's eyes lost their worry. "Hey, that's great! Didn't Uncle Guy say something about his caretaker quitting? I guess he don't want to leave his place empty, huh? How long can we stay, Mom?"

Stormy started to tell him again not to call Guy Harris Uncle Guy, but then she changed her mind. What did it really matter? With luck, they would be gone long before Guy came out to Bolinas. If she didn't have to worry about paying rent for a while—and if she could find some kind of work in Bolinas—maybe, just maybe, she could save enough to keep them going for a while after they returned to San Jose. It all depended on how busy Guy's schedule was—and whether or not he had time to go to Bolinas during the next few weeks.

The worst that could happen was that he would throw them out—surely, he wouldn't dare charge her with trespassing, not when he was running for mayor and after he'd already evicted her once....

Having come to a decision, Stormy put Guy Harris out of her mind. "Okay, kids, finish your breakfast. We have quite a trip ahead of us."

IT HAD BEEN a long time since Arnold Story had been in such a temper. Oh, he'd been irascible all his life, no denying that, but the years had mellowed him. Not that he ever let anyone walk over him, of course. No, he'd always run the big daily newspaper he'd inherited from his father with an iron hand, molding its style to his own personal taste, setting its political slant, hiring the men—and a few women—who thought the same way he did.

His rivals had called him a dictator, and maybe that's what he'd been, but he'd always been up-front about where he stood, had never cheated or lied or held a grudge overly long.

Sure, he'd enjoyed the power of owning a city daily, the *San Jose Press*. He was as human as the next guy, wasn't he? That part he'd always admitted openly—so why the hell had Elsie, who'd been his greatest supporter during their thirty-five years of marriage, called him a little tin god this morning?

When he'd retired a year ago, at sixty-one, he'd had it all planned out. He and Elsie would take a trip or two, see the places they'd been too busy to visit earlier. And then he'd take up a sport like golf or fishing, and find himself an interesting hobby, maybe stamp collecting, to keep himself busy.

It had all seemed so clear-cut, and Elsie had been very agreeable, had gone alone with his plans. Nothing too physically strenuous at first, of course. The doctors had been very clear on that part. No stress, no hard physical activity, no long hours. A little golf, some deep-sea fishing or maybe a little bike riding—that was okay. They would lead the good life, he and Elsie, really enjoy their golden years.

So what the devil had gone wrong? For the past few months, Elsie had been acting—well, strange. Half the time, she was off somewhere at one of those silly charities she was so wrapped up in. Hell, it had been a long time since she'd even bothered to ask if he'd like to go along to one of her luncheon affairs.

And when he'd complained, she said that was because she knew he'd be bored. Which was true enough. The one time he had gone, he'd been petrified with boredom. Matter of fact, he'd tried several times to talk her into resigning from some of her clubs, especially since she always seemed to take on the hardest jobs, like chairman of charity drives or head of ways-and-means committees.

But she'd refused to give them up, and that had been the end of that.

If it wasn't so unbelievable, he'd say that she'd been avoiding him since he'd retired. Which was ridiculous. He was her husband—and she'd always been tickled pink those rare times when he could get away from the newspaper to spend a weekend with her.

The quarrel that had erupted this morning had come out of nowhere. They had been eating breakfast, and all he'd said was that he'd been eating so much oat bran lately that he felt like a damned horse. That's when Elsie had flared up and told him to grow up and stop acting like a sulky kid.

Naturally, he'd lost his temper and said a few things that—well, maybe he shouldn't have said. But she'd started it, hadn't she? And her cooking *had* changed since his retirement. Okay, the doctor had put him on that lousy diet, all those vegetables and fruit and salads. And Elsie, who did her own cooking, had been religiously following the food list the dietitian at the hospital had given her. But there was no reason why she couldn't jazz them up with some of her special sauces and butter and condiments.

Until his heart attack, luckily a very minor one, Elsie had always catered to his taste in food. But now—hell, sometimes he felt downright hungry when he got up from the table. He was a steak and potato guy, always had been, always would be. And for breakfast, he wanted his eggs and bacon. Now that was real food....

So okay, he'd lost his temper and maybe he'd gone too far, telling her she'd been neglecting him since he'd retired. She'd slammed down her napkin, jumped to her feet and yelled something about there being such a thing as too much togetherness. He'd yelled right back, demanding to know what the hell she wanted from him.

"I want you to leave," she'd said, shocking him to the bone. "I want you to go out to Bolinas and stay at the beach house until you get your head together. And for God's sake, find yourself a hobby. Take up knitting or shell collecting or *something*. You're driving me crazy, following me everywhere, even around the house."

"Well, I don't want to go to Bolinas," he'd growled. "So what are you going to do about that?"

She had looked him square in the eye. "Then I'm going to leave you," she'd said, and he'd known that she meant every word of it.

So he told her that if that's what she wanted, if she couldn't stand having him around, he'd be glad to move out. Only it wouldn't just be for a few days. If she wanted him back, she could damned well apologize and ask him to return. Until she did, he would be staying at the beach house.

He'd expected her to simmer down then, apologize, like she always did after one of their rare quarrels, but she'd just stared at him, her eyes very cool. Having made his threat, he wasn't about to back down. He had his pride, didn't he?

So he'd gone up to the bedroom they had shared for over thirty years, tossed some clothes in a suitcase, and then gone back downstairs, still fuming and ready to have another go at it, only to find that Elsie was gone.

She'd left a note, propped up on the table in the hall, addressed to him. He'd been tempted to just leave it there, unread, but curiosity got the better of him and he'd finally picked it up and opened the envelope.

"I think you need to do some heavy thinking, Arnold," the note inside said. "When you've decided to stop sulking just because you were forced to retire, we'll talk. Meanwhile, I think it best that you stay in Bolinas."

She hadn't added *love*, only her initial, and that angered him most of all.

So now he was heading out to Bolinas where he intended to stay until Elsie came to her senses. He had taken the old '49 Nash instead of the Volvo, which was his message to Elsie that *she* might have forgotten the length of their marriage, but he hadn't. After all, he'd held on to that old Nash, which had taken them to Mexico on their honeymoon, for sentimental reasons, hadn't he? Maybe she'd get the message and feel remorse for the way she'd been treating him.

Oh, he had no doubt that she'd come around, sooner or later. The thing was—he wanted it to be sooner. Maybe he had hung around her a little too much since retirement, but then—what else did he have to do? Already, after just a year, he was bored stiff with retirement—and she had always been happy to be with him before. In all their years together, they hadn't had more than four or five quarrels—and Elsie had always been the one who said she was sorry first.

This time—well, this time he wasn't going to be so quick to forgive her. After all, she'd said some pretty rotten things about him being spoiled and used to having his own way and having a little tin god complex. And that was just not true. Hadn't he always taken good care of her, given her a more than generous personal allowance, never complained about anything she spent? Hell, he'd even donated generously to her charities.

During those early years, when he was trying to get the newspaper back on its feet, he'd been adamant about her not taking a job. Oh, she'd said she wanted to go to work, that she would enjoy it, but he'd known she was just trying to help out financially.

And later, when the newspaper became such a success, hadn't he bought her that showplace in one of San Jose's most prestigious suburbs? She'd really been surprised—she hadn't said a word that day, standing there in the front of the house, staring up at all those windows and at the greenhouse, the tennis court and the swimming pool.

What was it she'd finally said? Something about needing a staff of twelve to keep it up. But he'd pointed out that she was a genius at organization, that she could run it with one hand tied behind her back.

It was obvious she'd forgotten a lot of things he'd done for her. Hadn't he gone on that South Seas cruise with her even though he'd been sure that it would be boring as hell? And it had been. All those dull people, their only interest playing cards and bingo, taking hula lessons or watching a fourth rate movie in the bowels of the ship, for God's sake! He'd been so glad when the ship returned to San Francisco that he'd told her that was it, that he never wanted to take another cruise.

Arnold shifted uncomfortably. Maybe he had gone overboard complaining about that trip, but he'd been honest, hadn't he? And he'd done his best to be a good sport. Elsie, of course, had enjoyed herself to the hilt, quickly getting acquainted with their fellow passengers, entering the various tournaments—and winning the bridge and cribbage ones. But then, she was very sociable, easy to please—until lately.

Well, she would simmer down. Whatever was bugging her, she'd come around and then he'd forgive her and they'd make up. He grinned suddenly. Making up—now that just might be the most exciting thing that had happened to him since retirement.

And right now, he'd better start thinking about getting some gas. Once he was across the Golden Gate Bridge and into Marin County, he would turn off at Sausalito and fill up for the ride over Mount Tam and along the coast to Bolinas.

STORMY and her two kids were sitting on a bench in front of a Sausalito gas station, their canvas suitcase and the box that held Magic nearby. A friendly woman trucker, who had been hauling a load of office supplies to the small bayside resort town just over the Golden Gate bridge, had picked them up at a gas station on Lombard Street in San Francisco.

Although she couldn't take them any farther than Sausalito, she'd dropped them off at another filling station, telling Stormy that maybe they could pick up a ride to the coast there, at least as far as Stinson Beach. The station attendant, although not too friendly, had promised to get them a ride, but they had been waiting for almost two hours now, and Stormy was beginning to wonder if he hadn't changed his mind about helping her.

At first, Tommy and Laurie had talked excitedly about living at the beach and all the exciting things they meant to do this summer, but they had been quiet for a while now and she knew that once again, they were having doubts. Did kids keep on forgiving you for failing them, for not keeping your promises, or did they eventually just give up trusting you?

And if they didn't get a ride, where would they spend the night? She didn't have enough money left for a motel room, even the cheapest kind. Would they end up sleeping on one of the houseboat wharves tonight?

She jumped nervously as the station attendant spoke near her ear. "That old guy over there is heading out to Bolinas," he said.

He pointed to a car so old that she wondered if it could possibly make the trip. It did seem to have had a lot of loving care because the paint sparkled like new in the sunshine. The man leaning against it, drinking a Coke, was gray-haired; he was wearing jeans and a sweatshirt and what looked to be work shoes, but if he did hard work, it was not with his well-manicured hands.

"Do you know him?" she asked the attendant doubtfully.

"Sorta. He and his wife tank up here when they're going out to Bolinas. They got a place at the beach, he told me once. He's an okay guy. Nice spoken, like that. But you'll have to hit him up for the ride yourself. I can't go bugging my customers about taking on hitchhikers."

He moved away to service another car, and Stormy told Tommy and Laurie she'd be right back, to come running with the suitcase and Magic if she waved to them. She wasn't too optimistic as she hurried toward the man. He looked as if he had a grudge against the whole world. Well, maybe that was just his natural expression. He could only say no.

"Excuse me, sir," she said, trying to sound pleasant and confident.

"You talking to me?"

"Yes, sir. I was wondering—I understand you're going out to Bolinas?"

"Maybe I am and maybe I'm not. What's your problem?"

"We—my kids and me—" she pointed to Tommy and Laurie "—need a lift to Bolinas."

"Why don't you take a bus?"

His gruff tone made her stiffen, but she forced a smile. "We've got our cat with us. They won't let you take an animal on public transportation." She hesitated briefly and then added, "I can pay for the ride."

"How much money you talking about?"

Mentally she reviewed the money in her purse. "Five dollars?" she asked tentatively, prepared to go up another five if she had to.

The man's lips twitched. "No charge. I'm going that way anyhow. You visiting friends?"

Tommy, who had come up behind Stormy, piped up before she could speak. "We're going to stay at Mr. Harris's beach house," he said importantly. "We're gonna make sure nobody rips him off."

The man eyed him. "If you're talking about Guy Harris, it's about time he got someone out there to keep an eye on things. I dropped him a postcard last week, told him his caretaker had split. Even at Bolinas, an empty house is vulnerable as hell to vandals."

"You live near Guy Harris?" Stormy asked.

"Next door—with a gully in between. Hope your kids are well behaved. I don't like noise. And that cat you've got in that box—you better put a bell on her 'cause I'm a bird fancier."

"Oh, I will," Stormy said quickly. "And I promise the kids won't bother you."

He grunted. "We better get going—you can put that cat on the floor in the back."

Stormy slid the cardboard box onto the floor in the back, then put the suitcase next to it. She motioned for Tommy to sit next to the driver's seat, and joined Laurie, who had been unusually quiet, in the back. If the man wondered about her seating arrangement, he said nothing. From his frown, she suspected he was having second thoughts, and she was relieved when he started up the car and pulled out onto the busy street.

"Gee, this is really a cool car," Tommy said. "It's a '49 Nash, ain't it?"

"Isn't it," Stormy said automatically.

"You know your cars, kid." The man sounded surprised.

"Yeah—say, I'll bet this one is worth a lot of money. You really took good care of it," Tommy said enthusiastically.

To Stormy's relief, the two of them talked cars for the next half hour. Although there was no air conditioning in the aging car, the wind that flowed through the windows was cool, and Laurie curled up against her and was soon asleep. She had her thumb in her mouth, but Stormy didn't remove it. In fact, she felt a little envious and wished she had a solace of her own.

And I do, she thought suddenly, her normal optimistic nature surfacing. *I have Tommy and Laurie....*

The ride, over beautiful Mount Tam and then north along the coastal highway, was surprisingly pleasant. The man, whose name was Arnold Story and who told them to call him Arnold, seemed bemused by Tommy's chatter. In fact, he asked the boy questions about school, about what he wanted to be when he grew up, and then listened with an interest that seemed genuine while Tommy listed several professions that he'd "been thinking about seriously."

Stormy, knowing how unlikely it was that Tommy would ever become a veterinarian or a lawyer or an astronaut, sighed to herself.

"You okay back there, ma'am?" the man asked.

"It's very comfortable. And thank you for giving us a lift. I really appreciate it," she said.

He grunted, which seemed to be his answer to a lot of things. Later, as they were approaching Stinson Beach, a resort town near one of California's state parks, Arnold looked at Stormy in the rearview mirror and asked, "How about some lunch? It's on me."

Stormy didn't need Tommy's anxious look to make up her mind. Pride was an honorable thing to possess, but sometimes you just couldn't afford it. "Thank you," she said, then added, "Is there a place within walking distance of Mr. Harris's beach house where I can buy some groceries?"

"In Bolinas—it's about two miles from Guy's beach house. You won't need much. Guy keeps his freezer stocked and there's a whole pantry full of canned goods and staples. Don't know why he bothers since he doesn't come out often these days. You'll maybe need eggs, fresh fruit and vegetables. I'd take a look first if I were you."

"Oh, I don't want to—" She stopped because, of course, this was the solution to one of her most worrisome problems—how to feed herself and the kids for the next few days.

A couple of minutes later, they pulled up in front of a seafood restaurant in Stinson Beach. It was obvious that Arnold was well-known there because he got instant service from a very pleasant middle-aged waitress. Stormy thought the looks she and the kids attracted from not only the help but from other customers were a little too curious, but then—what did she know about small towns? She'd lived in the middle of a city all her life.

Over an excellent lunch of shrimp and French fried potatoes and salad, Arnold was more talkative. Stormy listened with interest as he told them what he called "bits of Bolinas lore."

"You won't see any sign pointing to Bolinas," he said. "And if you do, it's because the county just put it up. It won't be there tomorrow."

The corners of his eyes crinkled, and she discovered he had a surprisingly nice smile. In fact, with his leonine head and strong features, his shock of thick white hair, he was a very attractive older man and she wasn't surprised that their waitress hovered around, refilling the coffee in his cup so often that he finally put his hand over it to stop her.

"People at Bolinas don't like tourists cluttering up their beaches and tossing around garbage," Arnold went on. "As soon as the county puts up a road sign, it disappears. It's something of a status symbol to the teenagers in the area, having one of those signs. You'd think the county would just give up, wouldn't you?"

"Are you a native of Bolinas?" she asked.

"No. I'm still a newcomer. We've only had our place there twenty-five years." At her involuntary laugh, he smiled again. "I was in the newspaper business before I retired. Always expected to make Bolinas my permanent home eventually, but Elsie—that's my wife—doesn't want to live out there. Too far from her good works, I guess." The sour tone was back in his voice.

Tommy swallowed his dozenth shrimp. "Did you deliver papers for a living, Mr. Arnold?" he asked.

Arnold's eyes twinkled. "You could say that."

"Does it pay good?"

"Tommy, that's a personal question," Stormy said.

"I'm sorry. I just meant—"

"I made a living at it," the man said, and then changed the subject and started telling Tommy about the bird sanctuary at Bolinas Lagoon.

They reached the small coastal town of Bolinas in late afternoon, after a spectacular drive along the rocky coast. The sun was still well above the western horizon, but already, as Arnold pointed out, a low fog was gathering out at sea and would soon be rolling in, blanketing the sky until well into the morning.

"The tourists should come here in the fall," he added. "Our best weather is in September and October."

The small town seemed to be sleeping in the sun as they drove through. Arnold pointed out the various businesses, including the grocery where she'd be shopping.

"The town's empty now," he told them, "but wait until the weekend. The tourists, most of them from San Francisco, descend upon the beaches here like a bunch of sand crabs. Luckily our settlement of beach houses is far enough up the coast that we don't get inundated, but we still get more than we want. Too damned many people know how to find us, but what can you do? This is a free country and the coast belongs to everybody."

After a short ride along a ridge of low hills where sheep grazed on lush, spring grass on both sides of a narrow county highway, he pulled off onto a gravel road just wide enough for one car. When he told Stormy this was Guy's private road, then pointed up ahead at a large redwood-and-stone house, she wondered if this was some kind of joke. Surely this couldn't be the place Guy had called a beach house.

Although very large, the two-storied building seemed to snuggle into a small hollow between two low hills, looking as if it had taken root there. The redwood siding blended into the stands of pine trees, some wind-distorted into enchanting shapes, that surrounded it on three sides, and the ice plants that crowded around its stone base, gave it a naturalized look.

"The place needs some attention," Arnold grumbled. "That caretaker Guy hired was worthless. Gone most of the time, doing what he called gigs. I was glad when he got that full-time job in a nightclub band in the city and pulled out."

"The house is awful big. It looks like a hotel," Tommy said.

He looked so uneasy that Stormy hid her own dismay. What difference did it make if the house was very large and obviously luxurious? They were only going to be here for a little while. Tommy and Laurie wouldn't do any damage—they didn't destroy other people's property. Besides, even if it had been the small, weather-beaten beach house she'd expected, Guy would be just as furious when he learned they were squatting here. Not that this mattered to her. The kids had been calling him Uncle Guy, right? Well, she'd really make him holler "uncle" if she ever got the chance.

Arnold let them off, unloaded their suitcase and gave the box that held Magic a long, hard look. He brushed off Stormy's heartfelt "thank you" so brusquely that she wondered if he regretted giving them the ride, afraid the children would intrude upon his privacy. Well, she'd see that they left him alone—and she'd put a bell on Magic, too, the first chance she got.

As soon as Arnold drove off, she let out the cat, who had been scratching frantically at the box lid. Magic stalked away to a patch of sand to do her duty and then followed them as they walked, single file, up the path. Stormy noted small signs of neglect—colonies of weeds among the ice plants, a pile of debris that had collected near one corner of the house, gouges in the redwood siding, a cracked window glass—but it wasn't until they were climbing the front steps that it occurred to her to wonder how they were going to get into the house.

Arnold had told her that the security system was broken—but that didn't help since she didn't have a key. Surely the caretaker had locked up tight before he took off....

It was Tommy who found the key under a large rock near the entrance. He grinned at her surprise. "That's where they always put the house keys in movies," he said matter-of-factly.

A couple of minutes later, they stood in the middle of a large, rectangular-shaped living room, silently staring around. Stormy had seen movie sets like this, but she'd never been in a house furnished so luxuriously. This was a beach house? So what did Guy's *city* home look like?

The walls, covered with a textured grass paper, were the color of cream, a perfect background for the modern art that decorated them. A collection of rattan sofas and chairs, tables and a magnificent buffet, all obviously top quality, gave the room a casual air. Although the wooden floor was bare, it had been stained a warm brown, and the ceiling-to-floor windows gave a magnificent view of the ocean.

But it was the books that filled one long wall that she stared at hungrily—as did Tommy.

"It's like a library, Mom," he said, his eyes gleaming. He moved closer to scan the rows of books. "Some of them are for kids—you think it's okay if Laurie and me read them?"

"Why not? But don't take them outside, you hear?"

"Aw, Mom. You know I'd be careful," he said indignantly.

"Indoors only," she said firmly.

Laurie touched a book with her fingertip. "*Little Women*—is that for kids, too?" she asked.

"It is. A little advanced for you, but maybe we can read it together. It was one of Grandma Todd's favorite books."

Tommy disappeared through an archway, but Laurie held on to her mother's hand, crowding up against her leg.

"Where's Uncle Guy?" she said.

"He's a very busy man," Stormy said evasively. "You think you'll like living here?"

"I think so. I know I'll like the beach."

"Hey, Mom, come in here," Tommy called. "Wait until you see what's in the freezer! It looks like the supermarket over at the mall."

Stormy found him in an outsized kitchen at the back of the house. With its oak cabinets and furnishings, yellow walls and calico curtains, it had a comfortable, rustic look, but the oak-fronted appliances, she noted, were modern, top of the line. Tommy was rooting around in a freezer that was large enough to hold a small whale. He came out with a half gallon carton of ice cream in each hand.

"Chocolate mocha and Rocky Road," he said with satisfaction. "Can we have some of both?"

Stormy started to tell him to put it back, but Laurie was looking so interested that she nodded instead. Why not?

She'd keep a record of the food they ate, and when she was on her feet again, she'd pay Guy back. Not that he deserved it.

"Well, kids," she said, expelling a long breath. "This is going to be fun, right?"

She wasn't surprised when both of them, their mouths already stuffed with ice cream, nodded vigorously.

STORMY HAD A HARD TIME getting the kids settled into bed that night. Tommy had discovered an eclectic collection of tapes, everything from '50s rock to Madonna, in a cabinet in the den off the living room, and he was fully prepared to listen to every one of them before he went to bed.

Luckily the novelty of having a room to himself diverted him, and once he was in bed, with a big down coverlet pulled up to his chin, he fell asleep even before she snapped off the lights.

It was different with Laurie. Although she was entranced with the bathroom off her bedroom with its thick, luxurious towels, nile-green tiles that matched its colored fixtures, she couldn't seem to get to sleep. She finally came trailing into the living room where Stormy was reading to ask for Magic. Although she had eaten well at supper, she'd had little to say, unlike Tommy who never stopped talking.

It was obvious to Stormy, who knew her daughter's fragility, that the whole business of being evicted, the uncertainty of this move to the beach, had affected her more deeply than it had Tommy. Or maybe he was better at covering up. Hadn't his bedtime hug been unusually long—and wasn't there something too adult about the way he'd accepted her edict that they eat the simple foods they were used to despite the profusion of steaks and roasts and turkeys in the freezer?

Change—her life had been one change after another, with never a chance to put down roots anywhere for long. Would it be the same with her children? Would a time ever come when they could stay in one place long enough to lead a stable life? She wanted that for them so desperately. Maybe somehow she could manage it—but how? Everything she and the kids owned would fit inside that old suitcase sitting at the foot of her bed.

Well, at least they had Magic, she thought as she watched the cat, who was purring loudly on Laurie's shoulder. She certainly added a bit of stability, of continuity to their lives....

She tucked her daughter back in bed, and she didn't say a word when Magic curled up next to Laurie's pillow. It was strange how Magic had come along just when she was needed the most, the very day she'd brought Laurie home from the hospital. It was almost as if the cat knew how much she'd been needed as a diversion those first months when every move Laurie made had to be monitored for fear she'd strain her heart. For hours, the cat had accepted Laurie's attention patiently, never squirming to get away, never protesting when Laurie held her too tightly.

Her name, Magic, was certainly appropriate. Why else would she have gone back to the bungalow last night, there to find out that everything she owned was gone? Without that knowledge, she would have still been at the motel when Guy came this morning to take them to breakfast—if he had bothered to turn up, which she now doubted. If she hadn't found out what a liar he was, she might have made even more of a fool of herself by thanking him again for his kindness.

Stormy had just finished hanging up her extra set of jeans and T-shirts in the bedroom she'd chosen for her heart, and she found herself wishing that there would be a miracle and Guy Harris would stay away all summer. Eventually they would have to leave, but surely she could hope for a few weeks, maybe even a couple of months, of peace here.

Of course, it was always dangerous, wishing for things that depended on luck or the actions of someone else. But then—maybe *this* time, it would work out and they would have their summer in the sun.

You are a dreamer, Stormy, she thought, suddenly annoyed at her own weakness. It would take money to keep them going—and she had only a few dollars in her purse. It always boiled down to that, didn't it? What would it be like, not to have to worry about money—or the lack of it? To have a job with a future, to not have to stop and consider the cost before you made even the smallest purchase? Right now, she only had eighteen dollars and sixty-five cents in her purse—and if Arnold hadn't refused her offer to pay him for the trip, she'd have had even less.

Her grand gesture, paying the motel bill, had been stupid. Guy Harris had owed her that much for his lies. But no, she had been so furious that she'd wanted to make a statement to him. And that note—well, she wasn't sorry about that. She just wished she'd said even more, really told him off....

In the morning, she would walk into town and start looking for a job. Maybe she could find work as a waitress, or in a gift shop, or maybe as a maid in a motel. With the tourist season already started, surely there were summer jobs—or would they all go to local people? This was a tightly knit community, according to Arnold—did that partisanship extend to not giving jobs to outsiders?

There was another problem—making sure the kids were safe while she worked. She would have to forbid them to go outside during her working hours. But they were used to that. After all, they were latchkey kids. There was the TV set she'd seen in the den, and the stereo and tape deck—and plenty of books, a whole collection of games, enough to keep them busy while she was away.

And when she came home, they would explore the beach, the tide pools and the meadows above on the hills. They would have picnics in some of those coves that Arnold had told them about, and while she had never learned to swim, maybe she could find someone to teach her, teach the kids so she didn't have to forbid them to go near the water.

And she would work all these things out when the time came, live day by day. For now she intended to take a long, hot bath, fix herself a cup of tea and then go to bed....

CHAPTER SIX

ALL HIS ADULT LIFE, Arnold had awakened early, instantly alert and ready for the challenges of the day. After a substantial breakfast, he would plunge into the day, submerging himself in work. He'd always been grateful that Elsie had been so understanding about the long hours that running a big city newspaper demanded. Being a sensible woman, she had kept herself busy with her charities and good works, with her gourmet cooking and gardening and other interests.

Oh, he'd always listened politely when she talked about her volunteer work and hobbies, but the truth was he'd only been pretending an interest. How strange that it was only now, since they were living apart, that he realized that in the main, he'd been indifferent to how she spent her days. Had she ever realized that he'd indulged her outside activities for the reason that she'd made so few demands upon his own time?

Looking back, he could see now that he'd always dominated their conversations, talking about the newspaper, the problems with personnel and competitors and recalcitrant news sources. Still, Elsie had never complained. She'd always understood that running a major newspaper took just about every bit of energy and drive he possessed.

Had she known that, for all his complaints about being overworked, he'd loved every minute of it, loved being something of a king maker in the county, even in the state, a force to be reckoned with? Which was why, he thought sourly, he never should have retired, no matter what his doctor had said.

"You've got to slow down, Arnold," Dr. Thomas had told him after he'd had that blasted attack.

And he'd listened. He'd been scared, never having had any experience with illness before in his sixty-two years on earth. Yeah, it had scared him and so he'd let the doctor and Elsie talk him into selling the newspaper and retiring. What he *should* have done was tell them it was his own life and he'd risk it if he liked. Better to die in the harness than to die from sheer boredom....

The golden years, they called them. What the devil was golden about them? Sure, he and Elsie had taken that obligatory cruise—Hawaii and the South Seas. But all he'd gotten out of it was an upset stomach from too much rich food and a blurred impression of too-sultry heat, too many strange faces and some guide's droning voice telling tired jokes about living in paradise.

So then he'd tried to take up a hobby, stamp collecting, which hadn't worked, either. What he hadn't known before he'd retired was that the chief value of hobbies was relief from hard work. Hobbies to fill time were a bore.

Lately he'd been trying to learn to sleep later in the mornings, figuring it would make his days seem shorter. So far, habit was too strong, and most mornings he was up before the sun rose.

Which was why he was sitting here on his patio this morning, drinking an unsavory cup of instant coffee and staring moodily at two pieces of slightly scorched toast, wondering what to do with the rest of the day.

Not fishing—or golf or cards. If he never saw another fishing pole or golf club or deck of cards in his life, it would still be too soon. When he thought of the crap he'd had to listen to from other retirees those first months after retirement, he wanted to throw up. It was always the same twaddle—complaints about their aches and pains, bragging about old stock deals or golf scores or what they'd done on the football fields forty years ago, what their kids and grandkids were doing now.

That nine-year-old Todd boy was far more interesting than any of those has-beens at the country club. Tommy was going to end up, as the saying went, either in jail or president. He was betting on president. But not of the country. No, as president of the board of some big conglomerate somewhere.

Not that the poor kid was going to get a fair start. Anything he did with his life he'd have to do on his own, starting at the bottom. Rock bottom, he'd say, from the way the three of them dressed and the state of that one piece of luggage.

Where on earth had Guy met the Todd woman, anyway? Something very strange about that. Well, Guy was getting a bargain if he was just paying her the going rate for caretakers. From his patio yesterday, he'd watched her hauling off dried leaves and cleaning windows and trimming back the ice plants around the house, scrubbing off the patio. Her youngsters had helped her. Being kids, they did as much playing as real work, but that was okay, too. Kids would be kids, even ones as well mannered as those two.

Too bad Elsie hadn't been able to have children. They should have adopted, maybe, but the years had slid past so quickly. He'd been so busy with the paper and she'd seemed content with her volunteer work. The problem was that she hadn't retired when he had. She was still going to meetings, planning charity balls, being involved—and who could blame her? What kind of company was an old ex-editor like him?

He brooded over the shortcomings of his life since retirement, his temper stirring. When he heard the sound of voices nearby, he muttered a curse. Kids—probably those boys from down the beach again. He'd chased them away a couple of times the past two days, told them to play somewhere else. But no, they liked using the meadow below the house as a ballpark. Well, this time he'd really give them hell. What was happening to the younger generation? No respect for other people's property these days.

He moved to the edge of the patio. Below, in the strip of meadow that separated the house from the edge of the beach cliff, two children were chasing what looked to be a ball of fur.

"You kids there," he called. "That meadow's private property. Get along home now."

At the sound of his voice, both of them stopped. When they turned to look up at him, he recognized them as the Todd children. The girl edged behind the boy, who grinned up at Arnold, obviously not intimidated.

"We're trying to catch our cat, Mr. Arnold," Tommy said. "We still don't have a bell for her, but Mom has to go into Bolinas again today and if they don't cost much, she's going to get one for Magic."

"What is she going into town for?" Arnold asked, surprising himself.

"She's looking for a job."

Arnold made a hurumphing sound. "Well, you kids run along. I'm eating my breakfast and I want some peace and quiet."

He went back to his coffee, but it tasted even worse lukewarm than it had hot, and he finally gave it up. He crumbled his toast and dumped it on the clover at the edge of his patio for the birds to clean up, then carried his mug and saucer back into the kitchen.

Two days of dirty dishes already filled the sink to overflowing. He looked at them in disgust, knowing he'd have to do something about them—and soon. Too bad the Todd woman wasn't available for housework. She was such a hard worker that he'd hire her in a minute....

Or maybe she *was* available. The boy had said she was looking for a job, hadn't he?

The idea of hiring a housekeeper was tempting. It wasn't that he was too lazy to do it himself, only that he had no idea how to go about it. He also detested clutter and unmade beds—and dirty dishes. Too used to living in a spic-and-span house. So maybe he would just stop by Guy Harris's place and talk to Stormy Todd when he took his walk this evening.

After all, why would Guy mind? It was obvious she could take care of both places with one hand tied behind her. And what was there about Guy hiring this particular woman that bothered him? Guy was—well, he was usually pretty conventional. He'd hired his last caretaker through a well-known employment agency. Which hadn't meant he'd found a good one. The fellow drank—the empty beer cans he'd hauled out of there would fill the local dump. After the guy had quit without notice, Arnold had dropped Guy a postcard, and now this woman had turned up.

Was something going on between Guy and Stormy Todd? It didn't seem likely. Guy's taste in women followed a certain pattern. He wasn't a stuffed shirt, far from it, but he did go for sophisticated women, never for young, dewy-eyed ones. He also was running for high office this fall, and not likely to do anything out of character. So it must be as Stormy had said: Guy had hired her to keep an eye on the place since he wouldn't be out here much this summer....

He heard a scratching sound at the door, and went to investigate. When he opened the door, two very blue eyes, slightly crossed, stared up at him from a mask of face. Her tail held high and regal, the Todd cat stalked past him, into the kitchen. Mesmerized by her insouciance, he watched as she made a slow circle of the room, stopping once to sniff the door of the refrigerator, another time to examine a spot in the floor where Arnold had spilled some milk earlier. When she jumped lightly onto the breakfast bar and sat looking at him, obviously prepared for a stay, he swore under his breath.

"Didn't anyone tell you that I hate cats?" he asked.

The cat opened her mouth but nothing came out.

"Well, that's a novelty. A female that doesn't make a lot of noise—you are a female, aren't you?" Arnold said.

The cat eyed the remnants of the omelet he'd fixed—and burned—for his supper the night before, made the silent meow again.

"You couldn't possibly be asking for food, could you? I have a hunch your owner feeds you when she doesn't feed herself."

The cat yawned, began washing her face with fastidious paws.

"I think it's time you left," Arnold said darkly. "I'm a dog man myself. Big, vicious, cat-eating dogs are my speciality. And I don't feed other people's cats. Besides, I have a hunch you're pretty particular about what you eat—and that omelet was a disaster. How come you ended up with the Todd family? I can't believe you get any gourmet cat food there."

He heard a sound at the door and turned to meet Laurie's green eyes. She ducked her head, but she didn't retreat, even when he frowned at her.

"Can I please have Magic, Mr. Arnold?" she asked.

"You're welcome to her. How come you call her Magic?"

"That was the name on her tag. She scratched on the door—this was the day I got home from the hospital—and Momma let her in, gave her some food 'cause she was so thin. We watched the Lost and Found in the papers but no one advertised for her."

Arnold digested this in silence for a few seconds. "Precocious, aren't you?" he muttered. "How old are you, girl?"

"I'm seven—and Tommy is precocious, not me." She took a step into the room. "Can I have my cat, please? I have to watch her so she won't catch any baby birds. After Momma gets a bell for her, they can hear her coming. It's okay if she catches mice but not birds. I don't know why that is. I like mice."

"I'll just bet you do," he said, amused in spite of himself. He picked up the cat and handed her to Laurie. "Better run along home now."

"Oh, that's not our home. Uncle Guy is letting us live there for now, but pretty soon we have to leave. We don't have a home since those men put our stuff out on the street and someone ripped it off. We're staying here until Uncle Guy tells us we hafta go."

"He's your uncle?"

She shook her head. "We just call him that. He gave me my doll—and Tommy that game. He's awful nice only Momma is really mad at him about something he did." She paused to sigh. "Adults are really funny sometimes, aren't they?"

"Indeed. Now I wonder—" He broke off as Laurie gave him a tiny smile and hurried off.

He stared after her, frowning. When he realized that once again he was speculating about the relationship between Guy and Stormy, he told himself that it was none of his business and stalked toward the back of the house to take his morning shower.

LATE THAT AFTERNOON, after he'd returned from his twice-daily walk along the beach, he picked his was across the gully and knocked at the back door of Guy's beach house. Stormy, holding a wooden stirring spoon in her hand, her face flushed, opened the door. She was wearing the same sweatshirt and jeans she'd worn when she had hitched a ride with Arnold, but they looked as if they'd been freshly washed now. The odor of something cooking wafted out from the kitchen and unconsciously, he gave an appreciative sniff.

"Oh, Arnold...do come in, won't you?" she said. Her voice was cordial enough, but there was wariness in her eyes.

"I came to ask—what's that you're cooking?" he asked.

"Beans and chicken wings and dumplings." She hesitated, then asked, "Won't you stay for supper? I don't have anything special but I did bake a pie this afternoon."

"What kind of pie," he asked hungrily.

"Cherry—there were some frozen cherries in the freezer."

"My favorite pie—thank you, I think I will stay for supper," he said, hoping he didn't sound too eager as he followed her into the kitchen. He'd always liked this kitchen because of its generous size and its cheery yellow walls and oak furnishings. Now, with the Todd kids greeting him as if he were an old friend, with the air filled with the odors of cooking, it was undeniably friendlier and homier.

Stormy filled a mug from the coffeepot and set it in front of him. "Laurie—add another place for Mr. Story," she said.

The fare was plain and simple—it was also very good. He ate as if he were starved, so much so that he felt embarrassed. "You're a wonderful cook," he said finally.

Stormy flushed; for a moment she looked almost as young as her own daughter and he wondered idly how old she was. *Young enough to be my granddaughter,* he thought.

"I'm just a plain cook," Stormy said.

"Momma learned how to cook when she was my age," Tommy confided around a mouthful of cherry pie. "That's when she was living with Grandma Todd. Grandma was very old and sick, so Momma had to do the cooking. I never met her 'cause she died when Momma was twelve and then—"

"Mr. Story isn't interested in that, Tommy," Stormy interrupted. "Finish your pie and then you two can run out and play on the beach for a while. But don't go near the surf, you hear?"

Arnold was finishing his second cup of coffee when he said, "I hear you're looking for a job. Any luck?"

"Not yet. The Beachline Motel did take my application for a maid job, but I have a feeling there isn't much work for outsiders in Bolinas."

"Your feeling is right. Which is something I want to talk to you about. How would you like to work for me?"

"For you? Doing what?"

"Housework—and cooking."

"How much cooking?"

"Just dinner. I can manage breakfast and lunch, but I like a good meal at night. And I need someone to take care of the house. As for pay..." He mentioned a more than adequate salary.

"That's an awfully good wage," she said slowly. The wariness was back in her eyes.

"It's worth it to me. Of course, I'd expect you to keep an eye on my place when I'm away."

Arnold wasn't surprised when she accepted. After all, if she couldn't afford to buy a bell for her cat, she must be very short on money. What he didn't expect was the extent of his own relief—and pleasure.

CHAPTER SEVEN

DURING THE WEEK following Stormy Todd's disappearance, Guy tried to figure out just what had happened—and why. It was obvious that at some point during that evening she had decided not to include him in her plans—which was her right, of course. But he would have sworn that she had relaxed her guard and no longer blamed him for the eviction debacle.

So why that brief, very hostile note?

Those last few minutes at the motel, as she was thanking him outside the door, she had looked so vulnerable, as if all her defenses were down. It had come to him that if he tried to kiss her good-night, she wouldn't protest. And wasn't it lucky that he'd restrained himself? What he didn't need at this point in his life was even the slightest emotional involvement with an unstable woman.

So he'd lucked out there. Not that he hadn't wanted to kiss her. She had looked—well, so damned kissable, with that lush, naturally pink mouth, that translucent skin and the ebony black hair tumbling over her forehead....

Not that anything serious could have resulted from a simple good-night kiss with the kids on the other side of the door, getting ready for bed. Those kids—okay, they had gotten to him. He wasn't ashamed to admit that. Laurie was so damned fragile, and the boy reminded him of himself as a boy—no, that wasn't really true. Tommy wasn't at all the way he himself had been at nine. Tommy had an uncomplicated friendliness, the assurance of an adult, of someone whose worth had always been accepted, while at that age, he, Guy, had been full of rage, carrying around a chip on his shoulder that wouldn't quit.

It was later, when he was in his early teens, that he'd wised up and realized that if he went on the way he was heading, he would end up in Juvenile Hall. So he'd learned to hide his—what had it been? Not disillusionment because first you had to possess a few illusions before you could be disillusioned. It was an inner resentment that he'd learned to hide, and certainly a fierce determination to win out over those who'd wronged him, to always, in anything he attempted, come out on top.

Well, he'd succeeded beyond his wildest dreams, and yes, what Stormy had said to him, her assessment of what made him tick, had given him quite a turn for the simple reason that he'd recognized how close to the truth it was. He *was* arrogant, impatient with those who hadn't fought their way out of poverty the way he had.

Maybe he should have told her about the years he'd worked at two, sometimes three, part-time jobs to put himself through school, and his long struggle to make it in the business world, about the hard times that can take the heart out of a man. No, it was best that he hadn't. It would have sounded like self-justification. And after all, her opinion of him wasn't important. The wisest course he could possibly take now was to put her totally out of his mind. And that's just what he intended to do.

During the next few days, Guy discovered this was easier said than done. The whole situation, the feeling that somehow he'd handled things wrong, kept him on edge. Even Marilyn, always so tolerant of his moods, finally had had enough.

"I don't know if it's something I did or something you did," she said, "but I'm tired of being yelled at."

This after he'd growled at her for an omission on his daily appointment schedule. Which, as it happened, had been his own fault because he'd forgotten to tell her about a planned working luncheon with several of his financial contributors, a group of fellow contractors. Feeling guilty, he'd apologized and was more careful what he said to her and to his campaign workers, not that it had improved his mood.

One thing he'd done the morning he found out Stormy had disappeared was to call Jeff Domini, an old friend who now headed the San Jose Police Department. Jeff listened to his story, and was diplomatic enough not to tell him he was a damned fool. Instead he promised to look into it, and see what he could find out.

The next day, he called to tell Guy that there'd been no police report of any kind of trouble concerning a Stormy Todd and her two children. Nor had she filed a complaint about an erroneous eviction action or the theft of her household goods, a possibility that had occurred to Guy as the reason for her strange note—and disappearance.

So it was obvious that he'd been taken in by a very devious woman. As soon as he'd driven away, she'd gone out, possibly to enlist the help of a friend, had arranged to have her possessions picked up and then had deliberately dropped out of sight. As to why she hadn't used the phone in her motel room to call her friend—maybe he couldn't be reached by phone. Since she had money enough to pay for her motel room, that particular suspicion he'd had, that she was broke, was obviously unfounded, too.

During the next two weeks, Guy managed to put the whole business out of his mind, except for those odd times when an image would emerge, unwanted, from his memory. Once, when he picked up a large bundle of handbills at campaign headquarters, he suddenly remembered how light Laurie had felt in his arms when he'd carried her to his car.

Another time, as he was getting into an elevator at City Hall, he caught the scent of herbal shampoo, the same one Stormy used, and he'd craned his neck, examining the women in the elevator. When he'd realized what he was doing, he'd felt like cursing.

He was walking through the lobby of the downtown hotel where he'd just had lunch with a journalist who was doing a series of articles on the local political scene, when he spotted an old friend, Arnold Story.

Guy greeted him with real pleasure. His admiration for Arnold went back to his college days, when he'd gone to work at Arnold's newspaper as a printer's helper. Arnold had taken an interest in him, had helped him later when he was just starting out with a brand-new architectural degree. Their relationship had deepened through the years, and it wasn't a coincidence that he'd decided to build his beach house on the lot next to the Storys at Bolinas.

"Well, Guy, I can't say you're looking great." Arnold Story said, and Guy reflected that Arnold always called a spade a spade. "Fact is, you look like hell. You been campaigning too hard?"

"I'm fine. Just a little tired—but retirement certainly agrees with you. That's quite a tan you've got. You been staying at the beach?"

"Yeah." Arnold looked a little embarrassed. "Elsie and I—well, we had a spat. I'm giving her time to cool off. Thanks to you, I've been eating well. Hope you don't mind me hiring your caretaker to do my cooking for me. You know I can't boil water without burning it."

Guy frowned at him. "Caretaker? Is he back? First I knew of it."

"Back? I'm talking about Stormy. She's a great cook—and good company, she and the kids."

Guy felt as if someone had slugged him in the stomach. "What the hell are you talking about?" he demanded.

Now it was Arnold's turn to frown. "Maybe you know her under another name. I just assumed Stormy was her real name but—"

"Oh, it's her real name, all right. How long has this been going on?"

"You aren't sore because I hired her to keep house for me, are you? She was looking for a job, only we both know the locals aren't too keen about hiring outsiders. So I asked her to work for me. Don't worry—she isn't neglecting your place. Looks better than it has in years."

It took Guy a few moments to digest this information. "How did you meet her?" he finally said, keeping his voice even with an effort.

"I gave her and the kids a lift out to Bolinas from Sausalito. They had their cat with them, couldn't take a bus, so they were hitchhiking. You should've flown them out in your chopper, Guy. Pretty dangerous, a woman hitchhiking these days."

There was more than a hint of disapproval in his voice, and Guy had to bite back a comment about damned fool men who picked up women hitchhikers. It was obvious that Stormy—and possibly the children—had gotten to Arnold.

Arnold glanced at his watch, said he had a dental appointment to keep, that he hoped Guy would find time to get out to Bolinas this summer.

"See you around, Guy," he added, and took off.

Guy stared after him. Oh, yes, Arnold would see him around all right—and damned soon. The only reason he hadn't given way to his anger was that he didn't want Arnold to alert Stormy that he was coming. How had she managed to fool Arnold, that hard-bitten newspaperman who had seen just about every scam in the book? Well, there was no fool like an old fool—or, come to think of it, a young one who thought he was a good judge of character.

Guy called his office on his car phone, canceling his afternoon appointments, much to Marilyn's annoyance. He didn't give her any reason, just told her he'd be in touch. Anger rode him as he went to his apartment to change his business suit for jeans and a cotton knit shirt. When he caught a glimpse of his face in the bathroom mirror, the grim lines etched around his mouth made him wince. Good thing the voters couldn't see him now, he reflected sourly, or he wouldn't get ten votes.

Okay, Stormy had taken advantage of his loose tongue. She had proven herself to be an opportunist of the first order, getting free rent for herself and her children for the summer—and probably eating well to boot from his freezer. He'd told Tommy that he doubted he'd get out to Bolinas very often this summer, if at all, and she'd used the information to her advantage. Hell, she must have planned it on the spot that evening.

Well, she wasn't going to get away with it. Not only was he going to toss her out, but he meant to tell her a few truths in the bargain. It was obvious she'd latched on to Arnold as her next victim, taking advantage of his problems with Elsie. God knew what she was planning. Did she realize that Arnold, despite that down-home speech he cultivated so well, was a very rich man? If so—what was her plan? Some kind of blackmail?

He had already called the airport where he kept the helicopter, and arranged for it to be serviced immediately. Half an hour later, when he got there, the chopper was gassed up and waiting for him. Although he sometimes used one of the local pilots on business trips, he was perfectly capable of piloting it himself. When he was airborne, he crossed the Peninsula to the coast, turned north, flying past San Francisco and the Golden Gate Bridge, then following the rugged Marin County coastline to Bolinas.

As he passed over the small coastal town, he noted how many cars were parked near the beach and along the coastal cliffs. The tourists had already begun their summer invasion, which would either infuriate or gratify the inhabitants, depending upon whether or not they owned businesses that catered to tourists.

A few minutes later, he sat the helicopter down on the flat strip of meadow that served as a pad and took the path that cut through the short stand of pine behind his beach house, approaching it from the rear.

No one was in sight, and when he went inside and turned into the kitchen, the silence told him the beach house was empty. Was it possible that she'd pulled out—no, there was Laurie's doll, the one he'd given her, sitting on the breakfast bar, and although the kitchen was immaculate, the odor of coffee still lingered in the air.

His eyes rested on several glass jars sitting on a sunny windowsill. Each contained a small sweet potato, suspended in water by toothpicks, each showing a few tiny green leaves. For a moment, he almost smiled.

But his amusement died a quick death. It was little touches like this that made Stormy so dangerous. Just how had she managed to fool Arnold with her unlikely tale of being hired as a caretaker? Like most newspapermen, Arnold was a cynical observer of life, not at all gullible.

Which should make me feel less like a damned fool for having been taken in so easily, he thought.

He went through the rest of the house. Everything was in order, unnaturally so considering two small children lived here. A few pieces of women's clothing—a pair of jeans, two cotton tops—hung in one of the guest room closets, rather than in the master bedroom, he noted.

"You're good, Stormy," he said aloud. All the moves of a genuine caretaker—except that she had no right to be here.

He heard children's voices as he went out through the front door. At the rock wall that bordered the cliff in front of the house, he paused, looking down at the beach below. Tommy and Laurie were standing there, at the edge of a tiny tide pool. Tommy was pointing out something in the water to Laurie, who was carrying Flame, the doll she'd told him was adopted.

Both of them were standing well above the waterline. Natural fear of the surf—or Stormy's orders? he wondered. Well, there was no denying that she was fiercely protective of her kids. And why did that realization intensify his resentment? That she had guts, what Arnold would call chutzpah, bugged him, too, although usually he favored strong-willed woman.

She had told him off properly when she'd thought he was criticizing her for taking minimum-wage jobs instead of going for something better. Yes, she certainly could stick up for herself. Which was another thing that irritated him.

And why the devil was he here, expending time he couldn't spare? This whole business was so minor in importance that he should have dispatched someone from the office to evict her. Was it because he'd been, despite his attempt to put her out of his mind, so damned worried about Stormy and her kids?

The suspicion was sobering; it revealed a weakness in himself he didn't like. It also reminded him that he was neglecting the errand that had brought him out here. He started down the broad wooden staircase that zigzagged to the beach, and had almost reached the bottom when Laurie looked up and saw him.

Her whole face lighted up with a smile, but it was Tommy who greeted him with his usual aplomb.

"Hi, Uncle Guy," he said. "Look what I just found."

He produced a small glass float. It was dark amber, square, with a short length of fishing net still hanging on it.

"That's a Russian float," Guy said. "They're pretty rare. You really hit it lucky."

"No kidding? Is it worth a lot of money?" Tommy asked hopefully.

"A few dollars—provided you can find someone who wants it," Guy said.

Tommy thought that over. "I think I'll keep it," he said. "With my games and other things gone, I got plenty of room for stuff like this."

"What do you mean, 'with your games and other things gone'?"

Tommy gave him a curious look. "Didn't you know? Those guys who ripped us off took everything, even Mom's old pictures of Grandma Todd." He glanced around at Laurie and lowered his voice. "They coulda left Laurie's dolls. I can see why they'd take my games, but what did they want with her old dolls, for gosh sakes?"

"When did this happen?"

"Why, that night you took us to the motel. Didn't Mom tell you? I thought that's why you let us come out here to stay."

"What exactly happened?"

"Well, after you left, Mom got worried about Magic, so she took a cab and went back to get her. She found her all right, but everything else was gone. They even ripped off those plastic drop cloths the sheriff's guy gave us to cover the furniture. It sure was lucky you asked us to come out here or I guess we woulda ended up in one of those shelters for homeless people. Mom lost her job, see, and after she paid for the motel room, there wasn't much money left."

The young-old look was back on his face as he added, "We're missing the last few weeks of school, Laurie and me, but we can catch up this summer, Mom says. She wrote the school for some lesson plans."

Guy digested this in silence. "Where's your mother?" he asked finally.

"She's at Uncle Arnold's house. She does his cleaning and laundry and cooking for him. You want me to go get her?"

"No. There's plenty of time. I want to hear more about what happened that night. Did your mother ever say why she didn't tell me about the theft?"

"I figured she did." Tommy sounded so uneasy that Guy decided it was time to change the subject.

"I'm going to walk into town. Anything you need?" he asked.

"I think I heard Mom say she needed some cookies," Tommy said carelessly.

"Cookies, it is. What kind?"

"Well, Laurie likes chocolate and I like coconut." He hesitated a moment. "And Mom likes the kind with marshmallow in the middle and chocolate on the outside."

Guy started away, then stopped. "I want to surprise your mother. Don't tell her I was here, okay?"

"Sure. She doesn't like surprises much, but I'm sure she won't mind this one."

On the way into town, Guy made a mental note to have a phone installed at the beach house—provided he decided to allow Stormy and her kids to stay for a while. He hadn't quite made up his mind about that, yet. Okay, he'd wronged her, misjudged her. That didn't make him responsible for her, did it? But if he did let her stay, he'd put in the order for the phone. Being out of contact was fine for a man who wanted peace, quiet and privacy, but with two kids living there, a phone was necessary in case of an emergency.

When he reached Bolinas, he sought out the pay phone in a filling station. But when he called Clyde Farris's office, he was told the man was out of town for the day. He dialed his office next and when Marilyn came on the line, he relayed the story Tommy had told him without giving its source.

"I'll see if I can locate Uncle Clyde," Marilyn said, her tone conciliatory. "It must have been some kind of clerical mix-up—you're sure that this isn't a scam of some sort? After all, the woman could be lying."

"She wouldn't deprive her children of their toys. If you reach Clyde, tell him I'll be calling him tomorrow morning."

He put the phone down before she could answer, mainly because he didn't like the strident sound of his own voice. Why was it that anything that involved Stormy Todd always seemed to throw him off balance?

Stormy was at the kitchen of the beach house, fixing grilled cheese sandwiches for the kids, when he returned from Bolinas. From the tenseness on her face and the protective way she moved between him and the kids, he knew that she was afraid of what he might say.

"Go play in your room," she told Laurie and Tommy. "I want to talk to Mr. Harris alone."

They didn't argue. In fact, they both looked so sober that Guy wanted to assure them that everything would be all right.

When they were out of earshot, Stormy turned back to Guy. "Okay, we've been squatting on your property. So what are you going to do about it? If you try to charge me with trespassing, I'll go straight to Claudia Benson and swear you tried to take advantage of me—"

"Shut up, Stormy, and give me a chance to speak."

To his surprise, she did just that. But she also folded her arms across her chest, her whole body tense, not giving an inch.

"I didn't know your furniture had been stolen until today. A truck showed up in the middle of the night, and the driver showed the guard what looked like an invoice signed by you. The note you left at the motel seemed to confirm that you'd arranged to have your stuff hauled away. You never filed a theft complaint—"

"It would have been a waste of time," she said. "And I'm not going to apologize for moving in here—or for the note. Maybe you didn't arrange for somebody to rip off my stuff, but you own the real-estate company that started this whole business. So I'm not leaving. I've got a job, working for Arnold, and I've already saved some money and—"

"You're welcome to stay all summer if you like," he said softly.

That stopped her. She blinked at him, and briefly, until she looked away, there was such naked relief in her eyes that he felt a restriction in his breathing.

"I need a reliable caretaker," he said, careful to sound brisk and businesslike. "I'll pay you a reasonable salary, of course. With my political campaign warming up, I'll probably be too busy to use the place this summer. If I do get a chance to come out, your culinary talents will be helpful. Arnold Story says you're one helluva good cook."

"Arnold told you that? When was this?"

"We ran into each other in the city this afternoon. He congratulated me for hiring such a reliable caretaker."

"I didn't exactly lie. I just let him think—"

"It's all right, Stormy." He sat the grocery sack he'd been holding on the breakfast bar. "I bought some cookies for the kids. I understand you've run out."

"Did Tommy tell you that?"

"He did."

"Tommy the con artist strikes again," she sighed. "I never buy store cookies—how many do you have in there, anyway? You must have bought the store out."

"He informed me that he likes coconut, Laurie chocolate, that you go for marshmallow. Personally I favor tollhouse. I got all four."

Stormy laughed, a rich, full-bodied laugh that made him aware again that he was playing with fire. He knew it was time to leave, but instead he found himself saying, "I could go for some of those cookies—and a mug of coffee. The salt air always makes me hungry."

She smiled at him. "How about some minestrone soup? I just made it this morning."

As Guy nodded, then watched her while she heated the soup, he reflected that while he no longer was angry, he hadn't changed his mind about one thing. Stormy Todd was dangerous to his peace of mind, and he wasn't about to let it get out of hand. What he didn't need was to become emotionally involved with a woman who was as different from him as day to night. Hell, she wasn't even his type.

Which was why, as soon as he'd eaten two bowls of Stormy's homemade minestrone, plus a large hunk of freshly baked bread and several cookies, he invented an important meeting in the city, and took off.

On the way back to San Jose, he came to a decision. Even if he found some spare time this summer, he wouldn't spend it in Bolinas. There just wasn't any point in taking that kind of risk.

CHAPTER EIGHT

DURING THE NEXT FEW DAYS, although Guy was as busy as he'd ever been in his life, he often found his mind wandering, drifting back to his encounter with Stormy.

For some reason he didn't try to define too closely, he hadn't told Marilyn or Larry Singer that he'd hired Stormy as a caretaker for his beach house in Bolinas. Of course, he knew it had something to do with his knowledge of the way they were bound to react, the unsolicited advice he was sure to receive.

Maybe, he thought morosely as he signed a stack of checks and then initialed his approval of several press releases, his reticence also had something to do with knowing that their advice would make good sense.

This whole situation with Stormy was a natural for rumors, if not out-and-out scandal. First he had evicted her, a young, attractive single mother, from one of his rentals. No matter that he'd had nothing personal to do with it, that his holdings were in a blind trust, or even that, according to Clyde Farris, it had all been a mistake, that a memo to the sheriff's office about stopping the eviction had been mislaid.

Because, of course, he *had* become personally involved, had taken them to a motel for the night and ended up hiring Stormy to be his caretaker at a remote hideaway on the coast. What the opposition paper, the *Bayside*

News, would do with that if they ever found out, he didn't like to think.

And yet—what else could he have done but offer her the job once he'd found out how he'd misjudged her? She wouldn't have accepted money from him, even though she'd lost everything she owned, was probably nearly broke. This he was sure of, that she had enough pride for three people. Well, he had his pride, too, and although he wasn't directly involved with what had happened, the whole business *was* still his responsibility.

So why, Larry or Marilyn was bound to ask, hadn't he simply arranged for Clyde Farris, who was responsible, to handle it—replace what the woman had lost, get her a job and find her a place to live? And then wash his hands of the whole crazy business?

But no, he'd acted like an impulsive fool, and was even more involved than ever. Which one of them or both was also sure to point out.

There was another danger here, one they couldn't possibly guess, not having seen Stormy in person. She was a very appealing woman, and okay, he was sexually attracted to her, an impossible situation. Which was why he was staying away from Bolinas and doing his best to wipe Stormy and the whole business out of his mind....

Arnold Story's call came as Guy was getting ready for bed after a particularly grueling day. He had already taken a shower and was towel-drying his hair when the phone in his bedroom rang. He cursed and almost let the answering service take it. Instead, for no reason other than that he was standing so close to the phone, he draped the towel around his midriff and picked it up.

"Yes?"

"This is Arnold Story, Guy. I hope I didn't catch you at a bad time."

"No, no—what is it, Arnold?"

"It's Stormy. She's got some kind of—well, I don't know what's wrong with her. She's been losing a lot of weight lately. Since she was only as big as a tadpole to begin with, she doesn't look good. I tried to talk her into having a checkup, but she says she's feeling great and besides, she doesn't like doctors."

"I don't understand. Why are you telling me this? She's an adult. She can make her own decisions."

"I'm not so sure about that. I think she's scared to go see a doctor for fear she'll find out something serious is wrong with her. Some people are like that, you know. I tried to talk some sense into her, but—well, she keeps making half promises but she still hasn't gone."

"I don't know what I can do—"

"You're her employer. You can order her to get a checkup. She'll listen to you."

Guy gave a derisive snort. "That's a joke, Arnold. She's an independent person. She'd resent my interference into her life."

There was a long silence. "I don't want anything to happen to that girl," Arnold said finally. "She and her kids—well, they mean a lot to me. She won't listen to me, but I'm sure she'll listen to you. Why don't you take a run out here and have a talk with her? As a personal favor to me?"

"I'm in the middle of a campaign—"

"Come on, Guy. How long would it take? Look, I'm worried about her."

So she really got to you, too, Guy thought—and then wondered about that "too."

"You're serious about this, aren't you? She struck me as someone who can handle her own problems. If she's really sick, she'd go—"

"But maybe she wouldn't. She's had a long run of bad luck, what with the kid being so sick for two years, and then being evicted from her house and losing her belongings. I think she just can't take anymore and she's afraid of what the doctor might tell her."

"What do you mean, 'the kid being so sick for two years'?"

"Laurie had rheumatic fever. It took a couple of years for her to recover. Stormy had to watch her every minute and make sure the kid didn't overexert herself. There was no way she could manage financially, not being able to work, so she had to go on welfare. Then, according to Tommy, they were evicted from the place where they lived and someone ripped off everything they owned. Which is why I have a hunch she's afraid to face up to any more trouble right now."

Guy took a deep breath, prepared to tell Arnold about his tight schedule for the next few days, and then, he heard himself say, "I'll be out there early in the morning."

He hung up on Arnold's "thanks," already regretting his promise. One rule he followed rigidly was not to get involved in other people's lives. Yet, here he was, butting in where he was sure it wouldn't be welcome. And yet—what if Stormy was really sick?

He finished drying his hair and went to bed, but it was a long time before he finally fell asleep that night.

IT WAS NINE O'CLOCK when the big blue helicopter, with the name Harris Developments painted on the side, settled down on the meadow behind Guy's beach house.

There was no question about sneaking up on Stormy this time. She and her kids must have heard the chopper because they were waiting for him at the edge of the meadow when he got out, a paper sack tucked under his arm. It irritated him that he read apprehension in her eyes as he strolled toward them. Hadn't she learned to trust him by now? Maybe that was why his voice was brusque as he told her, "I want to talk to you—alone."

She turned to the kids. "Mr. Harris and I have some business to talk over," she said. "Why don't you go plug in the electric kettle, Tommy, for coffee? And you can put out the coffee cake I made this morning, Laurie. We'll be along in a few minutes."

Guy handed Tommy the paper sack. "Here's a little something I got for you kids," he said.

Laurie smiled at him, and Tommy's eyes took on the predatory look that always amused Guy. Not to his surprise, they ran off toward the house, not looking back.

"Is something wrong?" Stormy asked then. He thought she braced herself but he wasn't sure.

"You tell me," he said.

"I have no idea what you—"

"What the hell are you thinking of, not taking care of yourself?" he demanded.

He saw the change on her face. "Arnold had no business calling you," she said hotly.

"Of course he did. He cares what happens to you. I'm taking you into town for a checkup. And in case you're about to say that you can't afford it, you're on the company's payroll—" he didn't add that her wages came out of his personal account "—so you're covered by health insurance. So get your gear together. The kids can come, too, and I'll keep an eye on them while you're having your examination. It's all been arranged with my own doctor."

"You have no right—"

"Don't you give a damn about your kids? What do you think would happen to them if you—if you let this business go too long? Or maybe you've got some relatives who would be glad to take them in and raise them?"

"You know I don't. But there's nothing wrong with me. Okay, my stomach's been bothering me a little, but I had a checkup at this clinic in town and they said it was indigestion. They gave me some antacid pills and they work just fine. Sometimes I forget to take them—that's all it is."

"When did you have that checkup?" he asked skeptically.

"In March. It isn't something new. I've always had a weak stomach that acts up when I'm—well, anxious."

"And a weak head. Come on, Stormy, you know you have to go for another checkup. Why are you giving me such a hard time?"

She was silent so long that when she gave in, it took him by surprise. "Okay—since you've gone to so much trouble. The kids will love riding in the helicopter. Tommy will probably decide he wants to be a chopper pilot when he grows up—along with a dozen other things."

In his relief, he grinned at her. "He told me he wanted to be a politician and run for mayor—like me."

"That was last week. Right now, he's considering a career as a newspaperman—like Uncle Arnold."

They exchanged wry looks. "Your appointment is at eleven," Guy told her. "I have no idea how long it will take, but I suspect several hours. Don't worry about the kids. I've been thinking about taking them to the Petting Zoo—or maybe into San Francisco to Fisherman's Wharf."

Fifteen minutes later, Stormy and her two kids, all wearing jeans and what were obviously new T-shirts, had gathered near the helicopter. Stormy's T-shirt was a very becoming soft green that accentuated her eyes. Although she wasn't wearing makeup, her tan gave her a healthy look. Since she was several pounds lighter than she'd been the last time he'd seen her, Guy found it hard to believe her story about indigestion and a weak stomach and forgetting to take her antacid tablets.

He saw that everybody was belted in before he activated the rotors. As soon as they were airborne, Tommy began asking eager questions and watching every move that Guy made. Before the flight was over, Guy mused, the boy was sure to come up with some better ways to operate a helicopter.

In the back seat, Laurie was very quiet; she clung to her mother's hand tightly, her eyes wide. Guy wondered how he could have missed it, the child's paleness and other evidence of recent illness. He knew he owed Stormy an apology, but he wasn't sure what to say.

Sorry I thought you were a deadbeat because you were on welfare? Sorry I misunderstood why you didn't work for two years? Sorry I'm always so fast to draw conclusions about other people?

He glanced back, and met Stormy's eyes. "We'll be there in plenty of time," he told her. "Is this your first time in a helicopter?"

"This is my first time to fly in anything," she said. "It must be great, owning your own chopper."

"Actually it belongs to the company," he said, feeling a little embarrassed—and resenting the feeling.

"Since you own the company, that makes it your helicopter, doesn't it?"

"Why are you so contentious, Stormy? Is it a reflex?"

It was a while before she answered. "What does contentious mean?"

"Argumentative."

"And *you're* so easy to get along with?"

"I'm a pussycat—except with you. Now why is that, I wonder?"

Unexpectedly she smiled. "I guess we got off on the wrong foot."

"I guess you're right."

He would have said more except Tommy asked him a question, and the moment passed.

IT WAS ALMOST FOUR when Dr. Johnson, an old friend of Guy's, called him into his office. Stormy, looking very pale, was sitting beside the desk. She didn't speak although she nodded tiredly.

"Well, I have good news and bad news," Dr. Johnson said, turning to Stormy. He was a stocky man, soft-spoken and comfortable to talk to, and Guy had often reflected that his friend must have been born with a silver stethoscope around his neck.

"The problem isn't anything life-threatening, which is the good news. But it also isn't indigestion. You have a small lesion in the lining of your stomach, Stormy, and it needs attention."

"Are you talking about an ulcer?" Guy asked, frowning.

Dr. Johnson nodded. "A still minor one. I'll give you medication, Stormy, but you'll also have to alter your lifestyle. No stress, a bland diet, plenty of quiet and rest. Some of my colleagues disagree on this and call that sort of remedy old-fashioned, but in my experience, it still has merit. The mind is a marvelous organ. It probably has more to do with how the rest of the body performs than most doctors are willing to admit."

He busied himself with a prescription pad, ripped several sheets off and handed them to Guy, not Stormy. Behind his gold-rimmed glasses, his eyes were very curious.

Guy wasn't sure he like the speculation he saw there. After all, when he'd made the appointment with John Johnson, he'd taken pains to explain that Stormy was his employee, not a personal friend.

"I'll see they're filled," he said aloud. "Is there anything else we—Stormy should know?"

For the next few minutes, he listened as his friend set up a routine for Stormy, who had said nothing, not even asking a question. It was at this point that it dawned on him that she wasn't surprised at the diagnosis. Which either meant she had guessed what was wrong or had been told about another ulcer at an earlier examination.

When he ushered her down the hall to the waiting room where he'd left Tommy and Laurie, she asked, "Did the kids give you a hard time?"

"They were great. I took them to the San Francisco zoo. I suspect I enjoyed it as much as they did. I thought Tommy would never stop asking questions."

She gave him a genuine smile. "Thank you—they don't get there as often as I'd like."

He started to ask her how long she'd known she had an ulcer, but they were already in the waiting room.

"Are you okay, Mom?" Tommy asked immediately.

"Everything's fine. I'll probably live to be a hundred. Just a little stomach problem, nothing serious."

"Hey, that's fantastic!" Tommy said. "That's what I told Laurie. 'You know Mom's got a weak stomach, so stop worrying' I told her."

"You was real worried, too," Laurie said reproachfully. She slipped her hand into Stormy's, leaning her head against her mother's arm.

Guy glanced down at his watch. "I'm taking you all out to dinner, but first I think you could do with a rest." He hesitated, then added, "Why don't we go to my place? It's not far from here."

TWO HOURS LATER, Guy was in his bedroom, having himself taken a nap and a shower, trying to decide what would be appropriate to wear for a family-style outing, when the doorbell rang. Although he had a full-time houseman, Kung Toy, who was recently married, had already left for the day, so he threw on a robe and went to answer the door himself.

The tall, slender woman standing there, her smile bright, took him by surprise. Marilyn—dammit, why had she picked *this* evening to drop in on him uninvited?

"Come in, Marilyn," he said, trying to sound welcoming. She lifted her face and he kissed her quickly, then ushered her inside.

"Has something important come up?" he asked pointedly.

"Not really. Since you disappeared so mysteriously today, I decided to spend some time with you this evening. Of course, if you have other plans—?" She eyed the terrycloth robe he was wearing.

"As a matter of fact, I was just dressing to go out."

"I see." There was frost in her voice. "Well, I'd better run along then. Some other time."

She started to turn away, then stopped, staring. Tommy had come up behind Guy; he looked Marilyn over, his nose positively wriggling with curiosity.

"Hello," he said in his adult voice.

"This is Tommy," Guy said, forced into introductions. "And this is my assistant, Miss Wright,"

"Hi. Are you going out to dinner with us?" Tommy asked.

"I haven't been invited," Marilyn said.

"I'm taking Miss Wright out tomorrow night," Guy said quickly.

Marilyn's eyes narrowed; she started to say something, but a sound in the hall stopped her. Even before Guy turned to follow her gaze, he knew it must be Stormy. Wearing one of his robes, a towel wrapped around her head, she came out of the guest bathroom and headed down the hall toward the bedrooms where Tommy and Laurie had been napping.

As if she sensed their eyes watching her, Stormy stopped, turned; at any other time, the disconcertion on her face might have amused Guy.

There was nothing to do but introduce the two women, adding, "Stormy came into town for a medical checkup and I invited her and her kids out to dinner."

Marilyn's smile was tight, too brief. "So you're the notorious—uh, famous Stormy," she said. "Somehow I pictured you differently. You must have had your children quite young."

Stormy regarded her with steady eyes. "Very young. We're sort of growing up together."

"I see. Well, I'll be running along. When will you be picking me up tomorrow, Guy? At the usual time?"

"Eight is fine."

"I'll be ready," she purred. "We'll make it a nice long evening, shall we? You need some relaxation—why don't we go to that new French restaurant that everybody is raving about?"

At his nod, she gave him a brilliant smile, then lifted her face. Although he was forced to kiss her, he made sure it landed on her cheek instead of her lips. Her eyes brushed Stormy's face as she wiggled her fingers at him and swept out the door, leaving the scent of her perfume in her wake.

Stormy caught her son's eye. "Will you tell Laurie to take her shower and get dressed? It's okay to wake her up if she's still asleep."

After he was gone, she turned to Guy. "I hope I haven't caused you any embarrassment, Mr. Harris."

Guy felt a sudden irritation. "I wish you'd drop the Mr. Harris," he said. "I'd even prefer Uncle Guy. And you didn't cause any embarrassment."

To his surprise, she giggled. "Sorry. It *was* kind of funny. She thought—" She giggled again, and it occurred to him that she'd carried off an embarrassing situation better than his elegant assistant had.

"That isn't surprising," he said. "You're a very attractive woman—and you're wearing my robe. She probably figured you just got up from a nap. How could she know that you'd been sleeping alone?"

He had meant it as a joke; the smile slipped off Stormy's face, and some expression he couldn't read replaced it. Suddenly he was acutely aware of the odor of the expensive soap he kept in the guest bathrooms, mingled with a scent that he was sure was all Stormy's own. Without thinking, he put his hand out and brushed a speck of bath powder off her cheek.

Her skin was incredibly soft, and he realized she was trembling. The scent, the slight tremor was like a powerful aphrodisiac. Careless of consequences, he bent his head and kissed her sweetly curved mouth.

He had known it would be erotic, kissing her, but he hadn't expected the almost savage surge of passion that swept through him. He put his arms around her, pulled her close, and was instantly lost in the wonder of her pliant female flesh blending into his own hard male body.

Nothing really earthshaking happened. He was a mature man, experienced in his relationships with women. He didn't lose control and start undressing her, didn't sweep her up and carry her off to his bed to ravish her. Although the temptation to do just that was so strong, he remembered in time that Stormy's children were there, that they might come out of their rooms at any moment.

But it cost him something, both in physical and emotional terms, to end the kiss and release her. He felt as if he'd been kicked by a mule, as if something incredibly desirable had been wrenched form his grasp. It didn't help that she seemed to be having just as hard a time returning to normal. Her eyes had a glazed, feverish look, and her mouth—oh, God, he had to stop looking at that mouth or he would really run amuck....

It took all his control to say, "Are the kids about ready? They must be starved to death. I was careful not to stuff them with junk food today. All Tommy managed to talk me into was popcorn and peanuts and ice cream."

It was make-do talk, a way to fill a void, and when she responded in the same vein, telling him that he probably was the one who felt deprived at the lack of junk food, he knew she'd regained control—if she'd ever really lost it.

He told himself her response to his kiss had probably been gratitude, but he couldn't quite make himself believe it. Whatever had happened, it had been mutual, just as that pulsating response had been real. Maybe abstinence had made her vulnerable—or simply had relaxed her guard for a moment and nature had taken over. Whatever the reason, he intended to be very careful in the future because *he* didn't have any such excuse.

He realized he'd been silent too long, and he rushed into speech. "I'm going to be watching what you order tonight. It's not too soon for you to start following that diet Dr. Johnson gave you," he said.

She gave him a tiny smile. "I don't think they serve broiled fish at McDonald's."

"No fast food tonight. I know a place the kids will just love. Trust me."

She looked at him searchingly. "I do," she said finally. "I do trust you."

And to Guy, her words seemed sincere. So why did he feel so blasted apprehensive?

CHAPTER NINE

STORMY LAY in the elongated rays of the late-afternoon sun, her thoughts drowsy, unfocused. It was good to relax, to not be forced to take advantage of a few minutes alone to make plans for the next day or the next week. Right now, she was thinking about Guy Harris, and while she was still wary of him, her thoughts were strangely pleasant

He was such a—what was that word? A paradox? So successful, and yet strangely down to earth at times. Or maybe the word was "earthy." Yes, that word suited him.

He also was good with her children. When Laurie had asked him if he had any kids, he'd shaken his head and said that since he'd never married, he'd never been blessed in that way. Laurie, her soft heart immediately touched, had looked at him sympathetically and then she'd told him, as artless as Tommy when he was working one of his scams, that her mother was unmarried, too, and that she liked babies very much and probably wouldn't mind having more.

Guy hadn't laughed. He'd nodded gravely, and then he'd asked Laurie a question about her cat, changing the subject. If he'd seen Stormy standing in the doorway, he'd given no sign of it.

A question slipped into her mind. What would it be like to be married to someone like Guy Harris? To live in a penthouse, vacation in exotic places, never have to worry about such fundamental things as rent or food bills or losing a job? To know that your children would have decent clothes, good food—and someday, a fine education? And how would it be to feel safe and secure, knowing you had Guy's love?

Well, there was no danger such a thing would ever happen to her. Two people couldn't be more different. She sighed, thinking how she must have looked to Guy's assistant, who was so beautifully dressed the evening she'd dropped by Guy's apartment and found her and her kids there.

His penthouse was as paradoxical as Guy himself. The kitchen was equipped with every gadget and appliance she'd ever heard of; the furnishings in the rest of the apartment were custom-made, starkly modern. And yet there were those wall paintings, like the primitives she'd once seen in a San Francisco museum, so at odds with the rest of the apartment.

And the books. When she'd passed the door of Guy's den and glanced in to see the floor-to-ceiling wall shelves filled with books, a collection that dwarfed the one at the beach house, she'd felt such a hunger, an envy that was foreign to her nature.

There'd been old books with worn leather covers, new ones with bright gaudy ones, sets of classics, whole shelves of architectural and political science books, and even a row of children's books, some of which, like *Rachel and the Seven Wonders of the World* she'd recognized from her own childhood when she'd haunted the stacks of the local library.

Her dream, when she was growing up in public housing, was to someday have a room filled with books. Although she'd had access to the public library, she hadn't dared sign out any books for fear the neighborhood boys would grab them from her and carry them off. She'd been safe to torment because not only was she so small for her age, but she had no father, no older sister nor brother, to be wary of, no one except her grandmother, the old woman they called "Crazy Sadie," who was even more frail than she.

So she'd done all her reading at the library, allotting herself an hour every afternoon after school. During that precious hour, she'd devoured everything in sight, gulping down words as if she was starving and they were forbidden sweets, hating the moment when she was forced to put a partially read book back in the stacks, knowing that she couldn't be sure that when she came back the next day, the book would still be there. If it had been checked out, then she had to wait, sometimes weeks, to find out what had happened.

But now—Stormy smiled up at the sky and wriggled her toes luxuriously in the warm sand—she had the leisure to read for hours at a time if she liked, time to draw her crazy little cartoons, as she'd been doing today, freedom to take one day at a time without thinking much of the future.

But the last thought was disturbing; it sent a small thrill of alarm through her. That kind of thinking was dangerous. These days in the sun were temporary, couldn't last, so it was foolish to grow careless, to fall into bad habits....

She dozed, and when she awoke, she sat up so suddenly that for a moment she felt dizzy. What had awakened her? She looked around—into Guy's intent stare. He was squatting beside her on the sand, wearing a cotton T-shirt over bathing trunks. The T-shirt read, Guy Harris, That's Me! and the caption was so playful, so incongruous with the intense, ambitious man she knew him to be, that she found herself laughing.

"I know I'm no Robert Redford, but I didn't know my face broke people up," he said, his tone rueful.

"It's that T-shirt. It doesn't suit you, Mr. Harris."

For some reason, he looked displeased. "Are you telling me to loosen up? I get that advice from my campaign manager all the time."

"Well, I do associate you with three-piece suits and a power tie," she said.

"Now what do *you* know about power ties?"

Stormy glared at him; she almost welcomed the rush of anger because it put things back in focus. "I can read," she snapped. "I might not have graduated from high school, but I'm not ignorant, no matter what you might think—"

"I didn't mean to insult you, Stormy. It was just a facetious—uh, joking remark."

"I know what facetious means, Mr. Harris."

"I did it again, didn't I? I'm sorry. Just chalk it up to—what would you probably call it? My overdeveloped ego?"

"I wouldn't say that," she said stiffly. "You've been very kind."

His face relaxed into a smile. "There—that didn't hurt, did it?"

She didn't smile back. "Of course, you *were* the cause of most of my recent problems," she pointed out. "And I earn every penny of the wages you pay me."

"You do indeed. The place has never looked better. I see you did some carpentry in the storage room, putting up those shelves. I've been intending to get around to them for ages. Where did you pick up that particular skill?"

"I learned how to handle a hammer when I was trying to keep that cottage on April Street from falling down on our heads," she retorted, and watched with satisfaction the flush that rose on his cheekbones.

"What is this? Trash Guy Harris week?"

"You asked a question. I gave you an honest answer."

A twinkle grew in his eyes—his very attractive eyes, she noted. For a moment, a memory slipped past her defenses. That kiss—why had he kissed her that evening in his penthouse? It couldn't have been because he was overwhelmed by her sex appeal. On a scale of one to ten she probably rated a four to a man like Guy Harris, whom one paper she'd read called "San Jose's most eligible bachelor."

And maybe what she *should* be asking herself was why she'd let him kiss her. Why hadn't she slapped his face or told him off? This was something she consciously hadn't allowed herself to think about for the past few days. No stress, the doctor had said...

"I think I've figured out why you're as prickly as a porcupine most of the time," he said. "You attack first, before the other guy gets a chance. And you can't stand the thought that I might think you were accepting a favor from me."

He raised his hand when she opened her mouth. "Let me finish. I'm just as bad. I keep assuming the worst about you. So why don't we declare a truce. No more prickles from you and no more suspicions from me."

She regarded him with thoughtful eyes. "Okay, no more prickles," she said, making up her mind. "But you be careful what you say, too."

"I'll be careful. Is it okay if I tell you that you looked like an old art nouveau print I once saw when you were standing in that tide pool a while ago, the wind blowing your hair all over the place?"

She felt her face grow hot, and automatically, she put her hands to her cheeks. Realizing he was smiling, she put them down again. A sharp retort rose to her lips, but she suppressed it and gave him a cool smile.

"Which print? *September Morn*?" she asked sweetly.

The surprise on his face delighted her. "Gotcha!" she crowed.

"Okay, you got me. It *was* September Morn." His grin was so infectious that she had to smile back.

"Where are the kids?" he asked idly.

"Arnold took them into Bolinas with him to pick up some groceries. They should be back any minute."

She rose, gathering up her beach towel. Since she didn't have a swim suit, she'd worn a pair of cutoff jeans and her oldest T-shirt to wade in the surf, and she was suddenly very much aware how the still-damp material clung to her breasts, especially since Guy was making no effort to hide his interest.

"Time to start supper," she said briskly, resisting an impulse to drape the towel over her shoulders. "I made meat loaf for the kids and me, but I can thaw out a steak for you."

"I stopped on the way to the airport and picked up a supply of steaks and roasts and seafood. When I put them away in the freezer, I realized it was still stocked with meat. I know you aren't vegetarians, Stormy so what gives?"

She brushed the sand off her legs, avoiding his eyes. When she pretended not to hear his question, he didn't pursue it. Instead he told her he was going for a swim. "To sharpen my appetite," he added. "And don't bother with a steak for me. I like meat loaf."

He stripped off his T-shirt, and she couldn't help noticing his superb physical condition. In his clothes, he looked a little stocky, but she realized now it was because of the breadth of his chest. As he trotted away toward the surf, she studied the hardness of his body, his well-developed thighs. Did he work out daily or was he into some sport?

Probably handball, she thought. Wasn't that the favorite pastime of men who were so busy making money that they didn't have time for polo?

She was smiling as she climbed the cliff stairway. Halfway up, it came to her that she'd been smiling quite a lot lately. Was it because she had no immediate worries? Or because of Guy's frequent visits?

If the last, it was time she faced reality. Her experience with men had been limited, but she did know how dangerous it was to get emotionally involved with one. Those first months after she'd met Eric, when she was sneaking out nights to meet him, she'd been deliriously happy, too infatuated to see that Eric's charm was all superficial, that he was weak and lazy, interested only in getting her into bed with him.

That was why he'd lied, of course, about not being married. She'd been so crazy in love that she hadn't noticed the signs that should have told her that it wasn't going to last. But up until the time she got pregnant with Laurie, even though the romance had gone out of the relationship, she'd been hanging on, hoping for the best, sure that eventually Eric would be the father to her children she wanted him to be.

Looking back, she could see how stupid and naive she'd been. Eric had never paid any attention to his son. Even after he started spending most of his time away from home, she'd still hung in there. Then she'd become pregnant again, and he had gone off one day and never came back, leaving her without any money, with the rent overdue...

Well, she could still give her kids a happy childhood. After all, in a strange, unconventional way she'd had one herself—up until Grandma Todd had turned...well, senile dementia, the doctors at the clinic had called it.

And that kind of happiness, of emotional security was something her own children deserved. Which meant she had to be careful in the future. She didn't want Tommy and Laurie to grow up with memories of a perpetually worried mother. To begin with, she was going to milk these days at the beach of every possible joy. And when, inevitably, they ended, she wasn't going to become desperate and unhappy, no matter what lay ahead.

No, she was going to remember how it felt to have fun, to not be worried all the time, and that's how she would behave. Who knows, she might even fool Tommy and Laurie.

As for Guy—it was stupid to relax her guard with him. He not only lived in a different world, but he was obviously not interested in her as a woman. And maybe it was dangerous to feel so carefree and happy. Eventually she would have to return to San Jose, and face reality again. But maybe she was wrong about being too cautious. After all, she didn't want Laurie and Tommy to grow up with only memories of perpetual trouble and hardship. So why *not* milk these days for every possible happy memory?

GUY was putting his T-shirt back on, after a brisk swim out to the breakwater, when he spotted the small sketch pad he had seen Stormy absorbed in earlier, when he'd been watching her from the cliff wall. It way lying near a clump of ice plants, along with a drawing pencil. Idly, he picked it up and began flipping through it.

There was no doubting that Stormy was talented—surprisingly talented. There were sketches of Tommy, absorbed in one of his games, looking like a small intelligent owl in his out-sized glasses, and Laurie, holding the doll she'd told him she'd adopted, could have stepped right off the page.

Then there was the cat—a subtle line here and there gave it the fey charm that made the name Magic so right. Although he wasn't a cat lover, he had to admit this was—well, tolerable. In fact, he was flattered that she'd accepted him, even though he still felt a little queasy when she settled herself in his lap, staring up at him as if she could see right into his brain.

And there was that little trick she had of staring at one spot on the living room floor—always the same spot—and when she did, the skin on his upper arms crawled. No wonder people used to think cats were the familiars of witches. He flipped to another page, to a drawing of Arnold Story, and his face sobered. He'd known Arnold since he was in his late teens. Over the years, they had become good friends, but it had taken him a long while to see past Arnold's reserve, to feel that he really knew the man. So how had Stormy done it so quickly, seen the kindness hidden behind his friend's irascible exterior, caught the recent unhappiness that Arnold concealed so well?

That business between Arnold and his wife—it must have cut much deeper and been more serious than Arnold had let on. And Stormy had caught it, that darkness of Arnold's spirit, with a few strokes of her pencil....

Guy went on, turning the pages, sometimes pausing to examine a sketch more closely. Intermingled with the character sketches were other, more crudely-drawn figures of a mother, a young boy, and a young girl, sketched in various situations, with bits of dialogue written in beside them. It looked as if Stormy was experimenting with a comic strip, using herself and her kids as models.

It was toward the end of the sketch pad that he found the drawing of an apartment. Not just the floor plan, but sketches of a kitchen, living room, three bedrooms, equipped with very simple but comfortable furniture.

The drawings had a completed look, as if they were the accumulation of much thought and planning, and he wondered how long she'd had this particular dream. She hadn't aspired to a house; she must have known this was impossible. In fact, the apartment was small, no "upgraded" touches, just the bare necessities. But she'd put a lot of thought into it, and his architect's eye saw that it was surprisingly practical, leaving room for the individual taste of its occupants.

His eyes lingered on the sketch of a wall of plants. Nothing exotic or expensive here. Just homey and practical and, he was sure, easy to care for, as were the rest of the apartment's furnishings. This particular dream was within her grasp—or would be with a decent job and a certain amount of luck. It was even something he could provide—but did he want to?

He came upon another sketch, this one of a man, and his whole body stiffened. Had he really looked like that to Stormy the evening he'd gone to April Street, righteously intent on setting an opportunist right? Of course, he didn't really have horns, like the man in the cartoon, but he had to admit she'd hit the frown, the wary eyes, right on the button.

He closed the pad and returned it to the spot beside the ice plants, suddenly aware that he'd been intruding upon another person's privacy. Some of the sketches were too personal, too revealing of Stormy's mind. And why, except for the caricature, were there no other sketches of him? Did she find him that distasteful?

Well, what did he expect? They were just employer and employee. He certainly didn't waste any time worrying about her personal opinions, any more than he did the personal lives of—say, his houseman or his office help....

ARNOLD KNEW, the minute he came into the house that he'd left so angrily and where he'd lived with Elsie for thirty-three years, that it was empty. He also knew that his annoyance because Elsie wasn't there to greet him was unreasonable. After all, he hadn't told her he was coming. How could he expect her to be home? Even if she'd known he would be dropping by to pick up some clothes, she probably wouldn't have canceled her club meeting or luncheon at the country club or whatever she was doing today.

The thought was so self-pitying that he shook his head in disgust. He was getting crotchety, just like Guy had said last week. And look who'd been talking! Now *there* was a guy, a young one, who was going to be as mean as a hound dog with a sore paw if he wasn't careful. What Guy needed was—well, just what was there, within his reach. He'd seen the way he looked at Stormy—and the way she looked back.

Despite the sexual tension that fairly sizzled the air between them when they were in the same room with each other, she still called him Mr. Harris, was unfailingly polite and formal with him. Which probably meant that she was very much aware of the social gap between them. Stormy was a high-school dropout, raised in a public housing project, and for all her appeal, was totally without sophistication, while Guy, with his fine education, was urbane, extremely ambitious—and very vulnerable to gossip.

So Guy was right to be leery. Sure, the chemistry between them last night, when he'd joined them for one of Stormy's meat loaf suppers, had been apparent, even to him. But life wasn't spent in bed. For a man like Guy, the important things were building a career, amassing a fortune, fulfilling ambitions and goals. Guy, of all people, would be aware of the pitfalls of letting his attraction to Stormy develop further. Another man, less controlled, might take a chance, but not Guy, who always knew exactly where he was going and how to get there.

So it wasn't going to happen, and he didn't know whether to be glad or sorry. Glad because the two of them would be risking so much if they drifted into intimacy, or sorry that real life wasn't a love song, a fairy tale with a happy ending. No matter how many good qualities Stormy had, she still wasn't in Guy's social class, wasn't anywhere near it. And she also wasn't someone Guy could make his mistress, tuck away on a side street while he went on with his life. She was too independent, too proud. So the best thing that could happen was for Guy to stay away and let her alone.

Arnold opened the refrigerator door, took out a container of lemonade, and poured himself a glass. He took a long gulp, not bothering to sip it first. It was only when he had refilled the glass, carried it outside and was sitting in the sun on the deck beside the swimming pool, that he realized the drink was sweet, just the way he liked it. And Elsie never added sugar to anything she ate or drank. Which was why she had that trim figure.

So what did it mean? Had it been habit, adding sugar when she made the lemonade? Or had she been expecting him today and fixed it the way he liked it? No, that was impossible. It had to be habit—or was she expecting a guest... say, another man?

The suspicion made his nostrils flare. Maybe that was why she hadn't had time for him after he'd retired. Of course, he had made such a point of telling her that he didn't intend to get in her hair—and then, or course, he'd done just that.

He should have pursued some hobby earlier, preparing for this day. But how could he have guessed that retirement would come so soon? He had expected to go on working until he was seventy—at the least.

Well, things had perked up for him these past weeks, thanks to Stormy and her youngsters. He'd always thought he didn't mind that he and Elsie hadn't had kids, that she was barren. But then, he hadn't known how interesting a kid like Tommy, with his inquiring, curious mind, could be. He hadn't known the satisfaction of being accepted by someone like Laurie, who looked like a fairy princess and whose heart was so easily touched.

And Stormy. She was the kind of daughter he and Elsie should have had—tough, able to take care of herself, and yet with so much empathy for anyone or anything in trouble.

She was a hell of a lot like Elsie in that way—and in being her own person, too. Right from the beginning, when he'd started courting Elsie, she'd let him know that she wasn't about to let him take over, that she was her own person. Only, thirty-six years ago, she hadn't used those words. Independent was the word she'd used. And he'd known that if he didn't win her, he would die of disappointment....

Did she ever think of those days, of the early years of their marriage? They had been so passionately in love—God, how they had loved to make love to each other! And then, so gradually that he wasn't sure how it had happened, they had grown apart. Would it have been different if they'd had a family? Or if he'd devoted more time to her and less to the newspaper?

"Well, this is a surprise, Arnold," Elsie said from the patio.

He looked around, and because it had been several weeks, he saw her with fresh eyes. Her hair was silver-white now, but her skin was still virtually unmarked by time, and her eyes were the same flawless blue as when he'd first met her in his father's office at the newspaper.

She'd been a file clerk, but it hadn't mattered. He hadn't cared that she was poor, from a less-than-respectable family, with an alcoholic father and a sluttish mother. He'd fallen in love—and that had been the important thing. And it had worked out—until lately.

"You're looking good, Elsie," was the only thing he could think to say.

"And you've been getting some sun," she said. "Haven't you picked up a little weight?"

"Five pounds. I've been eating very well, thank you."

"You've gained weight on your own cooking? Does that mean you've been eating junk food? You can't boil an egg without burning it."

"It's not my own cooking. Guy Harris's caretaker is a fabulous cook. Not gourmet like you, of course, but what she can do with a few simple ingredients, you wouldn't believe."

"She has you over often?"

"Every night. She and her kids really liven up my life," he said.

"I see. What's her name?"

"Stormy. And she suits her name. Fiery-tempered when someone steps on her toes, but she can be as sweet as honey, too. She's quite a gal."

"How old is she?"

He scratched his head; he discovered he was really enjoying himself. "I'm not really sure. She's older than she looks, I'd say. Then there's her kids. Tommy's as smart as a whip. Beats me at chess all the time. And Laurie—well, she's as pretty as her mother."

Elsie came out into the sun and sat down opposite him. Studiously she stared at a jade plant that filled a huge stone urn. "I'll have to tell Juan to spray that plant for mealy bug," she said absently.

"Tell him to dab it with alcohol—but not too strong a solution and not in the sun. That'll get rid of them," he said.

She gave him a curious look. "Where did you learn that? You never took any interest in gardening before."

"Never realized how fascinating it could be until Stormy got me interested. She's got a green thumb. She worked in a florist shop once and picked up a lot of tricks."

He risked a quick look at Elsie, discovered she was frowning. "You should see her plants. Knock your eyes out," he added for good measure.

"Oh? Is she into orchids?"

"Orchids? No, even more exotic plants," he said. *Like sweet potato vines and orange and avocado trees started from pits...*

Elsie didn't say anything for a while. He sipped his lemonade, humming under his breath.

"Did you come home for anything in particular?" she asked finally.

"I came to pick up some of my clothes. I need a new supply of underwear—say, where did you put those silk pajamas my sister got me for Christmas a couple of years ago?"

"You never wear pajamas, not since our—" She broke off, then changed it to, "I'll see if I can find them for you."

She bustled into the house and he grinned after her. So she remembered those pajamas he'd bought for their honeymoon, did she? And she wasn't happy that he had suddenly decided to start wearing silk pajamas to bed again.

But his good humor didn't last. After all, what difference did it make if she still had a small streak of jealousy left? It didn't really change anything.

"Here," Elsie said. She laid the pajamas, folded neatly, on the table near his chair. "Anything else you need, you'd better choose yourself."

I need you, Elsie, he wanted to say, but he didn't. He had his pride and she was the one who had asked him to leave, to go "cool off and do some thinking." So it was up to her to ask him to come back. And if he did, things were going to be different. By golly, they were.

He finished off his lemonade and set his glass down. "Well, I better get started."

"It's almost four. You shouldn't be driving those mountain roads after dark."

"Oh, Guy Harris is picking me up. We're taking his chopper. We'll be there long before dark."

"Oh? You two are pretty chummy these days, aren't you? I thought you didn't approve of his politics. 'A little right of the right-wingers,' I think you said."

Arnold rubbed his chin. "I could have been wrong about that. Seems to me he makes a lot of sense these days. Something is mellowing him—or someone."

"Now that surprises me. That business about him evicting that poor woman and her kids didn't sound as if he'd mellowed."

He stared at her. "What are you talking about?"

"It was in the *Bayside News*. Something about him having some woman's furniture put out on the curb because she was behind in the rent."

"That's a bunch of garbage. Guy can be a hard nose, but he isn't a monster. It was probably blown all out of proportion by that ass, Harvey Cummins. He's never gotten over losing that lawsuit."

"You're probably right." Elsie hesitated, then added, her voice a little too casual. "I might be coming out to the beach someday soon. I've been so busy lately that—well, I could use a little ocean air."

"You do look a little pale. A few hours of sun will do you good," Arnold said, managing a tone as casual as hers.

It wasn't until he'd gone upstairs to pack a suitcase that he allowed himself a satisfied grin.

ON THE WAY BACK to Bolinas in Guy's helicopter, he remembered Elsie's remarks about the gossip about Guy.

"What's this about your real-estate company evicting a young mother and her two children?" he asked.

Guy gave him a long thoughtful look. "You mean Stormy hasn't told you all about that episode?"

"Are you saying it's true, that it was Stormy and her kids who got evicted?"

"It was Stormy. How did you hear about it?"

"Elsie—and Tommy told me once that they'd been evicted. I put two and two together. How did it happen? I can't believe you had anything to do with such a dastardly deed."

But Guy didn't laugh at his wry remark. "It was one of those crazy mix-ups," he said. He went on to explain about a lost memo, followed by the theft of Stormy's possessions. "Stormy was so convinced that the police would do nothing to find her stuff that she didn't even file a complaint," he added.

"So you offered her the caretaker's job? You felt that responsible for what happened?"

"She blamed me when she heard about the theft. So she went out to Bolinas to do some squatting. I didn't know she was out there until you told me about your great new housekeeper and cook."

"And that's when you went out to Bolinas and offered her the job?"

"Actually I went out there to evict her. I didn't know about the theft until Tommy told me about it. I thought she'd put her stuff in storage."

"Well, it all worked out okay, didn't it?" He paused, thinking. "So what's going to happen now? You haven't got plans for something more personal, do you?"

Guy gave him a long, considering look. "Doesn't that come under the heading of mind your own business, Arnold?"

"Maybe so—but I hope you aren't. That girl is special. One of a kind. And I don't want to see her hurt. You don't have any staying power, Guy. You can only make things worse for her. And remember—it isn't just Stormy—there's her kids, too."

This time, the look Guy gave Arnold held anger. He'd seen his friend's temper before although he'd never been the recipient of it. Rather than carry it any further, Arnold was silent, knowing that he had no right to protest. But as the chopper began its descent to the meadow behind Guy's house, he made a decision. If he got a chance, he would talk to Stormy. And maybe he could convince her not to get too involved with Guy. Hell, he loved the guy—but that didn't mean that he was going to stand by and let her do something that could be the mistake of her life.

CHAPTER TEN

DURING THE NEXT DAYS, as summer arrived in earnest, the phrase "playing with fire" often came to Guy's mind. He knew it was unwise to see so much of Stormy and her kids, to impulsively drop in on them in his chopper, bearing food and gifts for Tommy and Laurie. Although at first Stormy accepted the latter without comment, he knew she had her reservations and he wasn't surprised when she eventually voiced them.

It was Sunday, and he was driving home after a difficult weekend—a series of radio interviews, a couple of which were openly hostile, a fund-raising banquet and two tiring strategy meetings, one with his finance committee and the second with his staff. Because he was tired to the bone, the thought of the sea breezes off Marin Coast was too tempting to resist. Not only was he sick of people who made demands upon him as if, by running for office, he was now available for any intrusion on his privacy, but the reproach in Marilyn's eyes whenever he made an excuse to avoid spending an evening alone with her was grating on his nerves.

It wasn't that he didn't enjoy her company. She was bright, vivacious and more than attractive, and he was proud to be seen with her in the fine restaurants of the Bay Area. But she wanted more from him, more than he was willing to give these days.

Why was it, he wondered, that he had lost all sexual interest in her? God knew sex was important to him—and Marilyn was one of the best bed partners he'd ever had. But he hadn't made love to her in months. Maybe he was beginning to burn out sexually at thirty-six. Or was it their relationship that had burned out without him noticing? Had it ever been anything but convenience and casual sex on his part?

Well, it was obvious that Marilyn hadn't lost interest in him. If anything, she was more aggressive these days, which was definitely off-putting. He had always admired her sophistication, and she was still the best-looking woman he'd ever been involved with. That new hairdo she was sporting emphasized her classic features, and the silky, very feminine dresses she wore to work, while appropriate for the office, flattered and emphasized the svelteness of her body. So why didn't all that perfection stir him these days?

And why, at the oddest and most incongruous times, did the mental image of a piquant face, a head of short, impossibly curly black hair, a too-thin body and a radiant smile, make his pulse leap?

Guy realized where his thoughts were heading and he caught them up short. Although Arnold's warning still smarted, he knew his friend had been right, and he'd been very careful not to let his attraction to Stormy get out of hand. But God, he was tired—and hungry tonight. Not for the fancy food of an elegant French restaurant, but for simple, unassuming food like, of all things, beans and corn bread and cole slaw and something tasty grilled on a charcoal barbecue.

He made up his mind quickly. What the hell—he'd built the beach house for just this kind of relief from the pressures of city life, hadn't he? Just because it was occupied right now, why should he spend the night in town? He was an adult. He could handle the problem of—well, whatever the problem was.

He stopped by a supermarket near the airport where he kept his helicopter, picked up chicken breast fillets, potatoes and fresh salad vegetables. At the last moment, he paused by the bakery section and chose a strawberry cheesecake. Feeling a little guilty because he hadn't called Stormy to tell her he was coming, he drove to the airport and was airborne in a matter of minutes.

The sky to the east was beginning to darken by the time the helicopter swooped over the row of beach houses north of Bolinas and settled down on the meadow. Although the sun was hidden behind the coastal fog, already gathering to the west, it was still very light as he walked toward the beach house. He deposited the groceries in the kitchen, then went looking for Stormy, found her on the beach, surrounded by children.

As he approached the group, he heard Tommy tell the other children, "Don't worry. My mom knows what to do. She's always taking in hurt animals and things."

Stormy, he saw now, was kneeling on the sand, cuddling a small puppy. It was whimpering pitifully, and from the glazed look in its eyes, he suspected it was in shock.

"What happened?" he asked.

Stormy didn't seem surprised to see him. Her voice was husky as she told him, "A dune buggy hit it."

"Yeah, and then they went on," Tommy said indignantly. "Is he hurt bad, Mom?"

"No, he's just stunned, I think. I can't find any broken bones or other injuries. Does anyone know who the puppy belongs to?"

Most of the children shook their heads, but one boy, who looked to be Tommy's age, said, "There were some

You may be the winner of the
MILLION DOLLAR GRAND PRIZE!

You'll love your elegant 20kt gold electroplated chain! The necklace is finely crafted with 160 double-soldered links and is electroplate finished in genuine 20kt gold. And it's free as added thanks for giving our Reader Service a try!

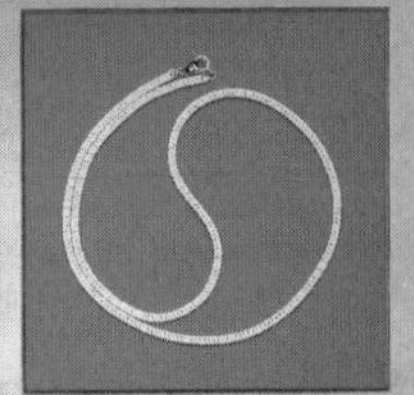

DETACH AND MAIL TODAY

Harlequin Reader Service®

Sweepstakes Entry Form

This is your **unique** Sweepstakes Entry Number: 3M 257316

This could be your lucky day! If you have the winning number, you could be the Grand Prize Winner. To be eligible, *affix Sweepstakes Entry Sticker here!*

If you would like a chance to win the $25,000.00 prize, the $10,000.00 prize, or one of the many $5,000.00, $1,000.00, $250.00 or $10.00 prizes…plus the Mustang and the Hawaiian Vacation, *affix Bonus Prize Sticker here!*

To receive free books and gifts with no obligation to buy, as explained on the opposite page, *affix the Free Books and Gifts Sticker here!*

Please enter me in the sweepstakes and, when the winner is drawn, tell me if I've won the $1,000,000.00 Grand Prize! Also tell me if I've won any other prize, including the car and the vacation prize. Please ship me the free books and gifts I've requested with sticker above. Entering the Sweepstakes costs me nothing and places me under no obligation to buy! (If you do not wish to receive free books and gifts, do not affix the FREE BOOKS and GIFTS sticker.)

134 CIH KA9D
(U-H-SR-08/90)

YOUR NAME PLEASE PRINT

ADDRESS APT#

CITY STATE ZIP

Offer limited to one per household and not valid for current Harlequin Superromance subscribers.

Printed in U.S.A.

campers here a couple of nights ago, and after they left, I saw the puppy running around the beach. I guess they didn't want him so they just left him behind."

Stormy muttered something under her breath. "Well, we can't leave him here. I think we'd better take him up to the house and fix him a place in the kitchen until he's better." She focused her attention on Guy. "If that's okay with you, of course, Mr. Harris."

"I'll carry him," he offered, and carefully gathered the dog up in his arms.

The other children followed him up the cliff steps and into the house. Some of them looked familiar, but he couldn't put a name to any of them. Strange—Stormy had only been here a few weeks and yet she seemed to know everybody on the beach.

It took a while to get the puppy settled in a padded cardboard box. First, he had to be fed—and since he ate like a glutton, gulping the food down as if he were starved, Stormy was confident that he was going to be okay. Then each child had to touch him, pet him, which he responded to with such appreciation that Guy reflected he was soon going to be one very spoiled pup.

After he fell asleep and the children went home, Stormy finally had time for Guy. The very fact that this irritated him was a warning. Was it possible that he was jealous of her attention to a blasted stray mutt?

He gave Tommy and Laurie the stack of books he'd bought for them, then told Stormy he was starved, how about him barbecuing the chicken fillets he'd brought? She began fixing a salad while he lit the barbecue and rolled potatoes in foil for baking. She seemed unusually preoccupied, as if she had something on her mind, and he wasn't surprised when she told him abruptly that she wanted to talk to him.

"Fire away," he said.

"It's the presents you've been bringing Tommy and Laurie," she said. "I know you mean well, but you're spoiling them. I heard Tommy tell Laurie yesterday that he hoped you'd bring him a new Nintendo game next time you came. They like you for yourself, you know. You don't have to be an Uncle Bountiful and buy their affection."

"I'm not trying to. I get a kick out of giving them gifts," he protested.

"I know you do. And it's very kind and generous of you. But you see, when we go back to the city, money is going to be tight. I don't want them to get used to things like—well, what you've been giving them. That summer dress you brought Laurie last week must have cost more than I'll earn in a week. You do see my point, don't you?"

He did—but that didn't make it easier to accept. "Of course," he said, and despite himself his voice sounded stiff. "I understand."

Her eyes sharpened and she started to speak, but Tommy came running up, eyeing the chicken fillets hungrily. "When we going to eat?" he demanded, effectively ending the conversation.

After dinner, Tommy talked the others into a long, involved game of Monopoly, which lasted until the children's bedtime. Not to anyone's surprise, Tommy ended up the winner, having bankrupted the rest of them.

Later, Guy found himself reading a bedtime story about a rather naive rabbit to Laurie, not really sure how it had come about since he couldn't remember volunteering. She fell asleep before he was finished and he turned off the bedside lamp, tiptoed out and went back downstairs.

Stormy was in the kitchen, cleaning up. When he offered to help, she refused his offer.

"I'm almost finished. I'll say good-night now unless—is there anything else you want?"

"No—oh, yes. How about having a drink with me when you're finished?"

She looked away. "I think I'd better go on to bed. Tomorrow is one of my cleaning days for Arnold. I want to get an early start."

"How is Arnold?"

She sighed and shook her head. "He puts up a good front, but I think he's a very unhappy man. The only time he smiles is when he's playing with the kids. He taught Tommy chess and they really get into some battle royals. Arnold's quite a favorite with Laurie. She loves it when he reads to her. Even so—well, I don't think retirement agrees with him."

"Does he ever talk about Elsie, his wife?"

"Very seldom. I think he expected her to come out last week, but she didn't turn up. I still haven't met her. Is she—nice?"

"Elsie's a sweetheart. They had a tiff, you know. It's obvious they haven't straightened things out yet."

"He shouldn't have retired. He's a man who needs challenges," she said.

"He had a minor heart attack, which probably scared him into retirement," he told her. "At the time, he seemed willing enough. He claimed he'd worked hard all his life and needed the rest."

"Well, maybe that's the kind who shouldn't retire, the ones who work so hard." She gave Guy an appraising look. "I can't imagine *you* ever retiring."

And do what? he thought. *Sit on the wharf and fish? Take trips to places I really don't want to see? Contemplate my navel? Is that how it's been with Arnold? If so—I feel sorry for the guy....*

"Well, retirement is the last thing on my mind," he said aloud. "Talk to me when I'm Arnold's age. And you're very perceptive about people. You should be working in a profession that utilizes it."

"Such as what?"

"Oh—psychiatry or maybe social work," he said glibly. He caught her frown and asked, "What did I say? You don't approve of psychiatrists?"

"I don't approve of social workers," she said.

"I'm sure they just do their job. After all, there has to be supervision or—" He stopped, a little too late.

"Or the taxpayers gets ripped off by deadbeats? Is that what you were going to say?" she demanded. "Well, excuse me if I don't bleed for them. It was social workers who put my grandmother in Napa. She begged them not to separate us, but no, they knew what was best. So they took her away and I never saw her again. She wasn't senile, no matter what they said. She was just frightened, afraid to leave our flat. And we were getting along okay. I never missed a day of school and—" She broke off and gave him an angry look. "I'll see you in the morning," she said and turned her back.

Guy retreated into the living room. He sat for a while, thinking over their conversation, then looked around for the book he'd been reading the last time he was there, one of Tom Clancy's spy thrillers. It was gone from the table where he'd left it, but he found it back on one of the built-in shelves, lined up with other books by the same author. As he plucked it off the shelf, he reflected that Stormy was almost obsessive in her neatness. Did she love cleaning and dusting and vacuuming and keeping things in order? Or was it simply that she wanted to earn her pay? And where in this room was there any evidence that children lived here? She hadn't known he was coming today. Were they only allowed to play in their bedrooms?

He tried to immerse himself in the book, but his mind kept wandering, and he finally gave up and went into the kitchen for a cup of coffee. He heard Stormy's voice even before he rounded the oak block table in the middle of the kitchen and saw her, kneeling beside the puppy. She spoke so softly that at first he couldn't make out her words. When he did, he wished he hadn't come in because they obviously weren't meant for other ears.

"There...don't you fret. Stormy won't let anything happen to you. I'd keep you myself only I don't know where we'll be living when we go back at the end of the summer. From the looks of those big feet, you're going to be a monster, and if we keep you too long, no one will want you."

The puppy whimpered and she stroked its back. "Tomorrow we're going to find you a nice home, and maybe by the time you're half-grown and not so cute, they'll be so fond of you that they'll keep you. It didn't work for me, but then I was past the cute stage when I got put up for adoption. It's different with puppies. People love puppies, even ugly ones. But behave yourself, you hear? Mr. Harris's a loner. He doesn't like animals—or anything else very much. He just might turn you out if you make a fuss."

She went on talking, but Guy turned quietly and went back to the living room to polish off a shot of Scotch, neat. Was that how she saw him—a loner who didn't like animals or anything else very much? He poured himself another drink, but when he realized what he was doing, he poured it out in the bar sink and went to bed.

GUY STAYED AWAY from Bolinas for the next ten days, but when he found himself with a free day and evening because of two canceled events, he weakened. After all, why should he let himself be chased out of his own place by a pint-sized woman with a biased opinion of him?

Stormy took his unannounced appearance with her usual equilibrium. Since he wasn't bearing gifts, she even seemed pleased to see him. He had almost defied her and brought the Nintendo game Tommy wanted, but he changed his mind. *Uncle Bountiful*, she had called him, a name that was especially irksome because he was aware it was appropriate.

Not to his surprise, Tommy looked disappointed when he realized Guy hadn't brought him a gift, but then he began talking about the puppy and how he was already growing.

"I thought your mother was going to find a home for him," Guy commented.

"She tried—but everybody around here already has a dog or they don't want one. Magic doesn't mind. She likes the puppy. Laurie and me want to keep Shag, but—"

"Shag?"

"Yeah. You know, for shaggy dog. He's going to be a monster, Mom says. You can tell by the feet. She says he'll eat us out of house and home if we keep him. I guess she's right only—well, maybe she'll get a job that pays a lot of money and then we can keep him. Dog food is real expensive—you know?"

"I know."

"Maybe something will happen that—" He looked at Guy with that appraising expression that made him look so adult. "You ever think about getting married, Uncle Guy?"

Tommy, the matchmaker? The thought amused Guy but he didn't smile. "No. I'm not in the market for a wife."

Tommy sighed. "Well, I guess some guys just don't like women," he said.

"I like women. I just don't want—" He broke off, and when he went on, it was about another subject. "How about a game of chess?" he said.

As they walked back toward the house, Tommy told him about a new game he'd been working on. They had almost reached the back patio when Laurie came running out of the house. She raised her arms for a hug, something she wouldn't have done a month earlier. In the sun, her skin had a delicate glow, and her cheeks had taken on warm color. She still looked like an angel, but now it was a very healthy angel.

"You haven't been out, Uncle Guy," she said reproachfully.

"I've been very busy," he said.

"That's what Mom said. 'Mr. Harris's so busy running for mayor that I don't expect him out again for a long time,' she said."

"Oh, she did, did she? Well, it looks like your mom isn't always right."

"Most of the time she is. Uncle Arnold says she's smart as a whip and it's too bad she never got a chance to finish high school," Tommy said. "Me, I'm going to college, maybe Stanford or maybe Harvard. I haven't made up my mind yet. I'll have to get a scholarship, of course, but that won't be too hard. I'm pretty smart."

"And modest, too," Guy murmured.

Tommy looked thoughtful. "I don't think I'm that. I guess I like to—uh, blow my own horn a lot. At least that's what Mr. Fredericks said."

"Mr. Fredericks?"

"My teacher at school. I don't think he meant it as a compliment."

"I'm sure you're right. People usually don't like to hear us brag about our own accomplishments."

Tommy sighed. "I know. But sometimes I get carried away. And how are people going to know how smart you are if you don't tell them?"

"They find out—sometimes, the hard way," Guy said, wondering where this conversation was taking them.

"Yeah. Well, other kids brag all the time. Mostly about the junk they got for Christmas and how much money their dad makes and what their mom paid for their stupid clothes. As if I care. And I don't care when they call me Welfare Tommy, either."

But you do care, Tommy, Guy thought, remembering how he'd hated being teased about being a foundling.

"The kids called me Orphan Danny because my middle name's Daniel," he said.

"They did? You were on welfare?"

"No, I lived in foster homes. I was an orphan."

"Ah, gee. That musta been a downer, not having any folks. I don't remember my dad, but Laurie and me's got a great mom. All my friends in San Jose liked Mom 'cause she never nagged them to be careful when they came over to the house. Of course, we didn't have much they could hurt."

His face lengthened suddenly. "I don't know why those guys did that, ripped us off. It wasn't as if they could sell our stuff and get a lot of money. It's like someone did it to be mean. Maybe they thought that if we didn't have any furniture we'd just leave town or something. But why would they want that?"

"Don't think about it, Tommy. Bad things happen, and when they do, you just pick yourself up and go on. If you let it bother you too much, you lose. If you don't, then you win."

"That's just about what Mom said. Only she did a lot of crying at night when she thought we was asleep. She hated it most that they took our toys and her books and Grandma Todd's photo album. This was the second time we got evicted, you know, only the first time Mom had already sold most of her furniture. This was after my dad split. I don't remember it 'cause I was only a couple years old. That's when we lived in the shelter for a while and then Mom got a job taking messages for people and we lived in that hotel until after Laurie was born. Then Mom saved enough so we could move into our own apartment, only we had to sleep on the floor and Laurie slept in a basket. Then someone gave us a mattress and we got the other stuff one thing at a time. I guess we'll have to start all over again when we go back to the city."

He blinked his eyes, looking like a sad little owl. Guy wanted to comfort him, but he didn't know how. "Where's your mother?" he asked.

"She took some soup and stuff over to Uncle Arnold. He's sorta under the weather, I guess."

"He's ill?"

"Not really. Just—you know, feeling down, Mom says. I'm going over there after supper and play chess with him. Maybe I should let him win this time. He don't much like it when he loses."

"You do that," Guy said, suppressing a grin. "What say we start dinner and surprise your mother?"

They chatted amicably while they put together a casserole that had been a staple when Guy was skimping on expenses—cheese and macaroni and slivers of frankfurters—and made a huge salad and spread garlic butter on slices of French bread. When Laurie awoke from her nap, she joined them in the kitchen, setting the table and laying out silver in neat rows. By the time Stormy returned, dinner was ready, needing only to be served up.

Whatever Stormy thought about Guy taking over culinary duties, she said nothing. In fact, she put away a surprising amount of the casserole and salad. Afterward, the kids did the dishes and she and Guy, at his insistence, retreated to the living room. The wind, stirring the raw silk curtains at the open windows, held a mellow warmth. For once, the evening fog was still hovering off the coast and the night sky was clear.

Stormy curled up in one corner of a sofa, sipping the wine he'd poured for her. "How is the campaign going, Mr. Harris?" she asked politely.

"Great. I might even win," he said. "And I think it's about time you call me Guy."

She didn't answer him and he wasn't surprised when she changed the subject. "How come you have the evening off?"

"Happenstance. A money-raising banquet was postponed—it's that flu that's going around. I do have some things to do tomorrow, but not until eleven. Thought I'd take advantage of the hiatus to get in a little swimming—and rest."

"I'll make sure the kids don't bother you in the morning so you can sleep in."

"No problem. I'll be up early as usual. I'm an early riser."

"I'd sleep until noon if I could," she sighed. "One of these days I'm going to stay in bed for a whole week!"

He looked at her in surprise. Somehow he hadn't expected this from someone who seemed so charged with energy. "No reason why you can't sleep late here. You don't have to follow any kind of schedule."

"I won't be here forever. I don't want to pick up any bad habits."

"You like living at the beach, don't you?"

"Of course. Doesn't everybody?"

"No. The salt air is hard on the skin and it practically ruins a hairdo. Or so I've been told."

"By your—by friends of yours?"

He had to smile at her choice of words. "By a woman friend I brought out here once. I come alone these days. This is my refuge from city life."

She gave him a troubled look. "I'm sorry. I hope the kids haven't ruined your refuge for you."

"They don't bother me," he said, and didn't add that it was their mother who bothered him—like right now. Her hair was a riot, as usual, and she was wearing no makeup, dressed in jeans and a T-shirt, both of which had seen much better days, but he was acutely aware of the flawless skin, the seductive curve of her mouth, even of her breath, which held the odor of wine and, of all things, apples....

"Why are you running for mayor?" she asked. It was so rare that she asked him a personal question that he dropped the glib answer he usually gave this particular question.

"My motive is a little self-serving. I'm primarily a builder, of course, and I don't approve of San Jose's antiquated construction regulations. If I get in, my first priority is to make some drastic changes in the way things are set up."

Stormy frowned at him. "I see what you mean about self-serving," she said.

"You misunderstood," he told her. "The building regulations in San Jose are out of step with the modern world. In my own projects, I've always followed the most rigid safety standards. I want to make sure other builders do, too. There are other aspects, too, little private empires that are flourishing among some groups of city employees, plus other bureaucratic bottlenecks that need to be cleared out. In order to prosper, the city needs a very large tax base—and yet industry is going elsewhere because they're tired of fighting against the tide."

"I wasn't going to vote for you, but maybe I'll change my mind," she said, so seriously that he found himself grinning.

"You do that." He drained his wineglass and stood. "I think I'll take a walk along the beach and then turn in for the night."

She rose, picked up their empty wineglasses and started for the kitchen. "Good night, Mr. Harris," she said over her shoulder.

She disappeared into the kitchen, and he stared after her, wondering why he hadn't asked her to join him in his walk along the beach. Well, it was all for the best. A walk through the moon-drenched night with Stormy Todd was unwise—very unwise. But maybe he'd take the puppy with him for company.

He went into the kitchen to get the puppy and found Stormy still there, washing the wineglasses they'd used. "I thought I'd take the puppy with me," he said.

"Oh, he'd love that—he needs to get out more but I'm afraid to risk it with so many dune buggies. I wish they'd ban them."

"I have a feeling you're going to keep him," he said.

"You're wrong." Her voice was firm. "I put some notices on a couple of community service bulletin boards in Bolinas. I'm hoping that someone will take him before he gets too big."

The puppy gave a sharp little bark, and her face softened. "He's already spoiled," she confessed. "If only I could put his breed in the notice, he might be more attractive to people."

"He's a Montesuma retriever," he said, deadpan.

"Really? I never heard of that breed. Are you sure?"

"Absolutely. It's an old breed, pretty rare these days. Fiercely loyal and good with children. Eats like a horse but you don't have to put that in your notices."

"I won't. How on earth do you know so much about dogs?"

"Oh, collecting bits and pieces of trivia is my hobby."

She looked at him suspiciously. "I think I'll look that breed up in your *Webster's*," she said.

He grinned at her. "A good idea."

He left, taking the puppy with him. As he trotted along the beach, the puppy at his heels, it occurred to him that he hadn't thought about the campaign all evening. But that wasn't why he felt so good. He had enjoyed teasing Stormy. For a minute or so, he'd even pulled it off. But not for long. She was sharp, street smart—and full of fascinating contradictions.

Was that why he enjoyed her company more than any other woman he knew?

And there it was again. Dammit, he should have more sense—he *did* have more sense. There was no future in any kind of relationship with Stormy except that of employer and employee. In a few weeks, she would be going back to the city and that would be the end of it. There was no question of her staying out here for the winter. Once the other cabins and lodges were boarded up, she would be alone. It was too isolated, too foggy and wet, too far from the nearest school.

Besides, he didn't want her here. It could only complicate his life. When the time came, he would give her a decent bonus—for a job well done. And then he would make sure she got out of his life for good.

CHAPTER ELEVEN

AS THE EARLY SUMMER weather grew hot and sultry, Guy's life fell into a pattern. Involved in the business of getting elected to public office, he met the demands of his advisors and election committee, attended rallies, appeared at fund-raising dinners, made speeches and gave interviews, always relaxed and unflappable, even when the cohorts of his rival heckled him about his political inexperience.

The source of his strength, he suspected, was not only his own natural resilience and determination, but the time he spent at the beach house in Bolinas whenever he could get away for an evening or even for just a few hours.

During this time away from the city, he put the campaign out of his mind. He ran along the beach for miles, usually with Shag at his heels, ate Stormy's simple meals, played games with Tommy and read bedtime stories to Laurie, and engaged in ferocious chess games with Arnold, winning as often as not because they were almost equally matched. He also played with Tommy, who more than held his own against him.

And during these visits, he watched Stormy. He watched her as she cooked his meals, cleaned his house, worked in the vegetable garden she'd started in a corner of the rear meadow. He lay on the beach, ostensibly taking a nap or reading a book, and watched from under the rim of the old baseball cap he favored as she played with the kids, building sand castles with Laurie or helping Tommy find shells for the collection he'd started, always completely absorbed in whatever she was doing, whether work or play.

And at night, whether in his penthouse in San Jose or at the beach house in Bolinas, he dreamed about her, erotic dreams that angered him because he had no control over them.

Outwardly their relationship was polite, impersonal. She treated him as an employer, allowing him his relationship with her children, but always there was a barrier between them, a thick wall that seemed impervious. Did she still not trust him? He didn't know, and he didn't ask. He didn't even ask himself *why* he didn't ask.

Sometimes, on the rare occasions when the two of them were alone, they talked together pleasantly, but never about personal things. There were so many questions he wanted to ask her—about her relationship with the children's father, about how she had survived those years when the kids were small and her daughter was ill. Was Laurie perfectly well now? She appeared to be in radiant health, her skin a golden tan like her mother's, her eyes bright and her cheeks so pink, but maybe that was deceptive.

He knew these things were none of his business, and yet he had a very personal reason for his curiosity. If Stormy had managed on her own with two kids, somehow staying afloat all those years, then couldn't his own mother have done the same? At the very least, she could have put him up for adoption. Why had she carried him for nine months and then tossed him away like a piece of garbage an hour after he was born? Or had she been the one? Maybe someone else had put him in that trash can. Well, that was something he would never know now. And wasn't it strange that it was only recently that he'd even considered the possibility that his mother hadn't given him up willingly?

Meanwhile, his other life—what he kept reminding himself was his real life—went on. If Marilyn and Larry wondered about his frequent trips to Bolinas when he had such a busy schedule, they asked no questions. Since he'd made it a point not to tell them that he'd had a phone installed at the beach house, there was little chance anyone would find out by accident that Stormy was staying there. Nor could he be reached for those time-consuming and aggravating questions that his staff could take care of on their own.

Then it was almost the Fourth of July and for a wonder, there was nothing on his calendar. A dinner party in his honor had been canceled at the last moment because of a death in the host's family, and a mix-up in dates took care of a county fair he'd been scheduled to attend in the afternoon. When he realized he'd have the day free, he called Stormy. Her husky voice, saying a wary, "Yes?" gave him such a rush of pleasure that involuntarily, he smiled.

"I'm coming out the Fourth," he said. "I thought I'd bring a turkey to barbecue since you don't seem to care much for steaks."

She hesitated, so long that he felt a stir of anger. "I'll be expecting you," she said, her voice cool.

He hung up, feeling aggrieved. After all, he paid her more than a fair wage, and never made any excess demands upon her. The least she could do was act a little pleased that he was coming. Sometimes the beach house at Bolinas seemed more like hers these days than it did his.

His mood changed when, on impulse, he decided to purchase a supply of fireworks in a nearby county that still permitted their sale. Prudently he paid by cash, not wanting Marilyn to find out, when his canceled check came into the office, that he'd spent a small fortune on something as fleeting as fireworks.

The kids were waiting for him, looking freshly scrubbed and wearing clean jeans and T-shirts in honor, he was aware, of his visit. As always, Laurie stood back a little, but when he'd finished greeting Tommy, she approached eagerly for a hug.

He left the fireworks, covered by a piece of tarp, in the helicopter when he unloaded the groceries. Tommy eyed the tarp, but he didn't ask any questions. *Stormy strikes again,* he thought with amusement and knew they had been lectured on greed—and Lord knew what else—in preparation for his visit.

He told the kids he had to go talk to Arnold for a few minutes, and then set them the task of taking some of the groceries he'd bought into the house. After they were gone, each carrying a sack of groceries, he took the path across the gully to Arnold's place.

His friend was in the kitchen, drinking coffee, when he rapped on the screen door. He waved an invitation for Guy to come in, then poured him a mug of coffee and sat it in front of him.

"This is a surprise," Arnold said by way of greeting. He eyed Shag, who had accompanied Guy, then went to set out a pan of water for the dog. "I thought you'd be up to your neck in your campaign."

"I have a free day so I bought some fireworks for the kids tonight," Guy said. "How about keeping them at your place until it gets dark?"

Arnold gave him a sardonic smile. "For the kids, huh? Or for Guy Harris's belated childhood?"

"Come on, Arnold. Would I get them for myself?"

"Or maybe for Stormy? The girl's crazy about them—as I suspect you already know."

"She isn't a girl. She's a grown woman."

"Yeah—that she is. If I were thirty years younger—"

"You've got a wife. But if you don't forget that pride of yours and go home and apologize, you won't have one."

Arnold set his mug down—hard. "Keep your nose out of my business," he growled. He got to his feet. "Where'd you stash the fireworks?"

"I left them in the chopper. I'd better go get them before Tommy starts snooping around."

"I'll get them." Arnold rubbed his chin, a sure sign that he was embarrassed. "Sorry about that remark I made about you minding your own business. There's more to that trouble with Elsie than an apology can clear up, but I know your advice was well-meant. And I hope you feel the same about some advice I'm going to give you. Don't start anything with Stormy. She doesn't need any more trouble."

"I'm not going to start anything with her. Where did you get that idea?"

"Well, you've got a thing for her—isn't that what they call it these days? But that isn't good enough for Stormy. She doesn't need a lover, for God's sake. She needs someone who cares enough to stick around—and that isn't you. You're too locked into success."

He was gone before Guy could retaliate and tell Arnold to mind *his* own damned business.

He took a walk along the beach with Shag instead of going back to the beach house because he was in no mood for company. For a long time, he sat on an outcropping of gray rock, staring out at the ocean. Was Arnold right? Had he been inching toward an affair with Stormy? She'd made it very plain that she wasn't interested—and of course she was right. Which made Arnold's advice way out of line, right? So why was he sitting here, wasting his time brooding over it?

He walked back along the top of the cliff, taking his time, and when he came in sight of the beach house, he stopped to lean against the trunk of a solitary redwood tree to study it, in no hurry to go inside. It was the house he'd always wanted—every inch of it had been carefully planned to suit his taste, his needs. And yet, it was sometimes months between visits—except this summer when he had been even busier than usual because of the campaign.

If he were honest—and it was about time that he was—he'd have to admit the truth, that it was Stormy who lured him here so often....

He wanted her. It was as simple, as complicated, as that. When he looked at that lovely, funny valentine of a face, when he knocked himself out, trying to make her smile, when he watched her from a distance or from up close, something happened to him. He wanted to make love to her, to possess her totally, to be one with her. It was sexual, of course, but infinitely more intense, more urgent than what he'd ever felt for any other woman.

And why *her*? Why Stormy? He'd always been attracted to elegant women before, the kind that made other men stare with envy when he walked into a restaurant or a party with her on his arm. Stormy would never cause that kind of stir. Her beauty was the quiet kind that grew on a man—and he'd yet to see her in anything but jeans or shorts. So why this obsession with her? Dammit—what *was* there about her that wouldn't let go?

Stormy came out of the house and shaded her eyes to look down the beach. She didn't see him, standing as he was in the shadow of the tree, and he was free to stare at her openly as she searched the beach with her eyes. Was she looking for him, he wondered.

She went back into the house, and a few minutes later, when he followed her inside, she was in the kitchen, putting together a salad from the vegetables he'd brought. The room smelled of yeast bread, and he knew that she'd remembered a remark he'd made about loving freshly baked bread. Although he came in quietly, she sensed his presence and her whole body stiffened before she turned to look at him.

"Everything's ready except the turkey, Mr. Harris," she said. "I went ahead and put it on the barbecue spit, but it needs at least two hours."

"How quickly we forget," he said lightly. "I do wish you'd remember to call me Guy."

She stared at him, her eyes darkening. After a long moment, she gave a stiff little nod, then returned to the salad. What was that he'd read once, that the sudden enlargement of the pupils when someone looked at a person of the opposite sex was a sign of sexual arousal? Maybe he'd been wrong, thinking she wasn't sexually aware of him. And what did his own eyes show when he looked at her? From the way he felt right now, they must be as black as midnight....

The kitchen door banged open and Tommy came barreling in. He snatched up a carrot stick, popped it into his mouth, chewed it vigorously. He got a carton of milk from the refrigerator, glanced at his mother's back to make sure she wasn't looking, and chugalugged a big gulp down without bothering with a glass.

"Hey, you want to play net ball with us, Uncle Guy?" he asked, wiping the milk off his mouth. "You, too, Mom. We need two more bodies. Uncle Arnold is going to keep score and that man from down the beach—you know, the redhead?—is my partner." He gave Guy a sly look. "You and Mom'll be on the other side."

"How much have you got riding on this game?" Stormy asked.

Tommy widened his eyes, looking wounded. "You know you don't like me to gamble."

"Uh-huh," Stormy said. "How much?"

"Just a quarter—with Uncle Arnold. And it isn't really gambling 'cause I already know we're going to win." He put the milk back in the refrigerator and went bustling off.

Guy looked at Stormy. "How about it? Let's teach that young whippersnapper a lesson, shall we?"

"What if he teaches us one?"

"He won't. The volleyball team I was on in high school won city championship two years in a row."

"Then let's go."

She put the salad away in the refrigerator before she went outside. Guy followed her, admiring the way her neat little buns moved under her denim shorts. The shorts were new, and he was pleased that she'd finally decided to spend a little of her wages on herself.

The way she hung on to her wages reminded him of a squirrel, socking away acorns for a long, hard winter. But then—had she ever had a winter that wasn't hard? Was that the basis for his fascination with her, for wanting to be with her all the time? Was it empathy because of all his own long, hard winters when he was growing up in a variety of foster homes?

The "man from down the beach" was a red-haired young jock with muscles that wouldn't quit. His name was Rusty, and it was obvious he was taken with Stormy because he couldn't seem to keep his eyes off her. When he socked a ball in Guy's direction, Guy took a savage satisfaction in grounding it just out of his reach.

Stormy winked at him when Tommy tried to convince Arnold, who was acting as referee, that it had gone out of bounds. But Arnold would have nothing to do with that. Tommy, giving up, shrugged philosophically, which didn't stop him from arguing just the opposite a few minutes later when Arnold declared one of his own sallies a foul.

Guy was lunging for a ball when, out of the corner of his eye, he caught a glimpse of something moving near his foot. He swiveled away to avoid stepping on Magic, and crashed into Stormy. Both of them fell to the sand in a tangle of arms and legs.

He knew he should roll away but the body under his was so soft and yielding that he didn't move. Stormy's eyes were very dark, her cheeks flushed, and he knew she must feel the telltale hardness of his instant erection against her thigh. He wanted—God, whatever the reason for this insane and inappropriate passion, he wanted to make love to her.

"Hey, you two okay?" Tommy called, and he realized that he was still lying on top of Stormy, that neither of them had moved.

He twisted away, sat up, then helped Stormy to her feet. She wouldn't look at him. She busied herself brushing sand off her legs, and the sight of her hands touching her own bare thighs was almost his undoing. If they had been alone, he knew he couldn't have stopped himself from kissing her, making love to her. But of course they weren't alone and the others were watching them, the eyes of the man from down the beach, knowing—and very envious.

"You look a little woozy, Uncle Guy," Tommy said, his voice concerned. "You sure you're okay?"

"I got the wind knocked out of me for a moment. Nothing serious," Guy said.

"How about you, Mom?"

"I'm fine. I'd better check on the turkey," she said. "I don't want it to burn."

She escaped up the hill and Guy, staring after her, wished he could think of some excuse to follow her.

THEY ATE DINNER outside, on the rear patio. Laurie had decorated the plank picnic table with the blue lupus and white narcissus that grew wild in the meadow, which gave it quite a festive air. The turkey was subtly flavored with lemon thyme, the homemade bread crusty, the salad crisp and cold. Even so, Guy found it hard to do the food justice. He was too aware of Stormy, of the way she avoided looking at him, of her silence.

No one else seemed to notice. Arnold ate with his usual gusto, praising every bite, and even Laurie, who was a light eater, put away so much turkey that Guy was afraid she'd get sick.

The fireworks, too, were a big success. Half the beach was there watching, drawn by the brilliant rocket sprays that lit up the night sky. Guy had no problem managing the fireworks, but he did regret that he wasn't free to stand beside Stormy and watch the delight on her face as the bursts of color exploded in the air.

Sleepy-eyed and yawning, the children finally went off to bed. Guy put the dishes in the dishwasher, while Stormy cleaned up the rest of the kitchen. For once, she hadn't refused his offer of help. She was so quiet, in fact, that he wondered if she was overtired. He knew that once the chores were done, he should go off to bed, but he was too keyed up and he decided to take a walk instead.

"Thank you for the fireworks," Stormy said suddenly. "They were spectacular."

"I'm a fireworks freak," he confessed. "I think the ancient Chinese had the right idea. They put high value on something beautiful that had absolutely no material value and was gone forever once it was over. A thing of beauty and all that jazz."

"Or conspicuous consumption, like this beach house," Stormy said, then gave him an apologetic look. "Sorry about that. It just slipped out."

"But you're right. That's what this house really is. I could get all the benefits of living at the beach in a one-room shack."

"But why should you? After all, you can afford this place. Why not enjoy it?"

There was no answer to that since this had always been his own philosophy. "How about a stroll along the beach? I have to walk off all that food," he said.

He waited for her refusal, so when she nodded, it took him by surprise. "Okay—but I don't want to get too far away from the house."

"Better get a wrap. Those sea breezes can get cool at night," he said.

She went to get the all-weather coat she'd been wearing the night she'd been evicted, but when they went outside, the wind had died and the air was so balmy that after they returned from their walk, they sat on her spread-out coat and stared out at the ocean, reluctant to go inside.

The restless water, its color drained away by the cold light of the moon, had a smoky look, and the phosphorous edges of the waves curled and uncurled, lulling Guy into a state of somnolence.

He stretched out on the sand, pillowing his head on his arms. He wasn't sure why he started talking about the campaign. Maybe because Stormy listened so intently, her eyes fixed on his face. When he finally ran out of words, she asked him, "Did you decide to become an architect back when you were a kid?"

"I was going to be another Mickey Mantle and play major league baseball when I was a kid. Then I was on a high school field trip to Stanford, and there was this architectural exhibition that included the blueprints for a new campus research center. I looked at all those intricate crisscrossing lines and suddenly they made sense to me. In my mind's eye, I could see the building that would someday be erected, and I knew then that designing buildings was what I wanted to do with my life."

"How did you become a builder?"

"I wasn't satisfied with the workmanship on some of the houses I designed. When one of my clients asked me to supervise the construction of a house I'd designed for him, I took on the job. It was so satisfying, seeing something I'd dreamed up becoming reality, that I've never looked back. It was one of those lucky breaks that happen. Funny how many of the important things in your life start that way."

"What's really funny is how often the breaks come to people who are prepared for them," she said, her tone dry.

He laughed, then asked, "Suppose you got that lucky break, and you could do anything you wanted. What would it be?"

She took her time answering. "Art. Drawing, I should say."

He nodded, remembering the sketch pad. "You should take some lessons."

"I will—someday."

"You won't always be so busy. The kids will grow up and you'll have time for other things—including personal relationships."

"If you mean friends—I would like that. The only friend I keep up with these days is an elderly woman named Abby Cornwall, who lived next door to us when I was a kid. If you mean something else, I'm not interested in—" She broke off.

"Men?"

"Yes, men."

"You obviously didn't always feel that way," he pointed out, and then was aghast at his own insensitive remark.

"You're talking about Tommy and Laurie's father, I guess. I was too young, only fifteen, to have much judgment when I met Eric. He was the younger brother of the foster mother I was living with at the time and several years older than me. He made me laugh—and he also made me feel important. So I ran away with him. I had Tommy ten months later."

"Was it a good relationship?"

"I wanted it to be. We had a lot of problems, but we stayed together for almost three years. Then I got pregnant with Laurie and that was too much for Eric. He wanted me to get an abortion and when I refused, he packed his things and left."

"How did you manage after he was gone, Stormy?"

"Not very well at first. But eventually, after Laurie was born, I got a job in a day nursery where I could keep the kids with me. Laurie was four when I read in the evening paper that Eric had been killed in a car accident—the papers said he'd been drinking. I didn't go to the funeral. I figured his family wouldn't want me and the kids there. We'd just be an embarrassment."

In the moonlight, her face had a pinched look, and he put out his hand to stop her. "Don't," he said. "I shouldn't have pried in your personal business."

"It doesn't hurt anymore. Time takes care of just about everything, doesn't it?"

"Courage, too. You've got a lot of that."

She gave him a long, level look. "Courage? Most of the time I'm running scared. I put on a good act, but—" She broke off, looking annoyed. "Now why did I say that? It isn't really true. And I don't know what got into me, talking so much about myself. You couldn't possibly be interested."

"But I am. It helps me to understand you better."

"Why would you want to do that?" she said, sounding puzzled.

"Because—God, you must know how I feel about you!"

The bewilderment on her face surprised him. Didn't she know how she'd gotten under his skin—or was this some kind of game she was playing? He met her eyes and he knew it wasn't a game. He saw something else there—a quickening, an awareness, a hunger to match his own—and suddenly, without thinking it through, he pulled her into his arms and kissed her.

She didn't try to get away. Her body, which looked so firm and yet was so surprisingly soft, seemed to melt into his, absorbing his hardness. The kiss deepened as he took complete possession of her lips, probing her warm mouth with his tongue, wanting all she had to give.

For a moment, when he touched her breast, she stiffened and he thought she meant to stop him, but then she relaxed, mutely giving him permission to explore her softness—and the taut nipples that gave so much away.

The kiss ended, but only so he could give his full attention to her breasts. He pushed up her T-shirt, unsnapped her bra, exposing her white breasts to the moonlight. In the gray light, her eyes had a silvery cast; her breathing was erratic, and a soft sheen of perspiration covered her skin.

He knew she was aroused, knew that he could have her, and briefly, he felt a trickle of shame for taking advantage of her vulnerability. But that didn't stop him from bending to kiss her breasts. How could it when his own body was charged with an overwhelming and irresistible need?

He undressed her quickly, then himself. She didn't help him—but she didn't stop him, either. For a long time, he fondled her, running his hands over her warm flesh. Although the effort not to take her immediately was hard, he made love to her slowly, skillfully, stroking the intimate places of her body, kissing her quickening flesh, suckling the hills and valleys that were so seductive, so enchanting.

Although he knew she must be sexually experienced, being the mother of two, it was like making love to a virgin, and he wondered if she hadn't slept with anyone since her lover's desertion. How was that possible, someone so sexually attractive as this woman? And how sweet her flesh tasted, how fragrant the natural scent of her body—she was all woman and like no other he'd ever made love to.

When she was fully aroused, trembling with need—and when he knew he himself could wait no longer—he took possession of her body. As he sank into the soft moistness between her thighs, he groaned aloud, as if he were in pain. He moved against her and she exploded in his arms, her whole body writhing against his. He felt the tremors start, deep inside her, knew that she had reached her climax, and his own body responded immediately, sweeping away caution, technique, everything but the rush toward satisfaction.

Afterward, he lay there, stunned and bemused. He had expected a lot, but maybe he'd also been afraid that reality wouldn't match up to those erotic dreams he'd had. No such problem. Making love to Stormy had been a total experience in pleasure. In fact, he felt rejuvenated, ready for more, as if he were a teenager again. How was that possible for an old campaigner like himself? What *was* it she did to him?

Beside him, Stormy stirred, sat up, and he half expected her to retreat into embarrassment. But she fooled him. She bent over him and kissed him, a warm and completely loving kiss.

"You were wonderful," he said, and to his surprise, his voice was unsteady.

"*You* were wonderful," she said, smiling.

He pulled her down on top of him and as he kissed her, he knew this wouldn't be a one-time thing. How could it be when the very thought of making love to her again made his bones melt?

And how was it that she was inexperienced, unskilled in the techniques of making love? The way she had hesitated to touch him, waiting until he'd put her hands on his body, as if she didn't know what was expected. Had her lover been one of those men who simply take their women without foreplay, who never try to arouse or satisfy? Was that the reason she'd been so susceptible to him?

And just what in the hell had he gotten himself into?

CHAPTER TWELVE

STORMY HAD EXPECTED to feel guilt, embarrassment, even shame, after her night of love with Guy, but it didn't happen. Was it because it had seemed so right, being in his arms, being possessed by this man—and possessing him? Whatever the reason, when she awoke alone in her own bed the next morning, but with the imprint of his body on the pillow beside her, a wonderful feeling of contentment filled her.

She hugged his pillow to her breast, breathing in the faint trace of his after-shave and his own musky male scent, and her heart soared with remembered pleasure of their lovemaking and its languid afterglow when they had lain in each other's arms, not yet ready to fall asleep, murmuring to each other.

She loved him. For the second time in her life, she had let down her defenses and fallen in love. Or was that true? The frenetic excitement she'd felt for Eric hadn't lasted through their wedding night. He'd been clumsy and rough and totally selfish, taking her without any concern for her extreme youth and innocence. To Eric, sex had been totally self-serving.

And she'd realized it, even at fifteen. It had killed the—whatever it was she'd felt for him. She'd stuck with him, enduring but never sharing his passion, for the simple reason that she was so hungry, so desperate for any kind of affection, for a family of her own, for roots.

But this, what she felt for Guy, was so different it wasn't even in the same league with that pitiful adolescent crush she'd had on Eric. And it was just as doomed. Oh, yes, she wasn't naive enough to believe it meant anything serious to him. It wouldn't last, couldn't last. There was a gulf between them so wide that it would be stupid to hope for more than a brief interlude of intimacy between two people who were drawn together through chemistry, accident, fate.

So she should end it now before she got hurt again. She already had so many problems lying in wait for her when summer was over. To add the heartbreak of unrequited love would be stupid. But oh, she wanted it to be different, wanted to be loved by Guy. How wonderful it would be if she could forget everything else and just enjoy this brief interlude of happiness....

Something intruded upon her thoughts, and she sniffed, trying to identify the aroma that wafted so enticingly to her nostrils. Bacon—someone was frying bacon in the kitchen.

Although she had conscientiously kept the menu for herself and the children pretty much the same simple food they were used to, not wanting them—or herself—to grow accustomed to a fancier and more expensive way of eating, she occasionally succumbed to a weakness for bacon.

It had been the Sunday breakfast of choice when she was growing up, always signaling a special day. Her grandmother had been a romantic, and having something special for Sunday breakfast had been one of their very few luxuries. Bacon and soda biscuits and scrambled eggs was still Stormy's favorite breakfast, although she had it only on holidays. And now the aroma was so tempting that she slid out of bed, then stood transfixed, staring at the image of her naked body in the room's beveled floor mirror.

She had filled out since her ulcer had healed, and her body reflected it. How—how *curvy* she looked, not at all boyish anymore. Her hair was glossy, even in its present tangled stage, which made her look a little bit like a Greek boy—no, like a Greek girl, she amended, and a laugh escaped her lips. Maybe she was part Greek—no one had ever told her who her father was. In fact, she was pretty sure that her mother hadn't known that particular lover's name—she'd had so many men.

Today, that thought didn't hurt. The way she felt right now, nothing could hurt her. Her skin glowed as if she were blushing and her eyes—when had they ever looked so large, so lustrous? Had this happened because she'd been enjoying the first leisure of her life—or was it the aftermath of the night she'd spent in Guy's arms?

The sound of the children—giggles and whispers—coming down the hall brought her back to the present. She hurried into her robe, and slid back into bed. The door opened, and when she saw the tray Tommy was holding so carefully she sat up, smiling. But it was Guy's amused face behind her children that made her heart swell, her breath catch in her throat.

"Surprise, Mommy," Laurie said excitedly. Her braids were lopsided, attesting that she'd done them up herself, and Tommy was wearing a strange mixture of clothing, a plaid shirt and striped seersucker shorts. Both of their faces were shiny, and she was sure that, under Guy's supervision, their teeth had been thoroughly brushed.

"I guess I overslept," she said guiltily.

"Oh, that's okay. We didn't need you," Tommy said cheerfully. "Uncle Guy helped us fix breakfast. He said you deserved to sleep in 'cause you had a late night."

She avoided Guy's twinkling eyes. If ever she saw an unrepentant smile, it was on his face. He also looked remarkably fit, certainly rested and relaxed. If she hadn't known better, she would have thought he'd just had a long, undisturbed night of sleep.

"So what's for breakfast?" she asked, trying to sound nonchalant.

"Bacon—just the way you like it," Tommy said. "Uncle Guy did that part. He said he didn't want to be responsible for grease-splattered kids. But I scrambled the eggs, and Laurie baked the biscuits. There was ten in that little round can and we ate the other seven so there wouldn't be no waste."

He sounded so righteous that Stormy had to laugh. "You two—no, you three, are something else," she said, shaking her head.

She began to eat with an audience watching every bite disappear down her throat. Guy finished the cup of coffee he'd brought for himself, then disappeared, saying something about taking a run along the beach. She couldn't help being relieved. It was hard to concentrate on her food with him watching. And why didn't she feel more guilty? Was it because, for just a little while, she could pretend that they were a real family, a family that included a father?

DURING THE WEEKS that followed, Stormy lived a double life. During the day, she was mother, cook, housekeeper, nurturer of not only her own two children, but one cat, a puppy, and several wounded birds the children from neighboring beach houses brought her, including a stubborn pelican that she had to force-feed at first to keep it from starving.

Then, on the nights that Guy was there, after the children were in bed, she was another person, a woman passionately in love. She had stopped worrying about tomorrow, and for the first time in her life, she thought only of herself, her needs, her hunger for Guy's lovemaking.

She had half expected the fire between them to cool down, but it didn't happen. When he came to her room at night, the sight of his nude, well-knit body sent her into another world, and she became the voluptuous woman she had never dreamed she could be.

His touch, even before he kissed her, sent her pulse leaping, turned the blood in her veins to hot lava. She tried hard to keep her perspective, to convince herself it was only sexual attraction, lust, anything but what she knew in her heart it was. Love. She loved him, even though love between them was impossible.

But she wouldn't let herself think of their inevitable parting. When he was away, as he was so often with election day, in early November, drawing closer, she never asked questions, never tried to find out if he'd missed her. When she heard the helicopter descending in the rear meadow, her heart would leap, her breathing quicken, and then she would start really living.

It was insane, dangerous, stupid. She knew all this, but still she allowed it to go on. In his arms at night, she burst into flame, not thinking, only feeling, and when he went away again, she never asked when he would be back because she didn't want him to feel she had any expectations of him, of their relationship.

She lost weight again. Her appetite, always unpredictable, seemed to have deserted her. While Guy was there, their lovemaking overwhelmed her need for food, and when he was gone, she missed him so much that she couldn't eat. Guy finally noticed her weight loss and when he questioned her about her ulcer, she could tell him truthfully that she'd never felt better in her life. Although he professed to believe her, he still worried, and one afternoon, near the end of August, he called to tell her that he'd made an appointment with Dr. Johnson to see her the next day.

"Just to make sure," he said brusquely.

She wanted to argue with him, but she knew that the best way to convince him was for Dr. Johnson to give her a clean bill of health. Besides, how often had anyone worried about her state of health since she was a small girl? So she told him it was probably the right thing to do, if only for the sake of her own peace of mind.

"And mine," he said. "Why don't we make it a family outing? Tommy and Laurie could use a treat. Dinner out and them maybe a movie or a show—say, the Ice Capades? We can stay overnight in my apartment and have breakfast before we return to Bolinas."

"Can you spare that much time?" she asked.

"I've already cleared my calendar," he said. "Not that it was easy convincing my assistant that I needed a whole day off."

"Oh—you mean Ms. Wright?"

"The same. She doesn't approve of—" He broke off.

"Of what?"

"Of a lot of things," he said.

He changed the subject and began telling her about a political rally he was slated to attend that weekend. Stormy couldn't help wondering if it was beginning to bother Guy that their love affair ate into his campaign time. Eventually his passion for her would cool—and then what? How would he handle the breakup of their relationship? In easy stages? A slow retreat from intimacy? Or would it be quick and clean? An offer of money, of a place to stay until she got on her feet, maybe even a job?

Well, if that turned out to be his scenario, he was in for a surprise. If she accepted his financial help, it would cheapen, make a mockery of the whole summer. And besides, she didn't need it. She had saved most of her wages, knowing how important it was to have a stake when she returned to the city. When the time came, she would walk away with at least her pride intact....

She realized Guy was telling her to be ready at ten the next morning, and some perversity prompted her to say, "There's no reason for you to give up a whole day for us, Guy. I'm sure Arnold will watch out for the kids. It isn't even necessary for you to bother picking me up in the helicopter. I can make an appointment with a local doctor and save you all that trouble."

"Don't go prickly on me," he said softly. "I want to spend the day with you and the kids and take you to the Ice Capades. I saw my first ice show after I was grown. I don't want them to wait that long."

"They haven't been deprived," she said tartly. "Before Laurie became ill, we always did something on the weekends, even if it was just a picnic in the park. You don't need money, just some planning, to have a good time. I haven't neglected them, Guy."

"Don't be so defensive," he said. "There's nothing romantic about poverty. I've been there and it's grubby and ugly and humiliating."

After he hung up, she turned over his words. He was right. Poverty was all the things he'd said, and yet, he was wrong, too. She hadn't felt poor when she was a child because she'd had her grandmother. Her mother, who had disappeared from her life so early, had come home only when she was between men or jobs, and yet, her childhood had been happy—until they took her grandmother away to Napa and then put her in that foster home.

So Guy was right and he was wrong. What had his own childhood been like? If things were different with them, she would ask him. As it was, she could only wonder.

Meanwhile—what was she going to wear tomorrow? She wanted to shine for Guy, make him proud of her. He was an important man in San Jose, easily recognizable. Anyone he escorted to the ice show and took out to dinner was bound to be noticed—and jeans were not appropriate attire for an evening on the town.

Laurie could wear the pretty summer dress Guy had bought her and Tommy was no problem because he would soon need school clothes and what she bought for him could serve two purposes. But she hated to spend money on herself. Maybe she could find something on sale at that boutique she passed when she went into Bolinas to the grocery....

ARNOLD WAS JUST GETTING READY to take a shower when the phone rang. He muttered an oath under his breath, threw his robe back on and went to pick it up.

"Yeah?" he said into the phone.

"Arnold?"

It was Elsie's voice. He straightened immediately and sucked in his stomach as if she could see him over the phone. "That you, Elsie?"

"Yes. How are you getting along, Arnold?"

"Oh, everything's great. And you?"

"I've been pretty busy." She hesitated, then added, "I was wondering—would you mind if I came out tomorrow? I don't want to interfere, of course, if you have other plans."

Mind? Was she crazy? He'd give his right leg to have her come out tomorrow! "Come on out," he said, trying for a casual tone. "I don't have anything in particular planned, nothing I can't postpone."

"Well, I don't want to be a bother—"

"I'll be expecting you. What say I pick up some grub at the market?"

"Oh, don't go to any trouble. A can of soup is fine for lunch."

"Lunch? You aren't going to stay overnight?"

There was a long pause. "I don't think that's wise, Arnold."

He wanted to curse, but he forced himself to laugh instead. "Don't worry. I'll sleep in the guest room—or you can, if you like."

"Maybe this was a bad idea—"

"It's a good idea. What time should I expect you?"

"I'll start out about nine. Should be there by noon, depending on traffic," she said. "And I'll think about staying. It *is* a long drive."

He cleared his throat. "I agree."

"Oh, by the way, I do hope I get to meet your housekeeper," she said so casually that he had to grin.

"I'll make sure you do. She's a great gal. Always accommodating and eager to please." Since this was a bit off the mark, he added, "'Course she's pretty independent, too. Doesn't let anyone walk over her."

"What does she look like—what I mean, is she blond or brunette?"

"Black hair, green eyes. Looks a lot younger than she really is."

"Oh?" Her voice was cool. "Just how old is she, anyway?"

"I never asked. Wouldn't be polite."

She said something, a single word, that he didn't catch, and then, "I'll see you tomorrow," and hung up.

He hung up with a grin, but it soon faded. Dammit, she wasn't coming because she wanted to make up. She was just curious to see the housekeeper he'd bragged about so much. Maybe that hadn't been a good idea. Soon as she saw Stormy, she'd know she didn't have a rival for his affections, not from a girl a third his age. Well, it had succeeded in one thing. Elsie was coming out tomorrow, and if he didn't blow things, this might be a new start for them.

He told Stormy about it when she came to clean his house that morning. For the first time, he really opened up and admitted that he'd handled things all wrong, made a pest of himself after retirement.

"That happens a lot," Stormy said when he was finished. "There were a lot of retired people on April Street, where I lived, and some of the men almost drove their wives crazy. The man would retire, and then he'd follow his wife around everywhere she went, even while she was doing her housework."

"What happened then?" he asked curiously.

"Well, they usually came to a compromise. You see, the man had retired but the woman still had her job."

"Elsie never worked a day after we were married," he growled.

"But she did. She was your housekeeper, cook, gardener, whatever. And that didn't end because you retired. Maybe you should have taken over some of her household chores so she could retire, too."

He gave a snort. "We have a gardener—and a full-time housekeeper. Elsie does the cooking, but only because she likes to."

"But maybe she'd like to divide the work. Why don't you learn how to cook? I'd be glad to teach you what I know."

"Elsie's a gourmet cook. She probably wouldn't eat anything I fix."

"And maybe she would. What else does she do with her time?"

"Volunteer work. She's always involved with some project to raise money for one of her charities. Her latest is a new organization that grants wishes to kids with terminal diseases. She's cochairwoman of the committee to raise money for it. They're having a rock-and-roll concert this year. Got some of the top groups to perform, I understand."

"I see." Her eyes were thoughtful. "Do all her charities involve children?"

"I suppose so—one leads to another of the same kind, I guess."

"Or maybe she deliberately chooses charities that deal with helping children. You're a businessman. You could be very effective helping her raise money. Or do you have too much male pride to play second fiddle to your wife?"

He glared at her. "Smart ass, aren't you? And just who asked your advice, anyway?"

She eyed him coldly. "You know something? You're a cantankerous, stubborn man, Arnold Story. I'm not at all surprised your wife threw you out."

She turned on the vacuum cleaner, drowning out his reply. He watched for a while and then went stamping out of the house, thoroughly disgruntled. For the next hour, he sat on the terrace, watching Stormy's cat, which had followed her to work, stalking a sea gull. She was wearing a bell, which gave out a merry little warning tinkle every time she moved, and from the way her tail twitched, she looked every bit as put out as he did.

Those things Stormy had said—what really irked him was his suspicion that they could be true. How did it happen that Stormy, who had never met Elsie and was young enough to be his granddaughter, had put her finger on something that he'd missed, the fact that all of Elsie's charities involved children?

No wonder she hadn't wanted to give them up. They were her solace, her compensation for the children she'd never had—and he was a monumentally self-centered fool for not seeing this sooner.

Tomorrow, when Elsie came out, they would have a little talk, and he'd hold on to his temper, no matter what came up. He would take Stormy's advice and offer to help out with her charities. Hell, to set things right between them, he'd even learn how to cook so he could spell her sometimes in the kitchen. Of course, she would not go for that. She loved cooking. If she didn't, she would've hired a cook years ago, wouldn't she?

HE HAD ALMOST FORGOTTEN what a good-looking woman Elsie was. For a sixty-year-old woman, she still had a lot of sex appeal. Which right at the moment, was a little embarrassing to Arnold. When was the last time he'd had an erection just from looking at a woman? His own wife, for God's sake?

Well, there was no denying that in that pink cotton dress, with her arms bare and her hair all soft and wavy, and her eyes so bright, Elsie was a knockout. Sometimes he wondered just what it was she saw in him. Even as a young man, he'd never had anything special in the way of looks.

He walked toward her, undecided whether or not to kiss her. In the end, he brushed her cheek with his lips, then stepped back, rushing into speech.

"The fog burned off hours ago," he said. "How about a swim?"

"I'll change into my suit," she said, nodding. Although she hadn't returned his kiss, he thought her voice was warm, certainly cheerful, and he felt a rush of optimism. Maybe it would all work out the way he hoped. The thing was to be very careful what he said for the next few hours....

After their swim, Elsie changed into shorts and a soft cotton top and joined Arnold on the terrace. He put a glass of unsweetened lemonade in her hand and sat down opposite her.

"So what have you been up to?" he asked, trying for casualness.

She sighed. "The rock-and-roll concert is over—it made a lot of money but it was quite a headache. My assistant dropped out at the last moment for what she called 'family problems,' and early on, if you remember, the cochairman resigned. He decided that rally in the stock market in March was more important. I don't understand why people volunteer and then don't follow through."

"It's more work than they anticipated so they drop out," he said shrewdly. "Besides, they know there's always someone like you around to take over if they quit."

For some reason, this annoyed her. "That's no excuse. I'm always glad when someone who's retired volunteers to work with me. At least they feel obligated to finish the job."

"I'm retired, but you've never asked me to help out," he said.

She gave him a quick look. "You aren't interested in volunteer work—you've made that very clear. And I have invited you to come to dinners with me. You've always been too busy."

"I'm not busy now."

"Are you saying—would you like to get involved?"

"Well, I might give it a try," he said.

He risked a sidelong glance. She wasn't smiling, but there was no denying that her expression was thoughtful.

"And I just might ask," she said.

Arnold had been to too many staff meetings not to know when to drop a subject while he was ahead. He stretched out his legs, feeling good. Strange how just having Elsie sitting here next to him made his day, he thought drowsily.

He nodded off, and when he awoke, the chair Elise had been sitting in was empty. He sat up, vexed with himself. Elise already suspected he was over the hill; his falling asleep on her would just confirm it. But no, she hadn't left the terrace. She was standing at the other end, her back to him. She was holding a pair of binoculars, and she was looking across the gully at Guy's house. He got up, but she was so busy with the binoculars that she didn't notice him until he spoke.

"That's Stormy, working in her garden," he said, making her jump.

She turned an accusing look on him. "Why she's just a baby, Arnold."

"She's in her twenties. I told you she looked a lot younger than her age. But don't let that fool you. She's a hard worker and really earns her pay."

"You seem to admire her quite a lot."

"There's a lot about Stormy to admire, even if she can be a smart ass sometimes," he said. He decided it was time to set things straight. "She's crazy about Guy Harris. Not that she doesn't hide it pretty well. Same with him. He's really gone on her."

It took her a few seconds to absorb this. "They're having an affair?"

"I don't know how far it's gone, but they act like lovers lately. And no, I don't approve. She's had a hard life, two kids to raise on her own, and no job skills. This thing with Guy—I'm afraid she's going to end up with her heart busted all to hell."

Elsie raised her binoculars to her eyes again. "She looks nice," she mused. "Not Guy's type at all. He goes for—well, women like that divorcée he was running around with last year."

"Yeah. Well, maybe it will all blow over. He *is* good with Stormy's kids. They call him Uncle Guy." He gave her a sheepish grin. "They call me Uncle Arnold. They're pretty fond of this old guy, both of them."

Elise smiled at him. "I'm not surprised. Kids always liked you."

He considered her words with suspicion. It wasn't true that kids always—or even usually—liked him. Sure, they behaved themselves around him. But that was because they knew they'd better. Maybe she meant older kids, those in their teens and early twenties.

"Well, I always took an interest in the young ones that came to work at the paper," he conceded.

"Like Guy Harris?"

"I worked his tail off. But that's the only way to learn a business, from the ground up. Too bad he went into the building trade. Would've made a good reporter."

"Uh-huh. But would he have become a multimillionaire?"

"He could have. I did."

"So you did." She smiled at him. "I'd like to meet your Stormy and her kids. Maybe we could invite them over for dinner tonight."

"Then you are staying over?"

"It does make sense. Besides, I don't have anything planned for tomorrow. What do you have in the way of food for tonight?"

He grinned at her. Things were looking up. Maybe it was time to go into his pitch—or maybe not. Maybe he'd just wait and see what happened next.

"I thought I'd leave that up to you," he said. "Why don't we have lunch in Bolinas and then drop by the supermarket?"

EARLY THAT AFTERNOON Stormy and the kids walked into town. While Tommy and Laurie ate tacos at their favorite Mexican fast-food place, she browsed through the boutique across the street. But the dresses she liked were too expensive by far and she finally moved on to a rather shopworn collection on a markdown rack. She was holding a limp-looking cotton shift up against her body when Arnold's deep voice hailed her.

"So how's it going, Stormy?" he said.

She looked at him in surprise. He sounded—well, jovial. In fact, he had a wide grin on his face. A smart-looking woman with silver-gray hair came up behind him, and understanding came to her. Arnold had made up with his wife—or at least she had come out to the beach to see him.

Arnold introduced them and Elsie looked Stormy over with more interest than seemed polite. Evidently what she saw was reassuring because her smile was warm as she asked, "Shopping for a dress?"

"Mr. Harris is taking me and my kids into the city for a medical checkup," Stormy explained. "I told him my ulcer was healed but I don't think he believed me. He's taking us out to dinner and then to the Ice Capades afterward and I'm looking for something to wear since I don't have anything that's suitable. I thought I'd find something here, but the ones I like are all resort-priced, I'm afraid. Guess I'll have to settle for one of these."

"Oh, my dear, don't do that!" Elsie looked Stormy over. "We're pretty much the same size except—well, your waist is slimmer than mine, but I do have this lovely shift that would look wonderful on you. The color is all wrong for me, which is why I left it out here last fall. Do me a favor and take it off my hands?"

"I couldn't," Stormy said stiffly. "Really, it's all right. I—"

"But I insist. You've been such a help to Arnold. I'm sure he'd be living in trash up to his armpits and half starved by now if you hadn't stepped in and helped out. Why don't you come over to the lodge for dinner in an hour or so? We have to pick up a few groceries and then we're heading back home."

She gave Stormy another warm smile and moved off down the aisle toward the door.

Arnold hung back long enough to say, "Take her up on the offer. It will keep her in a good mood. She's softening, Stormy. I think I can talk her into giving me another chance."

"Well, don't ruin it with your temper," she said disrespectfully.

He raised his grizzled eyebrows. "Me? Temper? Why I'm as gentle as a lamb."

Stormy was trying not to laugh when she caught the twinkle in his eyes. As he set off after Elsie, she reflected that at least in this case, there just might be a happy ending.

Later, when she tried on the cornflower-blue shift that Elsie handed her, she fell in love with the dress. It was simply made, with a dropped waist and plain round neck, but the material was so soft that it clung enticingly to her curves. Better yet, the color did great things to her tanned skin.

But it was hard to believe that the color was unbecoming to Elsie's silver hair and exquisite, pink-and-white complexion. Resolutely she put aside the suspicion that Elsie was finding this way to thank you for taking care of Arnold and gave into temptation. The dress was lovely, the nicest she'd ever had, and she was going to enjoy wearing it tomorrow—just as she was going to enjoy having dinner with Arnold and Elsie tonight.

As far as Arnold was concerned, it had been a great evening. If he hadn't been somewhat occupied with his plans for seducing Elsie after their guests had gone home, he would have called it an absolutely perfect evening.

The kids had been on their best behavior, justifying his praise of them to Elsie, and not to his surprise, Stormy and Elsie hit it off beautifully. It occurred to him, midway through one of Elsie's fabulous dinners, that the younger woman might well have been Elsie's daughter. She didn't look like Elsie, except that both women were diminutive, but there was something about them that was similar. Was that why he had taken to Stormy so quickly?

When Stormy and the kids left, he and Elsie stood side by side, and watched the light of their lantern bobbing as they crossed the gully. The sound of their voices came back to them and he heard Laurie say, "That lady's awful pretty, isn't she, Mom? I wish she was my grandmother."

Stormy's answer was lost in a gust of wind, but he knew she had agreed. As he did. He looked at Elsie, and something of what he was thinking must have shown on his face because she smiled up at him.

"You are pretty, you know," he said softly. "Pretty as a picture."

"I don't know how you made it as a journalist addicted as you are to clichés," she scolded, but her eyes were very bright.

Encouraged, he moved closer. "Pretty as a rose," he said, his voice so gruff that he had to clear his throat before he went on. "Pretty as a bride on her wedding day. Pretty as a rainbow. And I love you very much, Elsie."

He put his arm around her, and walked her toward the house.

And when they got inside, then what? he thought. God, this was worse than being a callow kid, trying to seduce his first girl. After all, it had been a long time since he'd gone through the courting thing. In the past, all he'd had to say, twitching his eyebrows like Groucho Marx, was a joking, "You wanta make out?" and she would smile and then—

"You wanta make out?" Elise asked softly.

He stopped breathing for a moment, and then his heart began to pound so quickly that he felt a stab of fear, one he'd lived with since his attack. He put it behind him, and suddenly he knew the right thing to do. He bent his head and kissed her, a lover's kiss, not the dutiful kiss of a husband, and her response told him it was going to be all right—at least for the night.

And it was, even though it was different. There was a freshness to the old familiar things they'd always done before. He touched her with a new awareness, renewed passion, and realized he was as excited as a kid. Elsie had always been responsive to his lovemaking, but always before, he'd taken the lead. Tonight, she seemed to be seducing him. She touched him in a different way, trying new things that astonished and delighted him.

Afterward, when they were lying side by side, their bodies touching, both exhausted from their prolonged lovemaking, he wondered if part of their trouble had been because their sex life had fallen into a rut. He'd never lost his passion for Elsie, never been tempted to stray, but had he taken her too much for granted? Whatever the reason, he knew that things were back to normal—or were they? Maybe Elsie was simply sexually deprived. After all, it had been several weeks...

And where had she learned those new tricks, like the way she'd kissed his nipples? She'd never done that before. And those other things she'd initiated—what was going on here? He loved it, of course—he hadn't felt so sexy in years. But there was no denying that it was a change.

He sat up and looked down at Elsie's sleepy face with sober eyes. She was lovely—not in the fresh, girlish way she'd been when they were first married. There was a fine network of wrinkles around her mouth, but then she'd spent so many years smiling—he wouldn't want her any other way. And although her body was slender, tight to the bone, it wasn't a young girl's body anymore, hadn't been for a long time. And yet—making love to her was precious and wonderful, a gift he didn't deserve. Why had it been so long since this had occurred to him?

"What are you thinking right now?" she asked and he realized her eyes were open, that she was watching him.

"That I love you. That I haven't been fair to you. That I want to change only I don't know how to begin. I'm a self-centered bastard—and I don't know if I *can* change."

Elsie sighed. "You dope. You've already changed. Don't you know that?"

"I don't understand—"

"Your offer to learn to cook. Your offer—well, almost an offer—to take an interest in my volunteer work. Next thing you know, you'll be offering to take me on that trip to Europe I've been pining for."

He grinned at her. "Oh, you are clever. Catch a guy when he's mellow. But you were right about me coming out here to do some thinking. I needed that time alone."

"Not alone. You had some help."

"You're talking about Stormy?"

"And her kids. They were a good influence, my husband. And if you were serious about helping me with my charity work, I'm going to take you up on that. But I also hope you find some other interests. And I'm not talking about sports. You're a dud at golf—and most of the things other retirees take up. What you need is something as absorbing as your newspaper was—but not as stressful."

Arnold rolled over on his back, staring up at the ceiling. "You're right. I've had something in the back of my mind for a while—no, I won't tell you about it, not yet. But maybe—well, I'll give it some more thought. Right now—would you believe that I'm horny as hell right now, Mrs. Story?"

"Oh, I believe it," she murmured. "Why do you think I've been rubbing my knee up against an interesting part of your anatomy for the past couple of minutes?"

CHAPTER THIRTEEN

THE EXAMINATION the next afternoon was brief and well worth the trouble because Dr. Johnson gave her a clean bill of health.

"I see you've been following the diet I prescribed," he said approvingly. "Now make it a lifelong habit and stay away from rich, highly spiced foods, especially junk food. And keep your life-style simple—as little stress as possible. The medical journals are turning away from the idea that the wrong food can cause ulcers, but there's no doubt that stress is a factor. Remember, Stormy—the fast lane just isn't for you."

Stormy didn't point out that she'd never been able to afford rich foods. Instead she nodded meekly and told him she would certainly follow his advice.

When they left his office, Guy asked her, "How come you didn't light into him when he made that remark about living in the fast lane? You would have blasted me for saying a lot less."

"Oh, he meant well. And his advice about junk food is good. He couldn't possibly know that has never been a problem with me. Of course—" she grinned suddenly "—the only reason I don't pig out on junk food all the time is that it's too expensive. I particularly love those big, fat doughy pretzels you smear with hot mustard."

Guy told her that his weakness was chili dogs and they were both laughing when they reached the waiting room where the kids were waiting.

Dinner, at an old-fashioned Italian restaurant that catered to families, was especially enjoyable because not only didn't she have to cook the food they ate, but the kids were on their best behavior, awed by the red-checkered tablecloths, the wax encrusted wine-bottle candles, the hearty food and, most of all, Stormy suspected, by the ferocious scowl of their mustached waiter.

True, Tommy managed to sip some of the wine from her glass while she was busy cutting Laurie's veal, but since he'd made a face and said "ugh," she pretended not to notice. Later, the Ice Capades was everything she'd hoped it would be—exciting, colorful, full of breathtaking routines and talented performers. She couldn't help noticing that Guy watched the kids more than he did the show, and she wondered what he was thinking when Laurie hid her face in his arm during a particularly scary routine. He'd said he hadn't seen an ice show until he was an adult, that he knew what poverty was. But surely he'd been adopted if he'd started out as a foundling.

She'd been too old to attract adoptive parents, but he'd just been a tiny baby—had the people who'd adopted him been poor? That didn't seem likely. Surely poor people couldn't pass the requirements to be adoptive parents.

Well, it was a puzzle, and it would have to stay one because she didn't have any right to ask him personal questions. Their relationship seemed to begin and end at the bedroom door. It was much too late to try to change the rules.

She was very quiet on the trip back to Guy's downtown penthouse apartment. No one seemed to notice and she was glad that Tommy, exuberant as always, carried the burden of the conversation with his very opinionated comments about the show they'd just seen. He had decided, he told Guy, to become a professional ice skater, but first there was the matter of the Olympics. Would training for them take a lot of money?

As she listened while Guy explained the complexities of becoming an Olympic athlete, she felt a deep sadness that the summer was coming to a close. Soon Guy would be plunging into the final months of his campaign and wouldn't have time to come out to the beach, even if he wanted to.

Every morning Arnold picked up a copy of the *San Jose Press*, which he passed along to Stormy in the afternoon. From the information about the mayoral race she'd read, she knew that Guy had more than a fighting chance of winning the election. Despite his frequent overnight trips to Bolinas, he had been campaigning vigorously, fulfilling all his obligations. Sometimes, when she caught a newscast that showed him speaking at a dinner or meeting—powerful, very confident, and also a little cool—she saw a different man from the passionate one who made love to her. Which one was closer to being the real Guy Harris?

Once, when she was cleaning the living room, she'd found a memo, written on notepaper, lying on the floor beside one of the rattan sofas. She'd read it before she'd realized it was a personal note, written to Guy by his assistant. In it, Marilyn had complained that he'd canceled an important social engagement with several of his key supporters, that she'd had the devil's own time explaining that away. She'd also commented that she'd be so glad when elections were over so they could spend more time—quality time, she'd called it—together, and then she'd signed it with "Love you, Guy."

The memo was dated the day after Tommy's tenth birthday, which they'd celebrated with a barbecue, and Stormy felt a pang of guilt, remembering that she had asked Guy if he could possibly attend the birthday party she was giving Tommy, that she'd invited Arnold and Elsie, as well as some of Tommy's beach friends.

Hadn't Guy hesitated a long time before he'd finally said he wouldn't miss it for the world?

Since the polls gave him more than a respectable margin of votes, it seemed certain that he would be San Jose's next mayor. And then he'd really be in the limelight. The slightest hint of scandal would be given full play by the newspapers, especially the *Bayside News*, which was committed to the incumbent mayor. It seemed very likely that he'd break off with her before election day. Which meant—well, what did it mean? That she should start preparing herself emotionally for the break?

After she put the children to bed in two of the penthouse's guest rooms, she returned to the living room. Guy poured her a glass of wine, then sat down beside her on the sofa.

"You were the best-looking woman in the restaurant tonight," he said. His eyes lingered on her mouth, then dropped to her breasts. "If it hadn't been for propriety, I would have ravished you on the spot."

She smiled at him, but she felt restless, emotionally detached from him. When she suggested they go out on the terrace to drink their wine, he agreed, even though she knew that he wanted to make love to her. For a while they sat sipping their wine and looking out over the city.

"I love this town," Guy said suddenly. "San Jose has all the ills of any big modern city—overcrowding, poor planning, gridlock traffic jams, crime—but it's my town. I want the best for it. Right now, it's at the crossroads—

everything that could make it one of the finest cities in the state is hanging in the balance. It needs capital growth, new businesses and industries, tourist attractions, all the things that make a city prosper. But it also needs guidelines to go by or it can become a sewer, full of decay. We need to encourage industry, not scare it away. And that means tax breaks and other inducements. We can't rest on our laurels—we have to be aggressive about attracting such revenue producers as conventions, big entertainment, tourists."

Stormy turned his words over in her mind. "I guess I have tunnel vision where San Jose is concerned, much narrower than yours. To me, the city is—well, the streets where I've lived, the walk-up flats and the housing projects, that cottage on April Street. It's the mom-and-pop stores where we had to buy our groceries when I was a kid because there weren't any supermarkets in the poorer parts of town—and if there were they wouldn't give credit."

She paused to take a sip of her wine, her mind locked into the past. "It's the city office where I went to apply for welfare," she went on. "The people I had to deal with there, the overworked, underpaid social workers, who develop skins so thick that most of them no longer see welfare recipients as human. To me, the city is the jobs I've had, the ones I'll have in the future, the people I've worked for, worked with, the neighbors I've lived next door to through the years, most of them living from payday to payday."

She gave Guy a long, sober look. "I can't see the big picture, Guy, so I'm glad you and others like you can. And I hope that if you get elected you won't get so bound up in the big picture that you forget about the little people who live on the edge all their lives, just a jump ahead of disaster."

She stopped, suddenly embarrassed by the passion in her voice. Guy studied her, his eyes as thoughtful and remote as if he were looking at a stranger, and she was sure she had offended him. She was too stubborn to apologize, especially since she'd spoken from the heart, but she knew it was time to change the subject.

"You've never talked much about what you plan to do if you win the election," she said. "Tell me about it."

Guy did just that, telling her his plans for consolidating some city civil service departments to save duplication and to institute reforms that would drastically reduce expenditures, help balance the budget and, eventually, reduce taxes. She listened silently, weighing the fervor in his voice, the fever in his eyes, and for the first time it was possible to see him objectively, not as an enemy or as a lover, but as a man who had a life apart from hers.

She genuinely loved the man who was her lover, but she hadn't understood him. She wasn't sure that even now, as he talked so forcefully about his plans for San Jose, that she did. This man whom she'd believed to be, so pragmatic was actually an idealist, with the fervor of a crusader. How could she have misunderstood him so much when they'd been so intimate?

Not that she agreed with all he said. In her eyes, he was too committed to the belief that money could solve most of the city's problems, something she doubted very much. But she loved the heart he'd hidden so well. It was big, generous, giving, and she felt a deep sadness that there was no place for her in the future he was laying out so confidently now. She wanted to be a part of his future, and yet she knew how impossible that was. She didn't fit into his life, could never fit in. Even the little she shared with him now was dangerous to him. When would he realize this and end it all?

When they went inside to make love in the master bedroom that was so modern, so masculine, she clung to him desperately, loving him with all the techniques he'd taught her until he gasped for breath and exploded prematurely into the final stage of passion. She held him then, incredibly sad, knowing that she would have to get used to being without him.

But not yet, not tonight.

When his breathing returned to normal, she ran her hand over his body, touching him intimately, arousing him again, even though he laughed and begged her for mercy. This time, they rose to the peak together and in the rush of ultimate pleasure, she forgot all her fears and worries, even her sadness.

When he fell asleep in her arms, she held him close for a long time, memorizing the feel of his body against hers, the warmth of his breath on her breast, the taut hardness of his thighs that fit hers so perfectly, despite the difference in their sizes.

Maybe this was enough, she thought. She'd been blessed by a deeply sensuous relationship with this man, the kind few women experience. Maybe to hope for more, that it would last beyond this one perfect summer, was just too much to ask....

IT WAS TWO DAYS LATER that Guy called to tell Stormy that he was sending his assistant out to pick up a speech he'd been working on and had forgotten to take back to San Jose with him.

"Look, honey," he said when she was silent, "I'm up to my ears in meetings or I'd come out myself, but I just can't get away. Things are speeding up and that means fourteen-hour days. I hope you don't mind if I cancel our Sunday barbecue. I'm sorry as hell—"

"Of course. I understand," she said, keeping her voice steady with effort.

"Marilyn will be out in a couple of hours. I'm sending her in the chopper."

"Can I have something ready for her—coffee or maybe lunch?"

"No, no. She'll just be in and out. Go on with your plans. I gave her my key in case she needs it—and she knows I left the speech in my den."

Stormy was in the kitchen preparing vegetables for supper when she heard the helicopter overhead. She was tempted to disappear into her room until Marilyn was gone, but she resisted the impulse. Guy must have told Marilyn that she was staying here, and after all, what did it matter what his assistant thought?

Marilyn obviously expected the house to be empty because she used Guy's key, not bothering to ring the bell first. Stormy stopped peeling a potato, strained her ears, a little puzzled when Marilyn's light footsteps crossed the entrance hall and turned into the living room. Hadn't Guy said the papers were in his den? It seemed to her that Marilyn was taking an inordinate amount of time to find what she was looking for.

A few minutes later, she heard the click, click, click of Marilyn's heels as she left the living room and went down the hall toward the den. It was obvious Marilyn was familiar with the layout of the house. She was his assistant, of course, but was she also the woman he'd brought out here who had complained about the salt air ruining her hairdo?

Marilyn's footsteps returned almost immediately. Stormy expected to hear them go out the front door again, but instead they turned toward the kitchen. Aware that she'd been standing there listening for the past few minutes, she busied herself with peeling the potato in her hand.

"I'm glad you're here." Stormy heard Marilyn's cool voice behind her. "I want to talk to you."

Stormy turned, trying to look surprised. "Oh? Did you find the speech?"

"Yes. Just where Guy said it was—in his den."

So why did you go into the living room?

"What is it you want?"

"I want to talk to you about your relationship with Guy. You do realize, don't you, that this whole situation is open to scandal?"

"What are you talking about?"

"If it leaks out that he's having a tawdry affair with the female caretaker of his beach house, it could be disastrous to his campaign. It's really so—so sordid. Man evicts young unmarried mother from his rental property, and then gives her a job and then—well, you know the rest of it. I'm sure that sort of thing wouldn't set well with his conservative backers—or the San Jose voters."

"Dirty minds are dirty minds," Stormy said shortly.

"I'm sure you're right. But with ethical conduct among politicians so much in the news these days, Guy's rival would just love to get hold of something like this. It wouldn't be so bad if you weren't—" Her voice came to an abrupt stop.

Stormy knew Marilyn expected her to ask her to finish the sentence, but she wasn't about to fall into that trap. "I'm sure you underestimate the common sense of most people," she said instead.

"You're willing to take the chance because what do *you* have to lose. But Guy is in a very vulnerable position. I'm sure he knows it—he's said a few things lately that—" Again, she stopped.

This time, Stormy couldn't resist. "That what?"

"That he'd like to get out of this relationship with you."

"Well, there's one way to find out if you're right," Stormy said coldly. "Why don't I pick up the phone and ask him? That way we'd both know for sure, wouldn't we?"

Marilyn's eyes narrowed. It occurred to Stormy that she'd never liked women with long, narrow eyes. Not that she'd like this pair of eyes no matter what shape they were.

"Are you sure you want to know the answer?" Marilyn asked.

Stormy forced a smile. "I always prefer to know the truth. If it hurts, so be it. I can live with that. But lies and rumors and half-truths really bother me. So I think I'll repeat this conversation to Guy the next time he comes out. You can be sure I'll let you know his answer immediately."

The transformation on Marilyn's face told Stormy that maybe she'd gone too far. For a moment, she was sure the woman would attack her. She braced herself, almost welcoming the chance to defend herself, but then Marilyn shrugged, and gave her a thin smile.

"You've very sure of yourself, aren't you? Well, most of Guy's women are. He has the knack of convincing them that they're important to him. But what really interests him is the chase. You've lasted a bit longer than the others, so I expect you didn't fall right into bed with him. Oh, I'm sure he'll be generous when he breaks it off, but like I told him once, you can hurt someone more with kindness than by just being honest. Well, good luck. I hope his parting gift is something special. He gave one of his women a trip around the world. Maybe he'll buy you a diamond ring—or a sports car. And it was nice meeting you."

She was gone, leaving behind a trail of her musky perfume.

Stormy sat down on a kitchen stool, her legs giving out from under her. It always happened this way, she thought absently. She could face just about anything and hold her own, but when it was over, she got weak in the knees. But she'd carried it off well, said nothing Marilyn could carry back to Guy—unless she lied. And somehow she was sure Marilyn was a very good liar. There had been that look in her eyes, too, as if she was laughing at some private joke. Well, there was nothing she could do about that. In the future, she'd stay out of Marilyn's way—and take each day as it came.

Stormy went to bed early that night, but was unable to sleep. She felt nauseous, out of sorts, and while she was pretty sure it wasn't the ulcer, she got up and took some of the medicine Dr. Johnson had prescribed, drank a cup of warm skim milk, then crawled back into bed.

Although she fell asleep almost immediately, her night was filled with dreams, ones she couldn't remember in the morning when she awoke. They must have been sad because there were tears on her cheeks as if she'd been crying in her sleep.

Was it because of the secret she'd been carrying for the past two weeks, the secret that no one else knew? Of course she didn't have official confirmation yet since she hadn't mentioned her suspicions to Dr. Johnson during the examination, but after all, she was the mother of two children. She knew all the symptoms—nausea, loss of appetite, soreness in the breasts. It didn't take an examination by a doctor to tell her that she was at least two months pregnant with Guy's child.

CHAPTER FOURTEEN

STORMY'S FIRST REACTION when she'd put two and two together, added up her symptoms, and realized she must be pregnant, had been disbelief. How could it have happened when they'd been so careful? In fact, Guy had quietly initiated safe sex, doing it so matter-of-factly that it had seemed an integral part of their lovemaking. But not that first time. No, they hadn't been aware of anything except the sweet demands of their bodies that first time.

A flush invaded her cheeks as she remembered that time on the beach, the way the sand, still warm from the afternoon sun, had cradled her body, how wonderfully erotic Guy's touch had been on her naked flesh. All her senses, every inch of her body had come alive, as if she'd just been reborn. She had been so happy that night while they were making love. Against all reason, she'd been convinced that Guy felt the same joy that she did.

That particular delusion hadn't lasted, of course. He had taken her with passion, with what seemed to be overwhelming need, but even during the most intense part of their lovemaking there'd been no talk of love, of any kind of commitment. Whatever he felt for her, it wasn't love—and now, when time was running out for their affair, she knew she was pregnant.

With the dregs of this knowledge like ashes in her mouth, she knew that she'd made another mistake, putting her trust in the wrong man again. She couldn't even blame Guy. She had made herself so available that he would have been inhuman to refuse what was offered so freely. So she had to accept the truth, that the seduction had stemmed from her own sexual needs.

Or was that really true? If she'd been thrown into the company of another man, even a man as attractive and seductive as Guy, she wouldn't have been tempted. It was Guy who had brought her out of her shell. She was in love with him, had been almost from the first. Nothing could change that. She wanted him as much now as she had that first time even though, God help her, it was more and more painful to accept him on his own terms, to be a mere appendage to his life, knowing that he would never want anything more than sex from her.

If their relationship continued after the election, she would see him only at his convenience. She would remain in the background, never sharing his public life, someone available when he needed a woman. Even if she were willing to play such a role, there was Tommy and Laurie to consider. They loved Guy, would accept him as a father without any reservations, but when they were older—what would they think of him as their mother's sometimes lover?

All too soon, Tommy would realize what was going on and he'd be ashamed. Yes, she knew this about her son, that he wouldn't want his mother to be the side-street mistress of a prominent man, even one he was beginning to think of as a father.

Stormy massaged her temples, trying to ease the pressure building there before it blossomed into a full-blown headache. Every time she thought of the dilemma that faced her, the helpless baby growing inside of her, she felt a little sick. She had already brought two fatherless children into the world. How could she have been so foolish, so careless as to have allowed it to happen again? True, she hadn't known Eric had never divorced his first wife when she'd married him, nor later when she got pregnant with Tommy and with Laurie. But for the rest of their lives, the word "bastard" would have a personal meaning to both her children. Could she do that to another innocent child?

And yet—what was the alternative? The baby existed, was part of her. There was no question of an abortion. That was against everything she believed. There was another solution, of course. She could bear the child and then give it up for adoption. But how could she possibly go through life always wondering where it was, who was raising it, if it was happy?

She knew this was the right solution for other women caught in the same trap, but not for her. No matter how difficult it would be, raising another child, she couldn't give it up. The baby had been conceived with love, even though that love was one-sided. It was part of her, part of Guy. That he didn't love her was painful, but something she could live with. Giving up her child was different. She couldn't live with that.

True, she hadn't provided much in the way of material things for the two children she'd already borne, but she'd given them all her love, even more fiercely because there was so little else to share.

They were both bright and well adjusted, and they didn't seem to miss the luxuries other kids took for granted. Or was that true? Tommy's preoccupation with money seemed a little—well, excessive for a ten-year-old. Had poverty twisted his values despite the fact that she'd never dwelt on her constant worry about money? Had he seen through her jokes about being broke, her cheerful comments about living on the edge and what an adventure it all was?

And now there would be three children, living on minimum wages—provided she found work that allowed her to keep the baby with her. Maybe she could find another job in a child-care center—could four of them live on those kind of wages?

There was another solution to the problem, the obvious one. Why did she find it so hard to consider something that was so logical? The baby was Guy's, too. Why shouldn't he help support it? He was a rich man and it was his own flesh and blood. She didn't expect fatherly concern, of course. He'd made it very clear that he had no interest in becoming a father. But he was a fair man, almost brutally so. Surely he would offer child support once the baby was born.

Soberly she considered what was so inevitable—and so hard to accept: that in the end, she had no choice but to go to Guy with her hat in her hand. It was the only solution, but she dreaded the confrontation with him. He would be furious. She knew this, knew that he would assume that she'd laid a trap for him. Well, she would make it very clear that she only expected minimum child support, enough to raise his child in modest circumstances.

It would be the end of their relationship, of course. A pregnant woman would on longer be a convenience to him or even, she suspected, desirable. Everything would change once she told him about the baby. Couldn't she postpone it for a little while, live out these last days as if the baby didn't exist?

And what if she was wrong? Maybe the nausea, the soreness of her breasts, her fatigue were all symptoms of stress....

As if to repudiate her words, she felt a rush of nausea. She made it to the bathroom, but just in time. Afterward, she washed her face with cold water, rinsed out her mouth.

When she crawled back into bed, she felt cold, shivery; she pulled the coverlet around her shoulders and huddled under its warmth. The sound of the surf outside the window, usually so soothing, had a sinister sound now, a perfect accompaniment to her bleak thoughts.

Face it, Stormy. You're pregnant, and you have to tell Guy, have to ask him for support, at least until the baby is old enough for you to go back to work. And if he turns against you, so be it. The baby comes first—and all the regrets in the world won't change that.

What would Guy's first reaction be when she told him? Would he do the "right thing" without blistering her ears with accusations? She was sure that he would take on the responsibility of the child, maybe even occasionally come to see the son or daughter he'd helped create. But she, the passion they'd shared, would be past history. Wasn't that the right description for an affair you'd outgrown?

She shuddered, fighting another wave of nausea. She won this time but only by forcing herself to think of something else. Guy would be out the first of the week, and that's when she would tell him. As for what happened then—that was out of her hands.

One thing she would not do. She wouldn't mention marriage. It would be too humiliating to see his face freeze, see his lip curl with disdain. No, she couldn't do that to herself. She loved him—that was the only thing that she was certain of.

If only he loved her, too.

GUY AWOKE before the alarm went off, then lay there planning the day ahead. As usual, his schedule was hectic, packed full of meetings, starting with a session with Larry, who was helping him write a speech for another fund-raising dinner.

The business of running for mayor was much more complicated than he'd anticipated even though he'd done an intensive study on it before making up his mind to run. For one thing, his opponent was lambasting him with every weapon in the political book, using rumors and innuendos, half-truths and out-and-out lies.

Since Guy's temper was a little ragged these days, it was sometimes hard to smile calmly, give one of his wry rejoinders in answer to the questions he was asked by the media. Not that he was worried. According to the latest opinion polls, his already substantial lead was increasing every day. Still—the pressure was mounting and he'd be glad when it was over. Maybe then things would get back to normal.

Thank God he had a place of refuge when the going got too tough. Right now, Stormy was probably still in bed, getting a final few minutes of sleep before the kids got her up. How he wished he was there with her. Just thinking about her, of curling up with her in that guest-room bed, made his mouth go dry.

These past few months, after they'd become lovers, the knowledge that she was there at the beach, waiting for a break in his routine so he could steal away to be with her for a few hours, was what kept him on an even keel. She was so practical and down-to-earth on one level and yet, when he made love to her, she responded so passionately, so generously.

Sometimes, because he was a realist, he tried to imagine life without her, but the picture never quite jelled. And maybe that was a mistake, depending upon a woman, on Stormy, so much.

He shook off his doubts. Later—someday soon, he would have to come to terms with this, but not now, not yet. Closing his eyes, he pictured Stormy as she'd looked the last time they'd made love, remembering the warmth of her smile, always so worth waiting for, her smooth, soft body, so warm and pliant, so eager.

And yet, she could be so—well, touchy, too, quick to bristle and take offence. How had it happened that he'd fallen under the spell of a woman so different from the ones he'd been involved with before? He'd always favored women who knew what the score was. Fragrant and thin and ornamental—yes, those were the kind he'd always sought out.

So how was it that Stormy, wary, prickly, never easily giving an inch, had gotten under his skin so thoroughly? She didn't agree with everything he said, didn't stroke his ego and tell him how marvelous he was, didn't play by the usual man-woman game rules, and yet, he couldn't get enough of her. Was he laying himself open for a big fall?

The thought was unpalatable; he thrust it away and rose to take his morning shower and dress for the day. His breakfast, the usual orange juice, whole-wheat toast, and coffee, was waiting for him when he went out on the terrace, along with the morning paper, lying folded beside his plate.

He had just taken his first sip of coffee when his eyes fell on the front page of the newspaper, the *Bayside News*. He choked, spewing coffee over the glass top of the terrace table. A caricature dominated the front page, one that he'd seen before—in Stormy's sketch pad. It showed a man with his nose in the air, his mouth open as if making some pompous speech, every feature exaggerated—including the horns sprouting from his forehead.

His eyes burning, he scanned the article that accompanied it. It was much as he expected—snide, full of innuendos that bordered on libel.

"One source, very close to Harris," it said in part, "claims that he took advantage of the incident during which Ms. Todd, an unmarried mother of two, was evicted from a house owned by Harris. Shortly after the eviction, during which Ms. Todd's possessions mysteriously disappeared, she turned up at his beach house in Bolinas, where she has been living ever since. Although ostensibly employed as a caretaker, it is rumored that the relationship has blossomed into something warmer...."

Guy crumpled the newspaper in his hand, then tore it into shreds for good measure. His thoughts were chaotic, angry, filled with a multitude of questions.

How had the newspaper gotten hold of that caricature—and the information about Stormy? Was it possible that she had sent it to them? But why—why would she do such a thing?

So many things suddenly took on a sinister aspect to him—the theft of her belongings for instance. She had left the motel that night, had been gone an hour—was that when she'd arranged to have her furniture picked up? The clerk Clyde Farris had sent to guard her belongings had sworn that the order the trucker had shown him had been signed by Stormy Todd, that there was no reason to suspect what seemed to be a legitimate trucker doing his job. Was that why she hadn't filed a complaint with the police about the theft of her belongings? Had it all been a ploy to give her an excuse to move into his beach house?

He hadn't checked into it because Stormy had been so convincing when he'd accosted her in Bolinas. He'd bought her whole story, had ended up offering her a job for the summer.

There was something else. Although she hadn't come on to him, she had let him make love to her that first time without the semblance of a protest. Had the whole thing been a plot to put him into an untenable position?

If so, Stormy had been clever as hell. She'd been very careful to let him be the aggressor. And he hadn't suspected a thing. Hell, he'd even felt guilty after they'd made love that first time because he'd been so convinced that he'd taken advantage of her. What a bloody fool he was!

He slammed his napkin down and jumped to his feet, so quickly that he sent his chair skittering out from under him. Kung Toy, his houseman, appeared in the doorway, is dark face startled.

"You want something, Mr. Harris?" he said.

"Yes. My coat and hat—sorry for the mess," he added perfunctorily.

"That's all right. Everybody makes mistakes," Kung Toy said, so good-naturedly that Guy would have smiled at any other time.

Fifteen minutes later, he walked into his office. From the carefully averted faces of his office staff, he knew they had seen the caricature and read the front-page article. Marilyn, who was standing by the receptionist's desk, gave Guy's set face a quick look and then followed him into his private office.

"I see you've read the morning paper," she observed.

"Call Masters at the airport and tell him to get my chopper ready," he said tightly. "And cancel my appointments for the day."

"For the whole day!" she said, alarmed. "You've been doing that too often lately—and this will be the second time you've canceled a luncheon with Judge Lanyard and his group."

"Just cancel the morning appointments. I'll be back by noon," he said. He opened the top drawer of his desk, and took out a handful of bills from the petty cash box. He didn't look at Marilyn as he left his office and headed for the elevator.

Before he left the building, he stopped at the newsstand in the lobby and bought another copy of the morning paper.

STORMY HEARD the helicopter overhead with mingled feelings. She was eager, as always, to see Guy, but there was the resolution she'd made to tell him about the baby the next time he came out, something she wished she could postpone. Knowing it couldn't be put off, she went to waylay the kids, who were already heading outside to greet Guy. She told them to take the puppy for a walk along the beach, that she had something important she wanted to talk over with Guy—in private.

Ignoring Tommy's groan and Laurie's reproachful look, she left the house and started up the path toward the upper meadow.

She met Guy halfway up the hill, and as always when she saw him after a separation, she felt a rush of pleasure. It wasn't that he was handsome; his looks were too unconventional for that. But there was no doubt that he was more than attractive with that shock of reddish brown hair, those dark brown eyes, and a smile that wouldn't stop.

But where was his smile today? Why did he look so grim?

She stopped in the middle of the path, taking in his stony expression, the ice in his eyes. Something was wrong—was it possible he'd found out about the baby? It didn't seem possible. After all, she hadn't confided in anyone yet....

Guy stopped, too, a few feet away; he made no move to kiss her. "Where are the kids?" he demanded.

"They took Shag for a walk," she said. "Is something wrong?"

"You can ask me that knowing what you did?"

So it *was* the baby... "It took two of us," she said, trying not to show her hurt.

"That's how you're going to play it?" he asked. "Well, it won't work. What I want to know is why? Why did you give that caricature to the *Bayside News*? Did they pay you more than you thought you could get from me? You're clever—I give you that—but you overplayed your hand. You should have waited for my offer. I even rented a comfortable furnished house in the city for you and the kids. And I was going to offer you a decent allowance, enough to keep you and your kids comfortable. I don't know what Harvey Cummins paid you but it couldn't match that."

She made a sound of protest, knowing she had to stop him. His words were cruel, meant to hurt—and they just didn't make sense.

"I don't know what you're talking about," she said.

He thrust a newspaper into her hands, then stepped back as if he was afraid she might touch him.

"You must be wondering just what they said," he said harshly. "That twist about your belongings disappearing so 'mysteriously' is a gem. And then you showing up at my summer place, 'ostensibly' working as a caretaker—very clever wording. Of course, we'll deny it all, but who is going to believe it? The facts are all correct—you can't win law suits over innunedos."

His words beat at her as she stared at the caricature on the front page of the newspaper, then scanned the article. She felt nauseous, realizing how damning it was. How had they gotten the caricature? Someone must have stolen it....

"—I do hope you got a good price for the caricature," Guy was saying. "It really is an attention-getter. By tomorrow, every bar in town will have one thumbtacked up behind the cash register."

Stormy looked up into Guy's hard, condemning eyes. Her heart twisted with pain, but also with anger. He didn't doubt, not for a moment, that she was guilty of selling him out. Was that how he saw her—a woman who could make love to a man at the same time she was setting him up for his enemies?

Her own disappointment was overwhelming. Had she really hoped, deep in her heart, that he would be happy when she told him about the baby, that he would love it, be a father to it? How self-destructive she was! Because she could never tell him about the baby he would father, not ever.

"I don't know anything about this," she said quietly.

"So you're a liar as well as a bitch," he said. "Now why doesn't that surprise me?"

She stared at him, struck dumb by his cruel words. Her silence, or maybe her stare, seemed to irritate him because he added, "I want you out of my house as soon as you can pack your things—and don't get any idea about helping yourself to anything that belongs to me."

Even though she knew that nothing she could say to defend herself would make any difference, angry words formed in Stormy's mind. Only her pride kept her from saying them aloud. Her shoulders held stiff and high, she turned and walked away, each step putting space between them.

When she heard footsteps behind her, she quickened her step, but she didn't look back. She didn't want him to know that she was crying. She went into the house, hurried through the kitchen, glad that Tommy and Laurie hadn't returned from their walk.

Behind her, Guy's footsteps stopped, but even so, when she went into her bedroom, she locked the door behind her. She needn't have bothered; a few minutes later, she heard the chopper taking off.

It took her longer than it should have to pack because her hands were shaking so badly she kept dropping things. When she finally went back into the kitchen, several bills and a handful of change, her wages to the penny, were lying on the breakfast bar. She wanted desperately to have the luxury of tearing the bills into tiny pieces and leaving them there for Guy to find, but she gathered up the money and stuffed it into her pocket instead. That kind of pride was for those who could afford it. The needs of her children had to come first, above her pride. There would be so many expenses—costs when they got there. Besides, she had earned that money—not for the passion she'd given Guy, because that had come from her heart and had been a gift, but for keeping his house clean, cooking his meals, doing his gardening.

She went to strip the beds, to gather up sheets and mattress covers and pillow slips. By the time Tommy and Laurie came back with Shag, she had already finished two loads of laundry and was putting fresh linens on one of the guest-room beds.

CHAPTER FIFTEEN

STORMY DIDN'T WASTE any time wondering why she was so determined to leave the beach house immaculate. She already knew why. All her life, she had derived a certain comfort from restoring order and cleanliness to her surroundings, welcoming hard labor because it served her so effectively as a safety valve against resentment and bitterness. When things got tough, the physical act of scrubbing and cleaning and dusting relieved the pressure, washing self-pity right out of her system.

This particular cleaning job had the added purpose of sending the message to Guy that she had earned every penny he'd paid her. It was even possible that he'd get another message, albeit a false one, that as far as she was concerned, being his lover had merely been a part of her caretaker duties.

If only that were true. It infuriated her, this knowledge that she would never be completely free of him. The baby growing inside her was a result of the passion they'd shared, making it impossible to ever completely shut him out of her mind, just as Eric, for all the pain he'd caused her, would always be a part of her because he had fathered Laurie and Tommy. Her only consolation was her determination that Guy would never know about the baby he'd helped create.

But for now, the physical act of scrubbing and waxing, of vacuuming and cleaning off shelves, straightening and dusting books and making sure that every dish and glass, every bed sheet or towel, was clean or freshly laundered, was good for her self-esteem.

Before she'd set Tommy and Laurie to work—Laurie to sweep off the entranceway and the patio, and Tommy to weed the vegetable garden she'd planted so hopefully—she had told them only that it was time to return to San Jose since Uncle Guy no longer required her services.

The disappointment on their faces, their unusual quietness, hardened her resolution to cope with her own disappointment, to rise above it, just as she'd risen above Eric's desertion.

As she made up the beds with freshly laundered sheets, she tried to think optimistically. At least, she wasn't without funds this time. She had saved every penny possible this summer—there should be enough to carry them over until she found a job. She wasn't worried about that part. There were always jobs in a city for someone willing to work for low wages. But could she live on it, now that there was a baby coming? There were so many things a baby needed—a crib and diapers and infant clothes. And what about medical expenses? She didn't have a speck of health insurance.

Maybe they could live in a free family shelter for a while and save rent money—no, she couldn't do that to the kids. She'd find a small apartment, if only a housekeeping room, in a low-rent district, get a job, work until the baby was born, and then—well, something would come up then. Something always did.

She was standing in the middle of the living room, inspecting the corners of the vaulted ceiling for dust, when Arnold came to the door and looked in at her.

"You couldn't be looking for cobwebs," he said in his gruff voice. "The cobweb never existed that could survive your trusty vacuum cleaner."

She forced a smile. "Did you want something, Arnold?"

"I thought I'd take the kids and that mangy dog of yours for a walk," he said.

She hesitated, then said reluctantly, "I'm sorry, Arnold, but we're moving back to San Jose as soon as I can hire someone to drive us in."

"But I thought you and Guy—why would you do a fool thing like that?"

"School will be starting in a couple of weeks. I'll need time to rent an apartment. I'm hoping to find something in our old neighborhood so Tommy and Laurie can go to the same school they did last year."

Arnold frowned at her. "That isn't why you're leaving. Did you and Guy have a fight? He was here this morning—I saw his chopper in the meadow."

"This job was just a temporary arrangement for the summer. You knew that." Despite herself, her voice shook slightly. Rather than show her agitation, she turned away and busied herself straightening a row of books she'd already straightened. She took out a book, couldn't think what to do with it, and stood there holding it.

She burst into tears.

Arnold took the book out of her hand, put it back on the shelf, then steered her to the nearest sofa. He handed her a facial tissue.

"In books the guy always produces a clean handkerchief," he said. "This'll have to do."

She laughed, and stopped crying. After she'd wiped her face and blown her nose, she told him, "I'll miss you, Arnold."

"No, you won't because you're going to see a lot of Elsie and me in the future. And you might as well tell me the whole story. What happened?"

But it was Tommy, his voice shrill, who answered Arnold from the doorway. "It's Uncle Guy. I guess Laurie and me get on his nerves, so he don't want us around anymore."

Shocked, Stormy stared at him. "Oh, Tommy—it has nothing to do with you."

"He's just like Dad. *He* didn't want us, either."

Stormy felt a wave of pity for him—and guilt. In her preoccupation with her own feelings, she hadn't realized that Tommy and Laurie might think they were to blame for being sent back to the city.

She opened her arms and Tommy blundered into them. He buried his face in her shoulder, and although his body shook with sobs, he didn't make any sound.

"Guy loves you and Laurie," she said softly. "This has nothing to do with you. It's strictly between Guy and me. Besides, you always knew we couldn't stay here forever."

He raised his tearstained face to look at her. "Won't you please make up with him, Mom? Maybe if you tell him you're sorry, he'll let us stay. We can go to school in Bolinas—it's only a couple miles walk. Won't you at least try?"

"He won't change his mind," she said. "And it's going to be fun, being back in the city. We'll find a furnished apartment, maybe in our old neighborhood so you can go to the same school—"

"I hate that school. Some of the guys make fun of kids on welfare—and Laurie feels the same way. We really love it here. Won't you please ask Uncle Guy to let us stay?"

Stormy took a deep breath. "I'm sorry, Tommy. You know that sometimes things just don't work out—"

"They *never* work out for us," he said angrily.

She tried to speak, but couldn't think of what to say. After all, Tommy was right. In his short life, how often had things worked out the way he wanted them to? She'd always tried to be optimistic with the kids, but Tommy was old enough to see the truth. Reality was a very cold companion when you're ten. Or even when you were twenty-five...

She started with surprise when Arnold cleared his throat; she'd forgotten he was there.

"I think I have a solution to your problem," he said. "You know I've been promising Elsie we'd do some traveling this winter. She's got her heart set on Europe and I have to admit it might be fun. I planned to hire someone to housesit for us while we're gone—these days, you can't be too careful. There's a guest cottage on the grounds. Two bedrooms, and a den that could make a third bedroom. It's small, but fully furnished and there's plenty of room for you and the kids. There's even a pickup truck you could use for transportation. It's just been sitting in the garage, getting rusty."

It had come too quickly. It took a few seconds before Stormy asked, "You're offering me a job?"

"Yeah, sure. You'd be doing us a big favor. Free rent and a salary, enough to keep you going. What do you say, Stormy? You want to take it on?"

Stormy felt a wave of relief, but it didn't last. Arnold's offer was too pat, too much of a coincidence. Did he really need a caretaker? The Storys already had a full-time housekeeper and gardener—why couldn't one of them act as caretaker? This was Arnold's way of lending her a helping hand, and she was grateful, very grateful, but charity was charity, even from a friend.

"Thank you for your offer," she said carefully, "but what I really need is a job with a future. I can't be a caretaker for the rest of my life and still give Tommy and Laurie the life they deserve. You understand, don't you?"

"I have some ideas about that, about a job with a future, I mean," he said. "I haven't said anything because I didn't want to get your hopes up, but—I might as well spell it out now."

"Spell what out?"

"You know those comic strips I borrowed from you? The one about the single mother and her problems?"

"Yes. You said you wanted to show them to Elsie to give her a laugh."

"And I did. Only she didn't just laugh. She got a few tears in her eyes, too. Which gave me an idea. I sent those strips to this old friend of mine, J.C. Landau, who lives in L.A. He used to be a cartoonist on my paper and now he's into the syndication business, handles some of the best cartoonists in the country. He was very much taken with your cartoon strip. It isn't anything certain. You'd have to satisfy him that you can sustain the quality, make it solid, develop the strip without exhausting the single mother theme. But there is a chance he'll give you a try. He wants to see more—say, enough for a ten-week run—to make sure the single mother concept isn't too narrow. It's up to you to convince him how timely that aspect is these days. How about it? You willing to give it a try?"

Stormy discovered she had lost her voice. It was too sudden, too frightening a concept to grasp.

Typically Tommy went right to the heart of Arnold's speech. "Hey, Mom, this J.C. Landau guy wants to see if you can keep making those cartoons funny before he offers you a contract."

"But I only do the strip to amuse the kids and to let off steam. I never thought—the comic strip field is very tough, the competition enormous. It just doesn't happen this way—besides, I don't know anything about presentations, roughs, that sort of thing. I've never had any formal training—"

"So you can learn. One of the political cartoonists who worked for my newspaper lives out my way. He did freelance work after he left the paper. He's retired now, but I'm sure I can persuade him to show you the ropes. The thing you have to sell is your own fresh view of the world. Since you know your subject inside out, you can show the life of the single parent with humor and still get across the plight of other women in your situation."

He took in her stunned expression and shook his head. "You aren't going to let this get away from you, are you, because you're afraid of failing?"

"But I've failed so many times, made so many mistakes—"

He said a word not appropriate for the ears of the young. At his quick apologetic look, Tommy grinned. "I've heard that word before," he said. "Used it, too, only not around Mom. She's kind of—you know, square." He gave Stormy a thoughtful look. "Uncle Arnold's right, Mom. You have to take a chance."

Stormy met his eyes. How strange that he should have so much good common sense at ten years of age. And he was right. She had to take this chance that had been given to her. So what if she did fail? She would survive—and meanwhile, she would have a breathing spell, long enough to have her baby, and put her life back in order.

"Of course, I'm going to give it a try. And I thank you for giving me a chance, Arnold."

"Don't thank me," Arnold said gruffly. "I owe you a lot—someday I'll tell you about that. But for now—why don't you get your things together? If we hurry, we can be in the city in time for you to get settled into the guest house before dark."

CHAPTER SIXTEEN

GUY WASN'T SURE just when his blind anger began to fray at the edges, but it happened very quickly, leaving a bitter taste in his mouth and a flood of doubts in his mind.

He had kept his afternoon appointments, as promised, and was in his office, winding up a strategy session with Larry Singer, Marilyn, and Jack Perl, his campaign publicist, when without warning, the realization that he'd been too hasty in condemning Stormy, that he hadn't given her a chance to refute his accusations, hit him.

He felt a flood of conflicting emotions—uncertainty, guilt, an almost overwhelming sense of loss. The anger returned but this time it was directed at himself.

The voices in the conference room faded as he fought against a need to curse—long and loud—and call himself a few appropriate names that would probably curl Marilyn's shell-like ears. He tried to tell himself that he'd done the right thing, the only sensible thing, casting Stormy out of his life, and yet...he prided himself on being a fair man. And a fair man would have given her a chance to answer his charges.

But no, he'd been so furious that he'd followed her into the house, not to ask for explanations but to drop that blasted money on the kitchen table and then storm off. True, she hadn't tried to defend herself. She'd stood there in the middle of the path, her face ashen, listening to him, and then, without a word, she had turned her back on him and walked away.

But what if he'd taken her so by surprise, hurt her so badly that she couldn't stand to look at him any longer? What if she were innocent and he'd just made the biggest mistake of his life?

He felt chilled, cold to the bone, although it was warm in his office. Somewhere in the room, Jack Perl was saying something about fighting the bad publicity about Stormy Todd, laying out a plan for a press meeting, but his words didn't seem important. All Guy was aware of was his own sick thoughts.

After a while, the publicist left, and Guy must have carried it off because the man was smiling as he went out the door. But Marilyn and Larry Singer had stayed behind and were both staring at him, their eyes hostile and accusing.

"What the hell's wrong with you, boss?" Larry demanded. "You agreed to everything that jerk said. You seemed to be in some kind of fog—"

"Leave him alone, Larry," Marilyn interrupted, her voice honey-sweet. "Can't you see he's upset about that Stormy Todd business?"

Upset? Yes, he was upset. The suspicion that he had let his temper, his stiff-necked pride, get out of hand, that he'd made a terrible mistake, was enough to upset him. But maybe it wasn't too late. Surely if he talked to Stormy, told her he was sorry, that he was willing to listen to her now, he could straighten things out....

"You'll have to excuse me. I have to make a phone call to Bolinas," he said urgently. "Personal business."

Larry's face lengthened. "You aren't going to do anything stupid, are you? You do know it had to be the Todd woman who gave that story to the *Bayside News*, don't you? Anything you say to her is just going to make it worse."

"I took it for granted she did, but I could have been wrong," Guy said.

"What do you mean, you could have been wrong?" Marilyn's voice was shrill. "Of course, it was Stormy. That was her drawing—" She broke off abruptly.

"How do you know it was her drawing?" Guy demanded.

"Why, I saw it when I went out to Bolinas last week. It was in her sketch pad."

"Stormy showed *you* her sketch pad?" he said, his disbelief obvious.

"Actually the pad was lying there in the living room and it caught my eye and I—well, I flipped through it," she said. "I remember thinking that caricature of you was appalling."

Guy wanted to pursue it further, his suspicions in full bay, but he was too conscious that time was getting away from him, so he dismissed Marilyn and Larry, not too politely, saying he'd talk to them later.

As soon as he was alone, he called the beach house. He let the phone ring half a dozen times, then hung up and called again on the chance that he'd gotten a wrong number. This time he let it ring several minutes before he gave up.

He tried to think calmly, logically. It had only been a few hours. She *could* already have left, but that seemed very unlikely. She would need time to pack, to arrange for transportation into the city. Maybe she was at Arnold's place. She would surely tell the Storys that she was leaving and say goodbye....

But no one answered at Arnold's lodge, and it was then that he called the airport and arranged for his helicopter to be gassed up and ready to fly.

GUY KNEW the house was empty even before he turned the key in the lock and went inside. For one thing, the door was locked. For another, all the blinds had been closed and there were no voices, no sound at all, as there would have been were Tommy and Laurie there. Even so, he called Stormy's name several times at the foot of the hall stairs.

When only silence greeted him, he turned into the living room. The long, rectangular room fairly shouted that it had just had a thorough cleaning. Nothing was out of place—there were no books or magazines on the coffee table, no newspapers in the wastepaper basket, and the collection of rare shells he kept on one of the bookshelves was lined up in perfect order.

He stared at the huge stone fireplace that dominated one of the short ends of the room. The hearth had obviously just been freshly swept and scrubbed. Logs, neatly stacked, had been laid out, ready for the touch of a match to start a fire.

He hurried through the rest of the house, found it to be in the same uncompromising order. Every washable surface had been recently scrubbed; there wasn't a speck of dust on any piece of furniture or a grain of sand on any floor. She had even hung fresh dishcloths on the kitchen towel rack. She couldn't have made it plainer. As far as Stormy Todd was concerned, she had washed her hands of Guy Harris, wiped him right out of her life.

"Damn you," he whispered, but it was himself he was cursing.

He searched the house again, this time noting that she'd taken the plants she'd started, the sweet potato vines in their mason jars, the citrus trees and redwoods starting from seeds, the ground ivy she'd grown from clippings. Without these homey touches, without the children's toys, the house seemed cold and unlived in, unearthly quiet.

He went outside, and found the same order. The vegetable garden she'd tended so lovingly seemed to reproach him now. Those neat, weed-free rows of vegetables, tucked in one corner of the rear meadow—they had added a special touch to the salads she'd served him and yet he'd never once complimented her on them. In fact, after they'd become lovers, he'd seldom complimented her on anything. Had he been afraid that she might take advantage of him if she ever realized how crazy he was about her?

He groaned aloud, feeling hollow inside, as if some vital part of himself was missing. He'd made a mess of it; how could he have said those things, lashed out at her so cruelly without giving her a chance to defend himself?

He returned to search the house for the third time, hoping against hope that he'd overlooked a note, anything that would tell him that she wasn't completely lost to him. For a long time, he stood in the doorway of her bedroom where they'd spent so many nights in each other's arms. She had taken everything that belonged to her, but he didn't completely give up hope until he opened a chest drawer at random and found the gifts he'd bought her.

He picked up a half-empty bottle of Joy that had been her twenty-fifth birthday present from him. She had loved that perfume; her eyes had looked like green stars when she'd opened the box and seen the exquisite bottle inside. When he'd found out later that she was hoarding the perfume for the nights when he was there, he'd insisted that she use it every day, even when she did her housework, telling her that when it was gone, he would buy her another bottle.

The sound of children's voices, down on the beach, aroused him, and he went outside, down to the stone wall that edged the rim of the cliff, hoping that it was Tommy and Laurie, even though he knew how unlikely that would be. As he watched several of the neighborhood kids at play, it came to him that he'd lost more than Stormy—he had lost her children, too.

And for what? He no longer believed that she'd given that caricature to the *Bayside News* reporters. Why had he been so sure earlier? Was there some self-destructive flaw in his own nature that had been expecting her to betray him all along? And now that he'd come to his senses, what was he going to do without her? He had thrown away the best thing that had ever happened to him, ruined the one relationship that could have saved him from a lifetime of loneliness.

Bleakly he turned away from the sound of children's voices and returned to Stormy's bedroom. Her presence was strongest here, even though she'd left no physical trace of herself, no discarded sock or broken belt, no hairpin or empty tissue box. He opened her closet and her scent, the perfume he'd bought her, reproached him. He shut his eyes, willing her to return, aching with loss.

He was closing the still-open chest drawer where she'd left his gifts when he spotted a small notebook, tightly lodged against the front of the drawer, held there by a large box of Joy bath powder, part of the set he'd given her.

He extracted it, read the inked-in words on the cover that said, Journal: Stormy Todd. Without any thought that he was invading her privacy, he stood in the middle of the bedroom with the notebook in his hands, and began to read.

It wasn't, strictly speaking, a journal. It was more like a financial record, listing every welfare check, every food stamp, every cent of charity she'd received over a period of several years. She'd even listed the hamburgers and fries he'd bought for her and the kids the night her belongings had been stolen.

Folded and paper-clipped to the cover of the notebook, he found a hospital bill. Laurie had been the patient—and the bill had been steep enough to make him whistle. He had already known why Stormy was forced to go on welfare; the size of the bill made him wonder how any single parent without health insurance or an enormous bank account could possibly pay such a bill.

Guy closed the notebook, put it away in his pocket. He already understood why she'd made such a detailed list of the charity she'd received from other people. He'd once kept the same kind of list—scholarships, student loans, grants, a cash gift from a professor who had bailed him out of a financial jam when he was a senior.

After he'd started on his first full-time job after graduation, he'd begun paying back every cent, with interest, even though, except for the student loans, it hadn't been necessary, hadn't even been expected.

Someday, Stormy meant to do the same—how could he ever have thought that the only thing they had in common was their sexual attraction to each other?

God, what an ass he'd been! He had let his prejudices blind him to so many things. Stormy had once accused him of intolerance toward those people who hadn't made it up the success ladder the way he had. It had angered him, not because it wasn't true, but because he'd suspected that it was.

And why hadn't she ever told him that the reason she'd gone on welfare was to assure Laurie medical care? Once she'd said that she never made excuses for what she did because to do so implied that you were at fault. Was that why she hadn't defended herself this morning? Did it also explain why she hadn't left him a message, not even another "Go to hell, Mr. Harris!" note? Because she'd done nothing wrong and was too proud to deny his accusations?

When Guy left, he took the notebook with him. He would give it back to Stormy when he found her. And if he didn't, if she'd gone out of his life for good? Then he would keep it as a reminder that he was a pigheaded, narrow-minded jerk.

Uncle Jerk, he thought, and didn't smile.

The evening after his return to San Jose, he went to Marilyn's apartment. It was so obvious now that he'd opened up his mind and let some fresh air in. He had noticed Marilyn's hostility to Stormy, but he'd put it out of his mind as unimportant. But had it been unimportant? Was it possible that her sly remarks about welfare mothers had influenced him more than he'd realized?

He had been tolerant of those remarks because he'd assumed they'd been spontaneous, stemming from female jealousy. Now he was sure they'd been deliberate, calculated. Marilyn wanted to be San Jose's first lady. Even if he had buckteeth and an extra eye, she still would have set her cap for him. Why hadn't he seen this earlier? How vain he'd been, thinking that her passionate response to his lovemaking was genuine. Now that he was ready to face the truth, it was obvious that it had been an act. After all, if she really loved him, how could she have leaked the fact that he was living with Stormy to the press, something that might well lose him the election?

It was getting dark when he reached Marilyn's apartment in one of the city's better condo complexes. For a brief moment, when she opened the door at his ring, he thought she looked disconcerted. Even so, she produced a seductive smile. She was wearing one of her white silk robes, looking as if she'd just stepped out of the shower, but he wasn't tempted to kiss her.

"I want the truth, Marilyn," he said when the door was closed behind them. "Why did you steal that caricature and turn it over to that rag?"

"What kind of lies did that bitch tell you?" she said, all innocence and hurt.

"I finally figured it out on my own. You took the caricature when I sent you out to the beach house to pick up my speech. Don't bother to lie. You gave yourself away when you let it slip that you'd seen the caricature last week."

Marilyn worried her lower lip with her teeth. He knew she'd decided not to brazen it out when she shrugged one slender shoulder.

"It was for your own good. That woman had you tied up in knots. I knew the whole sordid business was going to come out—it was just a matter of time. Since the story broke in the *Bayside News*, most voters will chalk it up to dirty campaign practices, and it'll hurt the mayor more than it hurts you. After all, you aren't married—and neither is Stormy. Never has been, I understand, despite those two kids. So it isn't a question of adultery. In fact, it rather humanizes you—you *are* a bit on the conservative side, you know."

"So you did it to help out my campaign," he said, his tone sardonic.

"Not entirely," she said coolly. "I was also jealous. You know I'm crazy about you, Guy." Her voice took on warmth and she moved a step closer. "I've missed you—we had a great thing going until *she* came along."

She laid her hand on his arm; her perfume filled his nostrils. "I only wanted to bring you to your senses, to make you realize how—how inappropriate your relationship with that woman was. The only thing you two had going for you was sex."

Guy disengaged his arm. "Well, your tactics worked. I said a lot of unforgivable things when I went out there this morning. Now, she's gone. I have no idea where she is."

Briefly there was a flash of triumph in Marilyn's eyes, setting his anger soaring again. "I'm going to find her, if it takes twenty-four hours a day," he went on, his voice tight, "and when I do, I'm going to beg her to forgive me."

"But that's insane! You don't have time for that. The election is just two months off and—"

"I don't give a damn about the election," Guy said coldly. "I also don't give a damn about you."

Marilyn's expression was a study of dismay—and anger. The anger won out and she was still screaming at him when he stalked out the door. He didn't dare stay around long enough to make it official and fire her because he was afraid that he just might forget that she was a woman and he a man, especially when she called Stormy a bitch for the second time.

GUY DIDN'T HAVE TO fire Marilyn. The next day, she came into the office very early, before anyone else was there, and cleared out her desk, leaving behind a wastebasket full of out-of-date memos and other discards. The note she left in the middle of the desk, addressed to Guy, said only that she was resigning to take another job, to send her termination check to her home address.

Guy was relieved when he realized she'd quit—and also surprised that she'd let him off so easily. He had expected that she would bring Larry into it, complicating things. Not that he still wouldn't have fired her. That kind of betrayal was unforgivable, all the more so since it hadn't been jealousy, borne from love, that had motivated it.

So he dictated a recommendation, citing Marilyn's efficiency and excellent business skills, her dedication to her job, and sent it and her termination check off by special messenger to her apartment.

He didn't enclose a personal note. She wouldn't expect it and besides, what could he say? That he was sorry she was gone? It wouldn't be true. The part of himself that found it impossible to forgive a betrayal would have been lying. Of course, he could say he was grateful that she'd spared him the chore of firing her. Now that *would* be true.

Oddly, despite his relief, he no longer was angry. He even felt regret that their relationship had ended this way, in a flurry of bad feelings. After all, they *had* been lovers; for a while, he had seriously considered marrying her. He'd even believed that her feelings for him were real, something he now doubted.

And yet—could all of it have been an act? She had responded to him so passionately. He was an experienced lover; some of the physical aspects of lovemaking she couldn't have faked. And if this were true—then she must be hurting right now.

It came to Guy suddenly how much he had changed. At one time, this possibility wouldn't have occurred to him or if it had, it wouldn't have mattered. Now—well, he'd learned a few things in the past summer, that where human emotions were concerned, there was no black-and-white, only various shades of gray....

He was also learning the pain of separation, the fear that comes from having to face the possibility that you would never again see the person you love. Not that he had any illusions that Marilyn felt that way about him. No, she didn't love him. But she had devoted her life to him for a long time—right now, she must be feeling pretty low....

In the end, he wrote Marilyn a letter. It was personal, warm—and kind. He thanked her for all she had done for him, told her that he was aware his own actions hadn't always been above reproach. He wished her the best of luck, and added that if she ever needed anything she shouldn't hesitate to call him. He signed the letter "Sincerely, Guy," dropped it in the mail slot and promptly put Marilyn out of his mind.

THAT MORNING, he cleared his calendar of all appointments for the next three days, putting the woman who was substituting for Marilyn into a near-panic. Luckily Larry Singer was off on one of his fund-raising crusades, so he didn't have to make any excuses. He'd already made an attempt to reach Arnold that morning before he'd left his apartment, only to be told by his housekeeper that he and Elsie were "out" and she didn't know when they'd be home.

Doggedly he kept phoning, and late that afternoon, Arnold called him.

"I hear you've been trying to reach me all day," Arnold said, his tone edgy. "What's up, Guy?"

"I'm trying to find Stormy. We had a quarrel—hell, it was more than that. It was a real blowup and she walked out on me, didn't leave any address. Do you know where she is?"

There was a long silence. "Sorry I can't help you, Guy," Arnold said finally. "The last time I saw Stormy, she seemed perfectly normal. What the hell happened, anyway?"

"I made a bloody fool out of myself," Guy said bitterly. "You must have seen that article about me and Stormy in the *Bayside News*?"

"I saw it. Pure garbage."

"Well, the caricature was Stormy's. I thought—hell, I thought she gave them that story. I started tossing accusations around, not giving her a chance to defend herself—and then I said something unforgivable and told her to get out. I know she can't forgive me but I have to know that she and the kids are okay. Can you understand that? I'm going out of my mind, worrying about them."

Arnold's voice was heavy when he said, "Then I'm sorry as hell for you."

"Yeah. Well, I deserve it, I guess, but—dammit, where could she be? She didn't leave a note—nothing!"

"Maybe she's just gone off somewhere to think things over. She'll probably get in touch with you—eventually."

"Maybe. She was hurt—God, I really hurt her, Arnold! I did something stupid. I followed her back to the beach house but instead of going to her and telling her I was sorry, I was still so furious that I counted out what I owed her—to the penny!—and dropped it on the breakfast bar, then stomped off and went back to the city."

"You're right. That was stupid—and pretty damned cruel, too."

"I know, I know! Look, if she should contact you, will you tell her—no, don't tell her anything. Just call me immediately and tell me where she is. I'll take over from there."

"Oh? You think it will be that easy?"

"Not easy. But I have to try to make her listen to me, forgive me. Will you call me if you hear from her?"

"Sorry, but I'm afraid I can't help you there. Elsie and I are just packing for that trip to Europe we've been talking about. Call it a second honeymoon. If we hit even half the places Elsie has in mind, we'll be gone for several months. I'll contact you when we get back—and I have to go now. Good luck, Guy. You're going to need it."

After Guy hung up, he sat for a while, staring at the phone. Arnold had been less than sympathetic—but how could he blame him? His friend knew Stormy's worth—and he must think he, Guy, was a real jerk for losing her.

To keep Larry off his back, Guy pleaded a bout with a virus and went home, leaving word that he would be incommunicado because of an attack of laryngitis. For the next two days, he exhausted every contact in the San Jose police department he had in his search for Stormy. When his efforts were unsuccessful, he knew he'd have to get private professional help.

The private investigation agency he chose was well-known and highly respected not only in San Jose, but all over Northern California. He had met the owner, a former San Francisco chief of police named Thomas Murphy, at a political banquet, and had been impressed enough to add him to his own private guest list for the dinner parties he occasionally gave to fulfill his social obligations. Even so, he felt embarrassed when he called his friend and told him he wanted to find a woman named Stormy Todd.

Tom Murphy asked him a few questions, then told him it shouldn't be too difficult to find Stormy Todd. "In cases like this, when someone wants to drop out of sight, they tend to seek help from old friends. I'll send a man around tomorrow to get more information about the woman. Meanwhile, I want you to jot down everything you know about her. The fact that she has two children will help. She'll be enrolling them in school the day after Labor Day, which will leave a record somewhere. Of course, I'm assuming that she returned to San Jose. If she moved elsewhere—that will complicate things."

The next morning, Guy was having his second cup of coffee when his houseman ushered in a short, stocky man. He introduced himself as Cal Haas, an investigator from the Murphy Agency, took a chair and accepted a cup of coffee from Kung Toy, added a couple of dollops of cream and three teaspoons of sugar. He jotted down notes while Guy listed everything he knew about Stormy. It was surprising how little there was.

When he ran out of questions, Cal Haas closed his notebook and tucked it away in his jacket pocket. "Well, this should get me started," he said briskly.

Guy found himself genuinely amused. He'd dealt with private investigators before, and they had all been very ordinary in appearance. This man, with his multiple chins, his stocky body, his froglike voice, could have stepped right out of a detective novel.

"Were you a policeman, like your boss?" he asked curiously.

"Army—MPs. When I got out, I decided I liked playing detective. Couldn't pass the physical for any of the city police forces, so I got on with the Murphy Agency. I like it—except surveillance gigs."

He gave Guy a shrewd look. "It ain't none of my business, so you don't have to answer this, but why are you looking for this Todd woman? She steal something that belongs to you?"

Guy almost told him he was right both times, that it was none of his business—and that yes, she had stolen something from him, one slightly battered heart. Instead he said, "I'm concerned about the way she left, without leaving a forwarding address."

"She was your—uh, girlfriend?"

"She's my friend. I'm very fond of her and her kids."

Cal finished off the coffee in his cup, and rose. "Well, I'd better get on with it. Don't worry. She'll turn up—most people do. I'll contact you as soon as I get a lead, which may take a couple hours or a couple weeks. It all depends on the breaks. First thing I'll do is talk to a contact of mine at city social services. Who knows? Maybe Stormy Todd went back on welfare."

Guy shook his head. "I doubt it. She was forced to go on welfare because of her daughter's illness. She went off as soon as Laurie no longer needed constant supervision."

Cal left, and Guy returned to his coffee. As he finished it off, he found himself hoping that the trail Stormy had left wasn't as cold as the coffee in his cup.

GUY RETURNED to his office the next day, only to find numerous problems awaiting him. The new secretary wasn't in Marilyn's class, and there had been several mix-ups in his appointments, a stack of letters to be answered, other distractions. Not the least of his problems was Larry. Not only was he incensed by Marilyn's resignation, but he complained about Guy's lack of responsibility.

"This is the final push, Guy! You're letting us down—and that article about the Todd woman didn't help. I thought we decided to jump on it with both feet, turn it around so it would end up hurting the mayor. But no, you won't even give any interviews about it, for God's sake!"

"Let it alone, Larry. I don't want to talk about it," Guy said wearily. He hadn't been sleeping well, and his head pounded ominously. "And I'm getting ready for that meeting with the real-estate group. I still haven't got my notes together for it."

"Yeah, well, you'd better have your wits about you when you meet with them. Those guys are your biggest campaign contributors. They'll have a lot to say about that prospectus you sent them last week. I've already had several calls and they aren't happy. Don't antagonize them, Guy. I know your intentions are good, but—give a little, you hear?"

Guy frowned at him. "I don't know what you're talking about. Antagonize them? How?"

"You know how the system works. You rub my back and I'll rub yours. They want some guarantees. Those reforms you're running on—I realize they're just campaign promises but be sure you make that plain to these guys. You know what I mean?"

Guy started to say that no, he didn't know what the hell he meant, but Larry was already heading for the door. Half an hour later, in his private conference room, he faced his major contributors.

"Sit down, gentlemen," he said, looking around the long, highly polished table. It struck him how ironic it was that these men, his largest campaign contributors, were also, in a business sense, his biggest competitors, the group that had first approached him to run for mayor.

For the first time, he felt uneasy. When he'd decided to run, before he'd started his campaign, he'd gone to them with a careful list of what he wanted to use as the issues in his campaign, and they had all backed him—enthusiastically. Now he sensed something different in their attitude. When he saw one man, a high-powered industrial builder, staring down at the memo he'd sent them, a strong feeling of uneasiness stirred.

"I hope you've all had a chance to read the memo I sent you," he said. He waited for agreements, nods, a smile or two, but all he got was an ominous silence. "I thought we should discuss it—I want to hear your ideas, too, you know. Contingent upon winning the election, this is a general idea of what I hope to accomplish during my term in office."

During the next few minutes, he got opinions—and none of them were favorable. His plan, which ranged from raising structural and fire safety standards for new housing to keeping heights within bounds to rejuvenating and strengthening the power of the city's building inspection department were all declared completely unacceptable, a disaster for the building industry.

"What the hell are you up to, Guy?" one of the men finally demanded. "We thought you were on the side of progress, of cutting through red tape so we could get on with the business of developing this city. If you try to implement these—these asinine so-called reforms, you'll set the industry back twenty years!"

After they were gone, none of them smiling, Guy sat for a while, trying to come to terms with what he'd just been through. How could he have missed it? They weren't interested in reforms, never had been. They had wanted one of their own in there to make it easy for them to exploit, expand, develop without restraints. No, they hadn't said that to him during those earlier meetings. They'd taken it for granted that as one of the boys, he knew what the score was. He couldn't even blame them. He'd thought he was so damned sharp—and all he'd been was naive.

Guy didn't sleep at all that night. He didn't even go to bed. There was too much to think about, too many decisions to make before morning. One part of him, stubborn and angry, was reluctant to give it up, toss in the towel, but another, much more pragmatic part, knew what had to be done. He had accepted their contributions without a qualm—he couldn't, in all honor, become mayor and then turn his back on them. The only answer was to resign from the race.

And there were a couple of advantages to it. Not only could he dissolve the blind trust now and take over his own affairs again, but he'd have more time to search for Stormy and her kids.

The next morning, he called a press meeting and resigned from the mayoral race, giving personal reasons as an excuse. His announcement, which took everybody by surprise, immediately caused more uproar and recriminations than he would have thought possible. Everybody, it seemed, was furious with him, including his political staff.

"You're never going to get any support, financial or otherwise, in this town again," Larry Singer, livid with rage, told him after the press conference. "Who'd ever trust you? You're dead as far as the party goes. It isn't as if you have a reason—"

"I have a reason, a very good one," Guy told him. "It just happens to be personal—and private."

Larry ran a nervous hand over his thinning hair. "It's that Todd woman, isn't it? You went ape over her. Well, where the hell is she? When are you going to bring her out of the closet? Or has she skipped out on you now that she got you out of the race?"

"She's gone, all right. I drove her away. And now I'm trying to find her—not that this is any of your damned business."

Larry's outraged stare pricked his conscience, and Guy added. "Okay, you put it all one the line for me and I'm sorry. I'll make it up to you financially. But my first priority right now is finding Stormy and her kids."

"And what if, when you do find her, she tells you to get lost?"

"I'll change her mind."

"And if she doesn't?"

"Then I'll have to live with it. I made a mistake, Larry. One way or another, I have to pay for it."

He knew Larry had given up when he flung out his hands in a disgusted gesture. "It's your funeral. But you owe a lot of people, including the volunteers who've been working their butts off for you, an apology. I'll tell you one thing—I think you're a bloody fool."

"And I think you're right," Guy said bleakly.

ALTHOUGH THE PINT-SIZE detective, Cal Haas, had warned that it might take as long as two weeks before he reported in, Guy found himself hovering near the phone, waiting for it to ring. To keep himself occupied, he spent the first few days after his withdrawal from the campaign getting his financial and business affairs back in order.

At first, he was just going through the motions, but his interest quickened when he began an in-depth study of the reports on the progress of the April Street project. Not entirely to his surprise, he discovered that the management, by Marilyn's uncle, had been less than satisfactory. Not only had there been unnecessary delays in razing the old cottages, but several important city excavation and building permits had gone astray.

Another factor, which had nothing to do with Clyde Farris's management of the project, was even more disturbing. When he looked over the construction plans and blueprints, they no longer satisfied him. Since they were the original plans, it was obvious that he was the one who had changed.

Was it because he was seeing the development through different eyes? All those luxury, upgraded features, the striking and innovative style, had been designed to attract wealthy and upper middle-class professionals back into the city. But it was the blue-collar workers, the lower middle-class, the elderly and the ethnic minorities who had been driven away because of rising rents, the inaccessibility of affordable housing.

And there was nothing here for them. Oh, he could see what was needed. A senior citizens' wing for the elderly, a section of co-op apartments for families of good character who also happened to be in the low-income category, perhaps a child-care center and a well-equipped playground—yes, that's what was needed. Call it penance for the way he'd failed Stormy and her kids. Call it a belated conscience. Call it anything you liked. It was something he wanted for the project.

Of course, there had to be a solidly profitable bottom line, or investors would go elsewhere and the project would never be realized. The trick was to initiate the new features he wanted and still satisfy even the most conservative, profit-conscious investor.

He was willing to invest his own capital, but even though he was a rich man, he couldn't come close to financing a development of this size. So how to sell the new concept to the wealthy businessmen and corporations who were potential investors? There were limited partnerships, of course, but since the new tax laws, they no longer were attractive to investors. Could he use the news value of such an innovation to gain publicity and draw in other investors, perhaps substitute many small ones for the present few major ones?

What about announcing a lottery for potential buyers of the lower-priced co-op apartments that would be available? The winners would have to qualify for a mortgage, of course, but he was sure they would sign up by the hundreds for a chance at reasonable housing in such a favorable location. To some, the savings on transportation alone would make those co-op apartments a bargain. After all, there were thousands of workers, living on low incomes, who were desperate for decent housing that they could afford, be proud of. And he could give it to them—a limited number to be sure, but then everything had to start somewhere.

So okay, he himself was convinced this was the way to go. The problem was how to convince others. He'd always gone for high profits, had built his reputation on the bottom-line principal as well as quality housing. Which was why he'd never had any problem raising capital for his developments. If he now came up with such controversial innovations as a senior citizens' wing and co-op apartments for low-income families in combination with luxury town houses, his financial backers would howl like a bunch of banshees....

No getting away from it. This idea of his was, to say the least, fraught with danger. But not impossible. No, it wasn't impossible. Just difficult as hell.

So he'd have to move carefully. One thing about this business, it would keep him busy. It might even save his sanity while he waited for news about Stormy and her kids.

ONE THING that kept Stormy going these days was her work, which never disappointed her. All her life, she had enjoyed using her natural drawing talent, an emotional outlet that cost only the price of a pencil and a cheap drawing pad. Secretly, she had yearned for other methods of expressing her talent—pastels and oils—but she'd restrained herself, knowing that if she succumbed to temptation, it would be far too expensive.

Now, for the first time, she could see a time ahead when she might be able to work with oils or pastels. But for now, her drawings were enough. There was so much to learn, and her teacher, Marvin Costa, was a hard taskmaster.

Although Arnold's friend permitted her to develop the story lines of her comic strip without comment, he allowed no compromise as to the quality of the drawings. Now retired, he had helped train and develop several top cartoonists, and he demanded that she follow his rigid standards. Sometimes, it was true, she didn't agree, thought his ways too structured, and then she dug in her heels and did it her own way. Grudgingly, slowly, he permitted her more and more latitude and the day finally came, three months after she started taking daily lessons from him, that he declared she was ready to begin preparing her sample strips.

She spent the next month developing a new story line, creating enough strips to cover several weeks, working on them doggedly, accepting Marvin Costa's sometimes caustic criticisms with a meekness that was contrary to her nature. When he finally declared them acceptable, adding that she would, by the nature of things, improve as she went along, Arnold set up a meeting with his friend, J. C. Landau, owner of Landau Syndication.

They met in Arnold's living room, and Stormy was grateful it was on familiar ground. So much depended on this meeting, she needed all the advantages she could muster. Meeting in surroundings she didn't find intimidating was certainly an advantage.

J. C. Landau was a small man, very dapper; he had the shrewdest eyes she'd ever seen in a man. She knew within seconds that his long friendship with Arnold would have no bearing on his decision. If he decided to take a chance on launching her strip, a very complicated and expensive business, it would be because he believed in it, not as a favor to an old friend.

After a few minutes of small talk, he got down to business. For a long time, he flipped through the panels she'd provided, stopping only occasionally for a closer look. Stormy, sitting rigid and tense nearby, fought against growing doubts. How could he possibly judge the comic strip with such cursory attention? Why had he bothered to come if he wasn't going to give her a chance? Had it been out of courtesy, after all, to Arnold, his old friend?

He came to the end and she braced herself for rejection. To her surprise, he was silent. He stared off into space, his eyes narrowed, and then, still silent, he turned back to the beginning and started through the stack of panels again. This time, he moved slowly, reading the captions, studying the drawings. To Stormy watching so closely that her eyes smarted, he could have been reading a telephone book. He didn't smile, didn't frown, and there was certainly no indication that the heroine's spunk and good humor in the face of a constant battle to keep her head above water moved him.

When he came to the final one, a six-panel spread meant for a Sunday newspaper, she had already given up hope and was struggling to keep her disappointment from showing. When he stood, stretching his back, and then said tersely, "Well, let's go with it," she was so surprised that she could only gape at him.

Arnold and Marvin Costa didn't seem surprised at all, which astonished her further. She'd had no idea they had so much faith in her work.

It came to her then that she was thinking like an amateur. Marvin and Arnold were professionals. They had assumed she knew they had faith in her work because why else would they go to so much trouble for her?

She found her voice finally. "You're offering me a contract, Mr. Landau?" she said, because she was afraid of making a mistake.

"I wouldn't take you on without one," J. C. Landau said dryly. "Do you have any idea how expensive it is to launch a new comic strip? And this one is very different from the usual run. A welfare mother heroine, for God's sake. It's going to take some doing to convince a bunch of hard-nosed newspaper editors that this one can be funny as hell."

Stormy had to nod. It *was* going to be a long process. But she wasn't afraid. She was going to give it everything she had, because if it was successful then she'd have security for Tommy and Laurie—and for the baby growing inside her.

THEY CELEBRATED that evening. There was every reason to. Despite a lot of wrangling, even a few hard words between J. C. Landau and the other two men, Arnold had finally negotiated a contract he was satisfied with. To Stormy, who would have accepted just about any terms, it seemed a miracle that Arnold had won out over a shrewd businessman like J. C. Landau.

Once the contract was signed, J. C. Landau was all smiles. "Call me J.C.," he told Stormy expansively. "No need to stand on ceremony."

After he took himself off to catch a plane back to L.A., Arnold declared a celebration was in order. Elsie agreed. In fact, she had already chilled a couple of bottles of champagne.

Arnold was in top form at dinner. He teased Laurie until she was dimpling with pleasure, exchanged good-natured banter with Tommy, was in such high spirits that his wife told him she wished he'd make a deal every day.

Her words seem to sober Arnold. He got very quiet, and for the rest of the evening, he was a little absentminded. Stormy wanted to thank him, wanted to tell him—and Marvin Costa, her teacher—how grateful she wàs, but there didn't seem to be an opening. In fact, they obviously didn't expect it. Didn't they realize what this meant to her, that the chance to make it as a cartoonist was the answer to her prayers?

Oh, she knew it wasn't going to be easy. She could still fail, fail miserably. What if people refused to accept her premise, that life, no matter how grim, could still be worth living, still be fun? Would they see past the necessary exaggerations, and understand that there was more here than a few laughs?

She hoped so. She would do her best to make them understand. But life was never pat. They could reject the whole thing and then she'd be back where she started. No, not back quite that far. If this strip failed, then she would try another and another until she did succeed. So much depended upon it—not only her own future but the futures of her three children.

And what a pity that she hadn't been able to give them the one thing they needed the most—a loving, caring father.

CAL HAAS'S FIRST REPORT to Guy was disappointing. Although it detailed the investigation he'd made, the interviews and record checking, the results were nil.

"I figure she musta moved out of the area, Mr. Harris," he told Guy. "If she was short on money, like you seem to think, it's possible she got a job where housing is part of her wages."

"What kind of job?"

"Housekeeper—maybe on someone's ranch or country estate. Could be some isolated place where they allow dependents because it's hard to get help. But don't you worry. I'm working on that angle. I'll keep in touch."

He hung up, leaving Guy feeling frustrated and not a little angry. Since there was nothing he could do to hurry things up, he threw himself into the April Street project. In the rush of reorganization, of hiring the best men he could find, of attending meetings and making numerous decisions, there were times when he almost forgot Stormy. But these moments were rare and short-lived. The worst time of all was when he returned to his empty apartment at night. He even considered getting a dog—or even a cat.

Although it seemed incredible, he missed Magic and that clumsy, oversize puppy. Had Stormy been able to find a place that would take pets? Or had she been forced to give them up? What was she doing now? Had she found a job yet? Or had she left San Jose, maybe even the state, as Cal Haas seemed to think?

It was more than three months now since she had disappeared. Where the hell was she—and why wasn't Cal making more progress?

CHAPTER SEVENTEEN

IT WAS THREE DAYS before Christmas, and Guy had spent most of the day in his office, consulting with his staff, with the project's funding committee, and with a journalist who was doing an article on him for the Sunday magazine insert of the *San Francisco Chronicle*.

Not everything had gone his own way, and he'd had to compromise more often than he was comfortable with, but all and all it had been a satisfactory day. And grueling, too. He was tired as hell, very much in need of a pick-up. Not yet ready to face the solitude of his apartment, he stopped by his favorite downtown bar, an out-of-the-way spot that catered to local office workers.

The bar, tucked away in a side street, was quiet, dark, friendly. The evening bartender, an old friend from Guy's college days who was also the owner, drew a draft beer and sat it in front of Guy as soon as he sat down at the bar.

"On the house," he said. "You look like you can use this."

Guy took a long drink, then sat the mug down, grinning at his friend. They had shared a room for a while, until his friend dropped out of school, while attending San Jose State, and there had been times, when they were both out of work at the same time, when they'd had to skip a few meals.

The bar was decorated for Christmas, including a fat, rather rakish-looking Santa Claus and, in one corner, a real tree covered with ornaments. Guy studied the Santa Claus with gloomy eyes. Did Laurie still believe in good old St. Nick? Somehow he was sure she did. At half her age, Tommy would already have figured out the inconsistencies in that legend.

No matter how rough things were for them, Stormy would see that they had some kind of Christmas. If he hadn't screwed things up, he would be part of the celebration. He'd never been crazy about Christmas, having had a scarcity of happy ones as a kid, but this one would have been different. Who knows? He might even have put on whiskers and stuffed a pillow inside a red costume and played Santa Claus for the kids.

And what kind of Thanksgiving had they had? Turkey and all the trimmings—or beans and rice? Maybe Stormy had taken them to one of the charity dining rooms for a free turkey dinner. If so, she would have made a record of it somewhere....

This year, wherever they were, Stormy would have to improvise Christmas decorations. Any she'd had would have been ripped off with her furniture. Clyde Farris had never admitted that he'd arranged for her possessions to be carted off, but Guy was sure Marilyn's uncle had been involved, probably to get rid of someone he considered a pest. Had he arranged for them to be put in storage somewhere or, which was more likely, were they in the city dump, buried under several months of garbage and trash? Whatever had happened, Stormy would probably never see her grandmother's photograph album again.

Well, maybe it was time to put pressure on Clyde Farris again. Why hadn't he done it sooner? Had he grown so hardened that he'd dismissed the loss of Stormy's possessions, because of their low value, as minor?

Tommy had told him that she cried at night because of the loss of her grandmother's photograph album. Had the pictures of her family meant that much to her? Funny—he couldn't remember her ever mentioning a mother or father, only her grandmother—and that rarely. She *had* talked a little about a friend—an old neighbor named Abby Cornwall. And then she'd added that the woman now lived in a rest home called—what the devil was that name? Stormy hadn't liked the name. Said it was too gloomy for a home for old people. It had something to do with shadows—wasn't it the Shadow Lane Rest Home?

He brooded over it while he sipped his beer, careful not to look receptive to conversation because he wasn't in the mood, not even with his bartender friend. When someone slid onto the stool next to him, he didn't look up.

"Hey, Guy—howzit going?" the man asked.

Guy regarded him, a journalist called Hal, with wary eyes as he said, "Everything's going fine."

"Sorry you dropped out of the election. I was hoping for some reforms. Well, there's always the next time," Hal said, and motioned to the bartender for a beer.

They drank together companionably for a while. An idea struck Guy, and he asked, "You ever heard of a place called the Shadow Lane Rest Home?"

"Sure. It's in Los Gatos. I interviewed this old lady there once—she was a hundred and eight, still going strong. How come you ask?" He gave Guy a sly look. "You thinking about retiring soon, Guy?"

"Someone mentioned it at a party. The name caught my attention."

"Yeah? Well, it's got the same name of the street where it's located. You know—Shadow Lane."

Guy drained his glass and slid off his stool. "Well, I'll see you around," he said. He waved to his bartender friend and left.

He called information from his car phone, asked for Los Gatos and quickly got the number of the rest home. When he dialed the number, the phone rang several times but he didn't hang up, sure that eventually someone would answer. He was right, but the woman's voice on the other end of the line sounded a little muffled and he suspected he'd interrupted her in the middle of a bite of dinner.

Yes, an Abby Cornwall was a resident there. Yes, she could have visitors. Visiting hours would start in a few minutes—who was calling, please?

He hesitated, then gave his initials and his last name. A few minutes later, he was in his car, heading toward Los Gatos.

GUY'S CAR PHONE RANG as he was turning off the highway into the outskirts of the prosperous little town of Los Gatos. He almost didn't answer it, but habit was too ingrained and he finally lifted it to his ear, said a noncommittal "Yes?" into the mouthpiece.

"This is Cal Haas. I think I have a lead."

With an effort, Guy kept his voice calm. "What kind of lead, Cal?"

"I checked out Ms. Todd's old neighborhood again—you know, the public housing project where she lived as a kid?—and this time I connected with an old timer who's been there since it opened. He gave me the name of a neighbor who lived next door to Todd's grandmother. Said she and the old lady were good friends. This neighbor—name's Abby Cornwall—is pretty old, in her late eighties. She lives in a rest home now—you want me to go have a talk with her?"

At one time, Guy would have told Cal that his information had come a little late, but now he only said, "I'll do it myself. Anything else?"

"Well, I tackled Social Services again—for the third time. Haven't been able to get any information out of them so this time I bent the truth a bit. I let the woman I contacted think I was an insurance agent, trying to settle a claim, and she finally got out Stormy Todd's file."

"Did you learn anything new?"

"Not from her. Frozen-faced type, very officious. But I did find out one thing. What you heard, that report on Stormy Todd the real-estate company passed on to you, saying she'd had some trouble with the welfare people? Well, it was true, all right. The thing is, she was only twelve when it happened. That's all I could get. You want to dig further?"

"Twelve? Stormy was twelve when this happened?"

"That's what I read." He gave a snorting laugh. "I've got this special talent, see? I can read upside down. Only the lady caught me and slammed the folder shut before I could get anymore. You wonder, don't you, what a twelve-year-old could do that they'd label fraud."

"Anything else?" Guy asked.

"Not much. She was taken out of her grandmother's care at twelve, farmed out to three different foster homes during the next three years, ran away from the last one. That's the sum of it. You want Abby Cornwall's address, I guess-"

"I already have it," Guy said. He hung up, feeling a sour satisfaction. Let Cal figure that one out.

But he felt depressed as he drove through the bustling downtown section of Los Gatos. Even if Stormy was still in touch with this woman, Abby Cornwall, it was doubtful she'd tell someone in her late eighties any of her problems. More likely, she'd put a good face on it, something she did so well . . .

The Shadow Lane Rest Home was set back from the street, fronted by a large, winter-weary lawn; its redbrick walls had a somber look, but the woman at the reception desk was friendly enough.

"Abby'll be so pleased to have a visitor," she said. "She does love company. She's quite a talker, that one."

She pointed out the way to Abby Cornwall's room, telling him to follow the yellow arrows painted on the walls, which would take him to the right wing. Guy followed the arrows along a long hall, up a staircase and down another hall. He found himself holding his breath, repelled by the faint odor of decay, the stronger odor of disinfectant. At the end of the second hall, he found the room he was looking for.

The door was standing partially open, and the sound of a radio talk show assaulted his ears as he knocked gingerly.

"Come on in," a thin female voice told him, and he pushed open the door.

A white-haired woman, seated by a window and dressed in a neat cotton housedress, stared at him with eyes that snapped with energy from across a small room sparsely furnished with a white metal hospital bed and a World War II chest of drawers.

A few minutes later, Guy had come to the conclusion that the receptionist was right. Abby Cornwall was indeed a talker. That she was confined to a wheelchair seemed not to bother her in the least.

"So you're a friend of Stormy's," she said. "Now isn't that nice. And you lost track of her, you say? Well, she does move around a lot—or at least she did before she got that nice place on April Street."

Guy hesitated, then said, "I'm afraid she's moved again. A new housing project is going up there. That's when I lost track of her and the kids."

"Oh, yes, Tommy and Laurie. It was such a tragedy when the little one caught that—well, can't think of the name of her ailment right now. Almost lost her, Stormy did. For a while there—well, we won't talk about that now. The boy—isn't he something? I told Stormy he was going to end up as rich as that Trump fellow. Did he ever get that watch for his mom?"

"Watch?"

"Why, yes. He's been saving for it for ages. Every penny he can earn—or talk someone out of. When he asked me how much the kind he wanted would cost, I told him he should settle for a cheaper one, but no, it had to be that one. Seems Stormy had stopped to look at this watch in the window of a jewelry shop, and he made up his mind then he'd get it for her someday. Only the best is good enough for his mom, you see."

A nurse came to the door, and stopped when she saw Guy. "Now you just go away, missy," Abby said crossly. "I got me a visitor and I don't want you hurrying him off, you hear?"

The nurse went away, shaking her head, and Abby gave Guy a triumphant smile. "You have to stand up to them or they'll walk all over you," she confided.

"You were going to tell me what Stormy was like when she was a girl."

"Did I say that? Well, I guess I did. She was a good girl. Which was a miracle when you consider that her mother was pure trash. Best thing ever happened was when that one went off with some fellow and never came back. Stormy didn't need her—she could take care of herself, all right. A lot of rough kids in the projects, you know. And her not having anyone to take up for her didn't help. She learned to fight back, wouldn't take no guff off them kids. Got knocked around a bit, but after a while, they left her alone. No fun tormenting someone who always fights back."

She stopped to shake her head. "She took good care of Meg—that was her grandmother. Saw she got fed and always had clean clothes to wear, after Meg went—" She made a circular movement in the air near her ear. "'Course, I helped her cover up the best I could. It wasn't too hard, fooling that social worker. She didn't come around but a couple times those two years. Had a big caseload, she said. Which was just fine with Stormy. It wouldn't have lasted nearly so long if that woman'd kept a closer eye on things."

"What lasted so long?"

"Why, letting on everything was just like it used to be. Didn't Stormy tell you? The old lady got—well, they called it some fancy name but I figure things got too much for her so she shut it all out. She just lost touch with reality, thought Stormy was her daughter half the time. Never caused no trouble, but she wouldn't go out the door, not even down the hall. They got a name for that, but I can't recollect it right now."

"Agoraphobia?"

Abby beamed at him. "That's it. My, you are smart, aren't you? All Meg wanted to do was listen to music on the radio or play with Stormy's old toys. She liked Stormy to read to her, too, but she only wanted kids' stories. Stormy was real scared they'd put her grandmother in one of them places for crazy people. So she just took over, bought the food and cooked it, never missed any school 'cause she didn't want one of them truant officers coming around. Not that they bother much in that neighborhood."

"What did she live on?"

"They was on welfare, had been even before Stormy's mother left for good. Stormy signed her grandmother's name on the checks when they came in every month and this man that lived in the project and had this under-the-table loan business cashed it for her. Charged her ten percent but it was worth it to Stormy. It went on for a couple of years before the welfare people caught on. Nothing they could do to Stormy, seeing as she was just twelve, but they were pretty upset with her 'cause it put them in a bad light. It's on her record and I always thought that's what kept her from getting adopted. 'Course, a twelve-year-old don't get adopted all that easy, anyway. People figure they've learned too many bad habits."

"How did she get away with it so long?"

"Well, she worked hard at it. When the social worker did come around, she said Meg was at the dentist or out shopping for groceries. There wasn't nothing physical wrong with Meg, you understand. Just had retreated back to when things were easier. She was happy, you know, living in the past. With me next door in case of an emergency, I couldn't see no harm in it."

She sighed deeply. "A month after they put Meg in that mental hospital at Napa, she got sick and died. Heart attack, they said, but I figured she just plain grieved herself to death. Stormy took it real hard. Wouldn't eat for a while, but she got over it. She's got a head on her. Too bad she turned right around and made such a mistake."

"Mistake?"

"Taking up with that truck driver fellow. Oh, he was good-looking, had a smooth tongue, and at first he treated her like she was a queen. I have to admit he fooled me, too, and I was a lot older than fifteen. The people Stormy lived with raised cain about her slipping out to see him, said they were going to put a stop to it, and so the two of them up and got married. When she come to tell me about it, she was so happy—always so hungry for, you know, a family and a place of her own."

"She *married* him?"

"'Course she did. What'd you think? I know things have changed lately, couples living together without getting married, but Stormy was kind of old-fashioned. Never went out with a boy until she met—what was his name? Can't think of it now. Anyway, she didn't want to be like her mother, sleeping around and bringing bastard kids into the world. So she wouldn't let him touch her until they got married."

"I thought—where did I get the idea she wasn't married to the father of her children?"

"Well, the way it turned out, she wasn't. He was a—what you call them? A bigamist. Seems he already had a wife and a couple of kids when he married Stormy, and never bothered to get a divorce. Only Stormy didn't find this out until he got killed in that accident. He'd already skipped out on her by then, left when she was pregnant with Laurie. She couldn't pay her rent, got evicted, and was living on the streets for a while. But she muddled through somehow, got a place to live and went to work at some child-care center. I woulda helped her but she didn't tell me about it until she was back on her feet."

She fell silent for a while, her eyes brooding. "Later on, after that man was killed and she found out they hadn't really been married," she went on, "she took back her maiden name. Got a lot of spunk, that girl. Never would take no help from me. Not that there was much I could do for her. Couldn't hardly pay my own rent and feed myself on what I got from social security. Stormy sure was happy when she got together enough money so she could move into that house on April Street. She even saved some money only it all went when Laurie got sick. Soon as her savings was gone, she had to go on welfare. Really hurt her pride, it did. But she's doing right well now. Got a good job and a nice place to live."

Guy took a long, steadying breath. "You have her address?" he asked carefully.

"She's living in—now where did she say? Slipped my mind—must have a yard because they've got a dog and cat."

"Did she tell you where she's working?"

"I don't believe she said. Likes it, I remember that. She must be doing well because she and the kids brought me a pretty silk head scarf and some chocolates when they came to see me Thanksgiving. She looked real pretty—had that special glow women get at certain times—if you know what I mean."

Guy looked at her with bleak eyes. Oh, yes, he knew what she meant. Stormy had met a new man—he only hoped she had better luck with this one than she'd had with the first two.

He knew it was time to leave, but he sat on for a while anyway. When he asked Abby how she liked living in the rest home, she gave him a blow-by-blow account of her feud with her next room neighbor, her voice so full of relish that he knew she could hold her own. When the nurse stuck her head in again and told him sorry, visiting hours were over, he rose. Abby told him to come back and see her, anytime, and he promised he would.

He stopped at the desk on his way out. "Does Mrs. Cornwall have any family?" he asked.

The woman who was filing away a stack of cards looked up with a smile. "It's *Miss* Cornwall—and no, she hasn't any family. Most of our guests don't. She loves company—I hope you come back to see her again."

"I intend to," he said, meaning it.

He went out to his car, but he didn't start it up right away. There were too many things he wanted to sort out first. Why hadn't Stormy told him that she'd married the children's father in good faith? Was this part of that asinine rule she lived by? Don't explain, don't excuse?

He drove away finally, heading for home, a late supper—and another restless night.

AFTER CHRISTMAS, in the complexities of reorganizing his office, in the rush of meetings and decision making, there were times when he almost forgot Stormy. But these moments were rare. At odd moments, sometimes inconvenient ones, her image would slip into his mind, haunting him. The worst time was when he returned to his apartment at night. Even though he turned on all the lights, the rooms seemed too empty and quiet, and he took to sleeping in one of the guest rooms, unable to sleep in the bed that he'd shared with Stormy the night he'd taken her and the kids to the Ice Capades.

The pace at work stepped up even more as construction began for the new development. Guy spent more time than necessary at the site, poking his nose into every aspect of the construction of the building that would become the development's community and administration center, and he suspected, getting into everybody's hair.

It was inevitable that the new project would attract attention. Suddenly he was being interviewed by not only Bay Area newspapers and city magazines, but even by the prestigious *Architects Magazine*.

He agreed to appear on a local public television station to explain the concept of integrating such a variety of housing into a single project. The interviewer, who specialized in controversial guests, paired him with one of the most conservative of Northern California's developers. Feeling something of a crusader, Guy plunged into the affray and came off so well that the program was picked up by a respectable number of the country's public television stations.

That other regional developers' noses were out of joint because of the publicity his project was drawing, he was well aware. When one of his competitors, a Sacramento developer, announced a similar project, he felt vindicated—and a little amused, especially since the company called theirs "the forerunner of a new concept in housing."

Then, in late January, the day of the dedication ceremony arrived. Unaccountably he felt depressed, despite the attention he knew it would receive from the press, and he couldn't help wondering if he was on the right track. Profit was the bottom line—and while there had been so many applicants for the lower price co-op apartments, there hadn't been as much interest in the luxury town houses where, he was so aware, the real profits lay.

He even questioned his motives for making the changes. Had he hoped that Stormy would hear about them and would realize that he himself had changed? That he wanted to find her and ask forgiveness? If so, it hadn't worked. Cal Haas, despite his conscientious efforts, still hadn't found any trace of her.

Dedication day dawned bright and fog-free, a Bay Area winter day at its best—clear and cool, but with the welcome warmth of the sun, too. The concourse in front of the administration building site was gay with flags that displayed the Harris logo, and the crowd that gathered was obviously in a festive mood. There were more people there than the firm's employees and their families and the city officials and representatives of the media he'd invited could account for, and he suspected that a large percentage were potential co-op buyers who hoped to strike it lucky in the drawing.

Standing on the small portable stage in front of the glass doors of the administration building, he nodded to several of his rival developers, to reporters and TV personnel and political figures. From the amount of nonalcoholic beverages that were being consumed, he knew they were enjoying themselves, even if the chief drift of the conversations he overheard was to question his risk taking.

His Honor the newly reelected mayor was there, smiling broadly and shaking hands, and undoubtedly gloating about his recent victory. Since he owed it all to Guy, he was lavish in his praise of the new project.

"Well, Guy, I can see why you're too busy to run for public office," he said, slapping Guy on the back. "Hope that continues."

"Don't count on it," Guy said coolly. He might have changed in some ways, but his old competitiveness was still going strong. "There'll be other elections, you know."

The mayor produced a credible smile. "Well, that's way off in the future." He glanced down at the thick gold watch on his wrist. "It's almost one—why don't we get this business on the road?"

Guy gave Al Barbour, his construction head, a signal, and Al rapped sharply on the temporary podium that had been set up in front of the building, getting the attention of the crowd. He introduced the beaming mayor, whose speech, unctuous and full of platitudes though it was, received generous applause.

Then it was Guy's turn. For a long moment, he stared around the crowd, wondering if they realized the grave chances he was taking. What would they say if he were completely honest and told them his change of heart had come because of his love for a woman, one who had once lived on this very site, on April Street?

"This is a special day," he said, impulsively discarding the more formal speech he'd prepared. "I would like to say that I have no doubts that what we are attempting here will work out, but that wouldn't be true. I'm a hardheaded business man, and it took a lot of courage to change my profit-above-all-else ways, but if this works, if this becomes a prototype for the future, then we all benefit. But for now, let's celebrate. Enjoy yourselves, have fun, believe that this will be a smashing success, the way of the future. Tomorrow, we go back to work."

There was a roar of applause, more than he expected, and he felt a sudden lift of his spirits. "I've been asked what the name of the project will be," he went on. "Originally we planned to call it San Jose Gardens, but that doesn't seem appropriate now. So we're naming it for one of the streets it replaced. From now on, it will be known as April Gardens—and I'm dedicating it to the person who inspired it, to Stormy Todd."

There was a buzz of voices as he motioned to Al to unveil the model. People crowded forward as the white muslin cloth covering slid off, revealing the clean lines of the town houses, the central courtyard and community center, the terraces and innovative planning that gave more privacy than was found in similar developments.

Al, his voice full of enthusiasm, pointed out the seniors' wing, conveniently located near transportation and the nearby shopping mall, and the family co-op units, an integral part of the whole. He was also careful to describe the luxury town houses, all of which had a superb view and the privacy that their eventual owners would be paying for, pointing out the custom features that made them unique.

Guy was glad that Al was so quick of wit when it came time for questions, especially since some of them, mostly from other builders, were obviously hostile.

"Well, Guy, you think you can pull it off?" a rival builder asked, coming to stand beside Guy. He was one of the old breed who had risen from a construction worker to become head of a large conglomerate, and as Guy met his shrewd eyes, he tried to look confident.

"Of course," he said coolly. "Would I invest my own money if I didn't?"

"Yeah, you do have a point there." The man rubbed his ear. "You're one of my toughest competitors. I've always admired your get-up-and-go. I would have voted for you if you hadn't dropped out of the race. Medical reasons, wasn't it?"

"Personal reasons," Guy said shortly.

"Well, I'll be watching this April Gardens project. If it does well—who knows? I might try something along those lines myself. Something has to be done about housing blue-collar people and the lower middle-class or eventually we're going to have riots in the street. Maybe it's time we all started thinking of ways and means. Good luck, Guy. I suspect you're going to need it."

He strolled off, leaving Guy staring after him. Had the man just been making small talk when he'd said he might try something like April Gardens himself or had he really meant it? And if it were the latter—who knew what had been started here today....

Al was beckoning to him, and he went forward to answer a question Al couldn't field. Later, he was talking to a tall middle-aged man who was interested in purchasing one of the luxury town houses, when he caught a glimpse of a black-haired woman, moving away through the crowd. For a moment, until he realized that the woman was much heavier than Stormy, he almost ran after her.

But the incident took the edge off the day. After all, no matter how the project turned out, he still was alone—and the way it looked now, he wasn't even going to get the chance to tell Stormy he was sorry for ruining everything between them.

STORMY WASN'T REALLY SURE why she decided to go to the dedication of Guy's development. After all, he was no longer a part of her life, certainly not a part of her future. Why should she be interested in anything he did? But when the day came, she saw the kids off to school, and then she changed into city clothes and took Arnold's pickup truck that she'd been using into town.

So many things had changed, she thought as she drove along the highway toward downtown San Jose. Her whole life was different now. There was the guest cottage, to start with. It might seem small to most people, but not to her. She had lived in a welfare hotel room with her kids, just after Laurie was born, in a shelter for homeless people after Eric had left her and she'd been evicted from their flat. She and Tommy had even spent a few nights on a bench in the Greyhound Bus Depot when there hadn't been room at the family shelter, moving to another bench every couple of hours so it wouldn't be apparent that they weren't waiting to board a bus.

Then, after she'd found a job at a day-care center, and borrowed enough money from a private charity to pay advance rent on a tiny studio apartment, she had thought that they were finally safe. But of course they hadn't been. No one ever was. This was something she had to remember, even though things were going so well for her right now that sometimes she had to pinch herself to believe it was really happening.

She owed most of it to Arnold, of course, and she would be eternally grateful. He and Elsie tried to downplay this, saying that she was the one who had brought him out of his shell so that he was willing to face retirement, and pointing out that when her comic strip began earning money, he would collect an agent's fee. She had insisted on this, and after a short resistance, he had agreed. In fact, he really wasn't in a retirement status now. He had taken on the agent's role for two young cartoonists, and he had his eye out for more talent.

The cartoon strip would be out in another week, and then it was a question of waiting to see how it was received. Everybody at Landau Syndicate headquarters was enthusiastic about it—and so was she. It might have originated as a safety valve for worry, but it was also funny. Very funny, she thought now, smiling to herself.

That new story line she was working on at present—how many social workers would recognize themselves as being like the one in the cartoon who advised Sunny not to get a job because she'd end up with more money if she stayed on welfare and food stamps?

So, with the future so bright, why was she so miserable? Why did she still cry at night and have a hard time getting down the sensible foods her pregnancy demanded? It was Guy, of course, but shouldn't she be over him by now? He had treated her with contempt, automatically believing the worst of her. Which had to mean that he had been totally wrong for her all along. So why was she going to the blasted dedication of his blasted town houses on the site of the place from which she'd been illegally evicted? It was enough to make her wonder about the state of her mental health....

She parked in the parking lot at the mall, three blocks from the building site, and walked slowly through her old neighborhood. How familiar it looked, these shabby streets that she'd walked along so often, and yet—it seemed so strange, too, as if she'd been away a thousand years.

There, on the corner, was the small mom-and-pop grocery store where she'd bought some of her food, even though it was much more expensive than the supermarket at the mall, because they would wait for their money at the end of the month when she was short of cash. What would the new project of luxury town houses do to their business? Bolster their trade—or send them into bankruptcy because wealthy people didn't shop at mom-and-pop stores?

A few minutes later, she was standing at the edge of a crowd of people, staring at Guy. Her stomach felt as if it had drawn up into a knot, and she found it hard to breathe. It just wasn't fair. Why wasn't she over him? How long could she go on missing him, wanting him?

Their baby would be born in April—why was she so sure it was a boy? How ironic that Guy, who had once told her that he didn't want children because he couldn't vouch for the quality of his genes, would never know that somewhere in the world, his son—or daughter—existed. She had intended to tell him he was going to be a father, but she couldn't take that chance now.

How could she trust a man who despised her? And what if he fought for the baby's custody? He was rich—he could hire the best lawyers in the state. And he just might do that. She, of all people, knew how ruthless he could be. So why the devil was she here, taking such a chance? Was it because, for just these few minutes, she wanted desperately to pretend that they were still lovers?

The speeches started, and although she was careful to stay behind other people, she couldn't keep her eyes off Guy. He had lost weight; there was a shadow in his eyes, even when he was smiling. Losing his chance to become mayor must have been traumatic. "Personal reasons" had been the excuse he'd given. Well, he seemed involved with his new development; maybe that's why he'd withdrawn from the race.

When he dedicated the project to her, she was so surprised that she sagged against a pile of cement blocks, trying to catch her breath. In a daze, she watched as the model of the project was unveiled. Just what was going on here? Why had he dedicated it to her? Was it some kind of sick joke? Or—was this a peace offering? Did this mean that he no longer blamed her for the newspaper article that had angered him so?

The model caught her attention. It was different from one she'd seen in his apartment. The architect began describing the various units, and now she realized how it had changed. Guy had included senior housing, co-operative apartments for lower-income families, and even a play yard, a day-care center and a social center that included an indoor pool. As the man talked about a lottery, giving families with lower incomes a chance to buy the co-op units on very small down payments and reasonable credit terms, she craned her neck, wishing she dared come closer.

When the crowds began to disperse, she knew it was time to leave. Questions flooded her mind as she hurried off toward the shopping mall parking lot. The few times Guy had talked about the development, he had called the units state-of-the-art town houses. He certainly hadn't mentioned senior citizen housing or co-ops for low-income families. So why had he changed?

Was it possible that it had something to do with her?

ALTHOUGH EVERYTHING had gone well at the dedication ceremony, including what seemed to be real interest in the town houses from, of all people, several city political figures, Guy made an excuse not to attend a luncheon with his office crew. They were all in such exuberant spirits that he didn't want his own mood to ruin their celebration.

When he opened the door of his penthouse, the air seemed cold, uninviting, something he was sure came from his own low spirits. As he looked around the living room at the bold, custom-designed furnishings, the primitive paintings that now seemed too coy and calculated, he knew that it was time for a change. Something quieter, less ostentatious, he decided.

In fact, the idea of moving into one of the April Garden town houses when they were finished was appealing. Maybe a change of residence would help dissipate this feeling of disenchantment with his life he'd had lately. Also, he'd be right there where he could keep an eye on things.

Since Kung Toy had already left for the day, he fixed himself a cup of instant coffee, carried it out onto the terrace. He hadn't had time to look at the morning paper at breakfast so he took it with him. He was riffling through it, hunting for the sports section, when he came to a full-page advertisement.

It announced the debut of a new comic strip slated to begin the coming Sunday, and as he stared at the sample strips, the skin on the back of his neck tingled.

There were five strips, a week's quota; they were skillfully drawn with full attention to detail. But it wasn't the drawing that arrested his attention. It was the fact that he recognized the characters.

The main character was called Sunny, which was also the name of the strip. She was young, a single mother of two, a boy nine and a girl two years younger, who lived in a run-down apartment building in what was obviously an inner-city neighborhood. The story line was simple, with that subtle twist of humor that the best of cartoonists must master to keep their material interesting. With a few strokes of a pen, the artist had created characters that radiated personality, individuality, and a warmth that was unusual for a comic strip.

For a long time, Guy studied the Sunny character. Her hair was black, a curly mop that gave her the look of a pixie; there was a mixture of naïveté and street smarts in the way she peered out of the strip. She had lost her job, was on welfare, and this first week's story line featured a running battle between her and an officious grocery cashier.

How she handled the woman's insults brought a smile to his face, and yet—he felt a jolt of something else, of empathy, as the cashier, smirking at other customers waiting in line, ordered the young heroine to have her food stamps ready in the future.

The heroine's responding quip was clever, cocky, and it made him smile, but he felt uncomfortable, too, especially when, in the next strip, Sunny's daughter innocently asked her what the word "deadbeat" meant. After all, that had been the word he himself had used when he'd heard Stormy Todd was on welfare.

He turned his attention to the advertising copy that accompanied the launch strips. The cartoonist, whose name was E. J. Williams, it said, lived in New York City, was the father of several children.

Guy wasn't fooled. E. J. Williams was a woman, Stormy—and this must be the "good job" her friend, Abby had mentioned.

He carried the newspaper back into the living room with him when he went to call Cal Haas to tell him that he was convinced that Stormy was the cartoonist who was launching a new comic strip.

IT WAS THE NEXT AFTERNOON before Cal reported in.

His news was disappointing. Despite his best efforts, he hadn't been able to crack the security at Landau Syndication's Los Angeles headquarters. The identity of the cartoonist, E. J. Williams, was being closely guarded. Cal was convinced that this secrecy was some kind of publicity gimmick, but Guy suspected it had more to do with the fact that Stormy was using her own children and personal experiences in the comic strip's story line.

After he told Cal to continue working on it, he hung up.

During the next two weeks, he followed the strip religiously. Although the family's problems and encounters with other people were presented in a comical way with the exaggeration that is the heart of comic-strip humor, there was also that hint of—not bitterness, but the refusal of those who have constantly lived on the edge to take anything, good or bad, on faith.

The strip that showed Sunny's boy coming home from school the day he'd been teased for being a "charity kid," was so close to Guy's own experiences as a foundling that he found himself wincing even while he laughed at Sunny's saucy advice. How true that those on the top, whether it be in the sixth grade or at the head of a multimillion dollar corporation, so often took advantage of those who were helpless, justifying it by putting the victims down as inferior or lazy or incompetent.

And wasn't it clever of Stormy to also show the other kind, a teacher who did his best to help his less fortunate students, not avoiding their problems or using them as ego boosters?

Once, when a social worker asked the heroine how often she entertained men overnight, he remembered his own assumption that "uncles" would be part of Stormy's life-style. His bias must have been all too apparent to Stormy. No wonder she'd been so prickly. And yet—she *had* fallen in love with him....

He was lying in bed, trying to get some sleep and finding it impossible. Maybe this was one of those nights when he would have to take two aspirins and one of the hot lemon juice toddies Arnold favored for insomnia.

Arnold—funny that he hadn't heard from his friend for months. Surely he and Elsie were back from their travels and yet he hadn't called....

It fell into place then, like the pieces of a jigsaw puzzle. He swore out loud, sat up, switched on the light. Not bothering with his robe, even though the apartment was chilly, he paced up and down his bedroom, putting it all together.

Of course! Why hadn't he seen it before? It must have been Arnold whom Stormy had turned to when she'd needed help. They had become good friends—and who else had the right contacts to get her comic strip seen by an important syndicate?

He reached for the phone, boiling mad, but common sense stopped him before he could tap out the numbers. This was not the time for an encounter with Arnold. If he got his friend up in the middle of the night, he'd already have a couple of strikes against him. Also, maybe by morning, he would have cooled down enough that his assurances that he only wanted to apologize to Stormy would be more convincing.

Somehow, he held out until morning. It seemed safe enough to call at seven since he knew that Arnold was an early riser. Even so, his timing was off. Arnold informed him, his voice tart, that he and Elsie had been still asleep when the phone rang.

Guy read the guilt in his friend's gruff voice and knew it would be useless to bother with diplomacy.

"Where is she, Arnold?" he asked.

"What are you gabbling about?"

"You know very well. Where are Stormy and her kids?"

"Hell, I can't tell you that. She doesn't want to see you. Haven't you done enough to her?"

"You have every right to say that, but you should know that I'm sorry as hell, Arnold. I love her, want to apologize and—and set things straight."

"The best thing you can do is leave her alone. She's finally getting her life together. She can't cope with you, Guy. You broke her heart."

"I've changed. So help me, Arnold, I've really changed. You could say I've seen the light."

"Until when? Until something comes up that arouses your suspicions again? Stormy is over you. Her life is busy and satisfying and—and happy."

"Happy? Like with someone else? Is that what you're saying?"

Despite his resolution to keep his emotions under control, his voice was full of pain—and anger. He was sure that he'd blown it for sure when there was a long silence on the other end of the line. But when Arnold spoke, his voice had lost its cutting edge.

"We've been friends for a long time, Guy. I want to help you. But I promised Stormy that I'd keep her whereabouts secret. She had a hunch you'd come around someday, looking for her. She isn't up to any more of this. She wants to start over, put the past behind her and that's how it's going to be. Goodbye—"

"Wait! Listen, I swear to you that I won't hurt her. Don't you understand? I'm talking about love, the kind that you and Elsie have. You know—for better or worse. Life has been hell these past months—I miss her and the kids, Arnold. I even hired a detective, trying to find her. Hell, one reason I dropped out of the mayor's race was that I wanted time to look for her."

"So that's it. I figured it was because of that article in the paper about you and Stormy. I did wonder why you felt it was necessary to quit the race. None of the other papers picked it up—guess they had more sense. Well, I see you've been busy. I saw the dedication of your April Gardens project on the news last month. I hear it's going to shake up the housing industry. Dedicating the project to Stormy was a surprise. Did you think it might soften her toward you?"

"It was just something I had to do," he said.

"She's hurting, Guy. You really blew it. I don't think you should—"

"Help me, Arnold. I want to marry her, be a real father to her kids."

"And maybe have some of your own?"

"That, too."

He waited, the silence pulsating in his ear. It seemed forever before Arnold spoke. "I'm probably making a mistake, but—hell, maybe you do deserve another chance. But I want your promise that you won't pressure Stormy. If she doesn't want to talk to you, you'll go away immediately. Is it a promise?"

"I promise," Guy said. "Where is she, Arnold?"

"She and the kids have been living in our guest cottage. We've been doing some traveling and she housesits when we're away. That comic strip she's doing has really taken off—two hundred and thirty-one newspapers have already signed it up. Even if you two do get together, she's not going to drop it."

"I wouldn't want her to, Arnold. I don't want a housewife. I want a helpmate."

Arnold chuckled. "You'll get both. Which will be a change from those cold-fish types you usually prefer."

Guy brushed aside his words. "Is she home now?"

"Probably. She usually works mornings while the kids are in school."

"I'm coming out there," he said. "I don't think I'll call her first."

"No, I wouldn't," Arnold said dryly. "She might not let you in."

Guy knew thanks was in order. "Thank you, Arnold," he said. "I'll never forget this."

"Well, you'd better forget it if things don't work out between you and Stormy. Elsie would have my hide if she knew about this conversation."

As Guy hung up, he discovered his hand was unsteady. It came to him that he hadn't felt this nervous in years. Was his decision to go see Stormy without preparing her the right way to handle things? Maybe he should call ahead—but what if she refused to see him?

No, the best way was to take her by surprise. The first look she gave him—surely, he could tell if he had a chance from that first look.

CHAPTER EIGHTEEN

ALTHOUGH STORMY had been working hard, developing a new idea for Sunny, which, when completed, would cover a month's run of the cartoon strip, she felt uneasy, out of sorts. For one thing, her concentration seemed poor today, even though she was satisfied with the story line, which featured the running battle between Sunny and her landlord, and was a well-balanced mixture of humor and human interest.

The landlord, a combination of two she herself had known, was sly, rapacious and miserly, but with occasional flashes of decency that made him very human. In this particular situation, he had begun to suspect that Sunny's boy, Timothy, was hiding a cat, thus breaking the building's no-pet rule.

The episodes involved a number of close calls as Timothy tried to keep the cat hidden until, eventually, the landlord was won over. The cat, of course, was the image of Magic, curled whiskers, slightly crossed eyes, crooked tail and all. Disguised as a baby, she smiled blandly from the panel Stormy was working on today, looking like an Oriental version of the Cheshire cat in *Alice in Wonderland*.

Stormy added a few lines of shading to the cat's fur, wasn't satisfied, and started over again. Still not satisfied, she laid down her pencil. Realizing she needed a break, she went into the cottage's sunny kitchen to fix herself some tea, hoping that when she returned to her drawing board, she'd be more productive.

One thing she'd learned in the past weeks was that when she couldn't work, it was usually because the material was not yet right and needed more thinking through. When that happened, she cleaned house or cooked up a storm or worked in the garden, hard physical work that left her subconscious free to work out the problem.

Working in the garden appealed to her today. Being city bred, she had always hungered to someday own a piece of earth on which to raise flowers and vegetables. That this particular dream might well come true sometime in the near future was a reason for rejoicing. So why did she feel so uneasy today?

She made herself think of the money she'd soon be drawing, of the savings that would accumulate in the bank. A few months back, who would have thought such a thing possible? Certainly she had every reason to be deliriously happy with things going so well for her and the kids, and the future as sunny as the name of her cartoon heroine.

The kids were thriving, enjoying their new life, their horizons expanding daily. Laurie had made several friends at school, and had found a place for herself where her sweet nature was appreciated. Tommy, too, seemed to have changed. His mind constantly challenged by the enrichment program at his school, he was presently involved in a science project that took most of his spare time.

And wasn't it ironic that it was the children who lived in this affluent neighborhood who got the cream of the county's enrichment programs and the best teachers?

The bitterness in this thought pulled her up short. After all, there were reasons for this that had nothing to do with partisanship toward the wealthy. For one thing, the teachers with the greatest longevity got their pick of the county schools. Naturally they chose places like Sylvanwood. Few teachers would choose to teach in government housing projects....

She laid out her garden tools and a sack of mulching material to use on her winter vegetables, with a feeling of anticipation. How wonderful to have a garden! A place to plant seeds and watch them grow, to weed and cultivate and nurture the developing plants, and then, when it was time, to harvest them for your own table! To eat the tender carrots, the juicy, flavor-packed tomatoes and succulent green peppers that you yourself had grown, to share them with good friends like Arnold and Elsie. Pure heaven.

Arnold and Elsie were another reason to feel on top of the world. They adored Tommy and Laurie, indulged them, but always stopped short of spoiling them. After an initial adjustment period, the kids had settled into their new life as if they'd always lived here. Only occasionally now did she catch that look that told her they were wondering why Guy never came to see them. And every time it happened her own disillusionment and sense of loss flooded back.

Well, the past was behind her. She was only twenty-five—and soon there would be another baby to fill any still-vacant corners of her life. She wouldn't forget Guy. How could she when she was bearing his child? But she wouldn't let what had happened destroy her, wouldn't let it change her goals or her trust in other people. Her name might be Stormy, but Sunny, the name of her cartoon character, was the person she wanted to be. Nothing bothered Sunny for long, not hostile landlords, officious social service workers or even ill-tempered supermarket cashiers. She always came through with a quip—and she always fought back.

What Sunny's creator had to remember was to not give in to bad feelings. What was it that song said? "Keep smiling, keep shining?" Yes, she would do that. She would raise her kids the best she could, be the mother they deserved, and maybe, just maybe, someday she could truly forget how it had felt to love Guy Harris, to make love with him....

She was putting mulching around a very young broccoli plant when she heard the doorbell ring. Since the gate was closed, it couldn't be a salesman, so it must be Arnold or Elsie—or both. Wondering whether to fix coffee or put water on to boil for tea, she dusted the mulching material off her hands, then rose, a little awkwardly, to her feet.

She was getting large now, and sometimes her back ached when she bent over too long. Soon she wouldn't be able to work in the garden, but by that time, her cauliflowers and broccoli and asparagus and other winter vegetables would be ready for the first warm days of spring.

She was smiling as she came around the corner of the house. When she saw Guy, standing by the front door, she stopped, totally stunned. He was wearing one of his dark business suits and holding an immense bouquet of hothouse roses in one hand, a brown paper sack in the other. He looked so ridiculous and out of place that for a moment, she almost laughed. He turned then, saw her, and when his eyes widened and his face lost color, she realized that she had waited too long, that she should have turned and run as soon as she saw him.

He came toward her and stopped directly in front of her. "I didn't know," he said. "Why didn't you tell me, Stormy?"

"And have you accuse me of trying to trap you into marriage by getting pregnant?" she said crossly. "I'm not a glutton for punishment."

"I wouldn't have said that," he said.

"Oh, I think you would have. In fact, I'm surprised you aren't tossing insults at me right now."

"I came here to apologize, Stormy, to tell you how much I regret my—my stupidity."

"Now *that* does surprise me. I can't remember ever hearing you say you were sorry before."

He groaned, looking miserable. "It doesn't come easy, but I'm learning. I want you to listen to me—I know I don't deserve it, but I'm asking you to listen to me. Will you do that much?"

A small pain started in her chest. She rubbed it absently, trying to think. He wanted her forgiveness—but what about her love? And those showy flowers—why hadn't he brought her violets or daisies, something homey and low-key? But then—he wasn't low-key. He was flamboyant, bigger than life, while she was down-to-earth, with plain tastes—and looks. Like the peacock and the peahen.

"I can't explain what happened that day," Guy was saying. "It was as if another man took over my body and said those rotten things."

"Or like a nasty little boy took over?" she said. "One who'd been badly hurt by women?"

It took him a minute to answer; his face was strained and his eyes had a hot, anxious look. "I brought you a gift," he said.

"I see them. Hot-house flowers—just what I need," she said, suddenly angry again.

"No, not just the flowers." He put the brown paper sack in her hands. "Open it. I think this belongs to you."

She opened the sack, looked inside, and her breath caught in her throat. "But—but where did you get my grandmother's photograph album?" she stammered.

"In the warehouse where the rest of your belongings are stored. I put pressure on Clyde Farris. He finally admitted that the truck driver who picked up your belongings was one of his security men."

"Why would he do such a thing?"

"Because—well, he hoped this would get rid of you for good. Without any household goods, you wouldn't need an unfurnished place," he said, his voice grim. "He claims he intended to turn them back to you once the cottages had been razed."

Unexpectedly, Stormy's eyes filled with tears. "That was so cruel. What a cruel man he is."

"I know. He doesn't work for me any longer. If I have my way, he'll never work in San Jose again." He gave her a long, steady look. "I should have looked into it earlier, Stormy. I'm very sorry—what else can I say?"

Try saying you still love me, want me, want the baby I'm bearing, she thought. She knew that all she had to say was that she forgave him, but she discovered she wasn't yet ready.

"How did you find me?" she asked instead.

There was a hunger in Guy's eyes, and the bouquet of roses he was still holding trembled in his hands, giving his anxiety away.

"I've been looking for you since the day you left. It only took me a few hours to come to my senses and realize what I'd done, how wrong I'd been. But when I went out to Bolinas, you were gone. I almost went crazy. The private investigator I hired didn't have much success, but I finally remembered the name of your friend, Abby Cornwall and I went to see her. She told me that the last time she'd seen you, at Thanksgiving, you had that glow women get at certain times and I thought—"

He paused briefly, his eyes bleak, before he went on, "Anyway, that proved to be a dead end, although I learned a lot from Abby that—that made me understand you better. Then I saw the advertisement for your cartoon strip and that's when it came to me that Arnold must have helped you get started, possibly opening a few doors for you, and if so, then he must know where you were."

He gave her a rueful smile. "When I first started looking for you, I called him to ask if he had any idea where you were. He didn't exactly lie to me—he told me you seemed perfectly normal the last time he'd seen you. Which is why I just might tie him up by his heels and leave him twisting in the wind the next time I see him."

Stormy had to laugh, and with the laugh, something tight and wary inside her began to dissolve. She had been given a second chance—did she dare take it? She could be making another mistake. Guy was a very complex man and although she was sure he loved her—could the differences between them ever be resolved? But then—when had anything ever come easy to her? Or to Guy?

Life meant taking chances—and God, she did have so much to gain....

"You'd better make your peace with him," she said softly. "Elsie and Arnold are going to be our very best friends."

For a long moment, he stared at her, and the expression on his face was so revealing that her eyes began to smart. The roses fell to his feet; in a few strides, he reached her. He picked her up in his arms, held her up against him. "My God—I'm going to be a father!" he said.

"Indeed you are. And I think you'd better put me down before old Judge Graves who's watching us from his upstairs window next door calls the police."

He didn't put her down. He carried her into the cottage, setting her down only when she insisted. He looked around, his eyes lingering on the profusion of plants that dominated a bay window of the living room. "I missed those sweet potatoes," he said.

He turned his attention back to her. "I love you, Stormy. Why was it so hard for me to tell you that?"

"You'll have to answer that."

"Because—because I was afraid? Because I couldn't bring myself to take a chance of being disappointed? Is that why I didn't ask you to marry me? I wasn't about to give you up—I'd already rented a comfortable house for you and the kids in the city."

"Are you sure you can handle it now?"

"I can handle it. When I thought I'd lost you and the kids—" He stopped and gave her a tormented look. "I haven't lost you, have I? You are going to marry me, aren't you?"

She felt a perverse desire to punish him—just a little—so she only smiled. "I'll think about it."

His face relaxed. "You're a witch. Did I ever tell you that?"

"I think the word was *bitch*," she said.

He groaned. "Lord—what a fool I was. I was crazy—I knew in my heart that you wouldn't deliberately do such a thing, and yet—"

"And yet, you reverted to your old suspicious ways." She hesitated, then because she had to be honest, she added, "You weren't totally to blame. I should have defended myself, pointed out a few truths. It was Marilyn, wasn't it? She stole the caricature and gave it to that newspaper, hoping to break us up?"

His mouth thinned and for a moment, she saw the old Guy. "We had it out. I didn't have to fire her. She cleared out her desk and left. I haven't seen her since."

"And did you call her names, too?"

"No. What she did couldn't really touch me, because I didn't love her. I reserved my yelling for the one person in the world who could break my heart."

She met his eyes and some of the old doubts stirred. Right now, he was so reasonable, so humble, but how long before the old Guy emerged?

"You're having doubts, aren't you?" He touched her face. "I don't blame you. I can't promise that we'll always be happy together, but I do make you this promise, Stormy. If you'll take me back, if you'll marry me, I'll never stop loving you—and I'll always put you and our family first. I've changed—not just concerning you. I don't have the same ambitions I used to. Oh, I'll always be a workaholic, but it will be in a different direction. Do you believe me?"

She nodded. "I saw your new project, April Gardens, the one you dedicated to me. I was there dedication day. The model had changed since I saw it in your penthouse because you'd added a senior citizens' wing and an area for lower income families. So yes, I can believe that you've changed."

"You were there that day and you didn't let me know?"

"No."

"Why not, Stormy? Arnold must have told you I had been looking for you."

She hesitated. "I'm not really sure. I wasn't ready. I had too much to figure out on my own. Besides, I knew I couldn't bear it if—if you took my pregnancy the wrong way. I was still too raw inside."

He hugged her so hard that she gasped. He pulled away, his face pale. "Oh, God—did I hurt you?"

"Of course not. I'm not made of cobwebs. I'm a perfectly healthy, mature woman. My doctor told me so." She gave him an oblique look. "In fact, he told me that my partner—he was being tactful, you see—and I could have relations for at least another month."

He laughed then, an exultant, excited laugh. "You are a witch. And I love you, want you, mean never to give you a chance to run away again. I'm going to be a possessive husband, forever running off bedazzled men. Can you put up with that?"

In answer, she put her arms around his neck.

He carried her into the bedroom, and she felt so ridiculous that she was laughing as he deposited her in the middle of the bed. The laugh got lost as he kissed her, as gentle as a breeze at first, and then, as his breathing quickened, the kiss deepened, grew passionate and demanding. It felt so good just to be in Guy's arms that she almost regretted the surge of passion that started up inside her.

Guy helped her undress, and she knew she should be embarrassed, her pregnancy all so apparent, but the wonder in his eyes as he touched her round abdomen, filled her with a deep, almost primitive satisfaction and pride. No matter what disappointments, tragedies or great moments of joy lay ahead for her and Guy, she knew that this moment, when Guy first touched the baby he had fathered, would always remain bright and clear and untarnished in her memory.

Then he was kissing her, and everything else faded except the joy, the rightness of being made love to by Guy.

Harlequin Superromance®

COMING NEXT MONTH

#418 RESCUE FROM YESTERDAY • Marisa Carroll
Book I of the Saigon Legacy
Simon McKendrick needed nurse practitioner Annie Simpson to smuggle a valuable pearl necklace into Vietnam—ransom for Simon's brother and sister, who were being held captive by a corrupt government minister. Simon promised he'd protect her, but Annie suspected Simon could be pretty dangerous himself....

#419 TIGERS BY NIGHT • Sandra Canfield
Everyone was worried about Jake Cameron. He'd been ordered to take a break from police work and had volunteered to watch over preemie babies...tiny Peter Bauer in particular. Falling in love with Peter's widowed mother Robin, however, proved an impossible complication. Sooner or later she would have to know he had killed her husband....

#420 HEART OF THE WEST • Suzanne Ellison
The Living West—Book I
Teacher Mandy Larkin and steam locomotive owner Joe Henderson both believed in the value of remembering the past and learning from it, but in order for their love to survive, it looked as if they were going to have to forget about the past altogether....

#421 THE MARRIAGE PROJECT • Lynn Patrick
Gillian Flannery's marriage project worked fine with her high school students. But when she was assigned a partner herself, her "marriage" to John Slater quickly ran into trouble. Between his bickering daughters and his meddling ex-wife, John's home life resembled a war zone. Did Gillian really want to get caught in the cross fire?

HARLEQUIN'S WISHBOOK
SWEEPSTAKES RULES & REGULATIONS
NO PURCHASE NECESSARY TO ENTER OR RECEIVE A PRIZE

1. To enter and join the Reader Service, affix the Four Free Books and Free Gifts sticker along with both of your other Sweepstakes stickers to the Sweepstakes Entry Form. If you do not wish to take advantage of our Reader Service, but wish to enter the Sweepstakes only, do not affix the Four Free Books and Free Gifts sticker to the Sweepstakes Entry Form. Incomplete and/or inaccurate entries are ineligible for that section or sections of prizes. Not responsible for mutilated or unreadable entries or inadvertent printing errors. Mechanically reproduced entries are null and void.

2. Whether you take advantage of this offer or not, your Sweepstakes numbers will be compared against a list of winning numbers generated at random by the computer. In the event that all prizes are not claimed by March 31, 1992, a random drawing will be held from all qualified entries received from March 30, 1990 to March 31, 1992, to award all unclaimed prizes. All cash prizes (Grand to Sixth), will be mailed to the winners and are payable by check in U.S. funds. Seventh prize to be shipped to winners via third-class mail. These prizes are in addition to any free, surprise or mystery gifts that might be offered. Versions of this sweepstakes with different prizes of approximate equal value may appear in other mailings or at retail outlets by Torstar Corp. and its affiliates.

3. The following prizes are awarded in this sweepstakes: ★Grand Prize (1) $1,000,000; First Prize (1) $25,000; Second Prize (1) $10,000; Third Prize (5) $5,000; Fourth Prize (10) $1,000; Fifth Prize (100) $250; Sixth Prize (2500) $10; ★★Seventh Prize (6000) $12.95 ARV.

   ★This Sweepstakes contains a Grand Prize offering of $1,000,000 annuity. Winner will receive $33,333.33 a year for 30 years without interest totalling $1,000,000.

   ★★Seventh Prize: A fully illustrated hardcover book published by Torstar Corp. Approximate value of the book is $12.95.

   Entrants may cancel the Reader Service at any time without cost or obligation to buy (see details in center insert card).

4. This promotion is being conducted under the supervision of Marden-Kane, Inc., an independent judging organization. By entering this Sweepstakes, each entrant accepts and agrees to be bound by these rules and the decisions of the judges, which shall be final and binding. Odds of winning in the random drawing are dependent upon the total number of entries received. Taxes, if any, are the sole responsibility of the winners. Prizes are nontransferable. All entries must be received by no later than 12:00 NOON, on March 31, 1992. The drawing for all unclaimed sweepstakes prizes will take place May 30, 1992, at 12:00 NOON, at the offices of Marden-Kane, Inc., Lake Success, New York.

5. This offer is open to residents of the U.S., the United Kingdom, France and Canada, 18 years or older except employees and their immediate family members of Torstar Corp., its affiliates, subsidiaries, Marden-Kane, Inc., and all other agencies and persons connected with conducting this Sweepstakes. All Federal, State and local laws apply. Void wherever prohibited or restricted by law. Any litigation respecting the conduct and awarding of a prize in this publicity contest may be submitted to the Régie des loteries et courses du Québec.

6. Winners will be notified by mail and may be required to execute an affidavit of eligibility and release which must be returned within 14 days after notification or an alternative winner will be selected. Canadian winners will be required to correctly answer an arithmetical skill-testing question administered by mail which must be returned within a limited time. Winners consent to the use of their names, photographs and/or likenesses for advertising and publicity in conjunction with this and similar promotions without additional compensation.

7. For a list of our major winners, send a stamped, self-addressed envelope to: WINNERS LIST c/o MARDEN-KANE, INC., P.O. BOX 701, SAYREVILLE, NJ 08871. Winners Lists will be fulfilled after the May 30, 1992 drawing date.

If Sweepstakes entry form is missing, please print your name and address on a 3"×5" piece of plain paper and send to:

In the U.S.
Harlequin's WISHBOOK Sweepstakes
P.O. Box 1867
Buffalo, NY 14269-1867

In Canada
Harlequin's WISHBOOK Sweepstakes
P.O. Box 609
Fort Erie, Ontario
L2A 5X3

Offer limited to one per household.

 LTY-H890